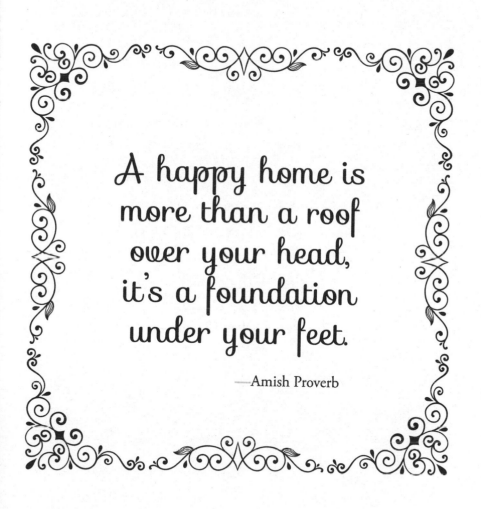

A happy home is more than a roof over your head, it's a foundation under your feet.

—Amish Proverb

The Buggy
BEFORE THE HORSE

TRICIA GOYER

New York

Sugarcreek Amish Mysteries is a trademark of Guideposts.

Published by Guideposts Books & Inspirational Media
110 William Street
New York, NY 10038
Guideposts.org

This is a work of fiction. Sugarcreek, Ohio, actually exists and some characters are based on actual residents whose identities have been fictionalized to protect their privacy. All other names, characters, businesses, and events are the creation of the author's imagination, and any resemblance to actual persons or events is coincidental.

Every attempt has been made to credit the sources of copyrighted material used in this book. If any such acknowledgment has been inadvertently omitted or miscredited, receipt of such information would be appreciated.

"Katie's Amish Fudge" on page 259 was provided by Katie and Heini's Cheese.

Scripture references are from the following sources: The Holy Bible, King James Version (KJV). The Holy Bible, New International Version®, NIV®. Copyright © 1973, 1978, 1984 by International Bible Society. Used by permission of Zondervan.

Cover and interior design by Müllerhaus
Cover illustration by Bill Bruning, represented by Deborah Wolfe, LTD.
Recipe provided by Katie and Heini's Cheese
Typeset by Aptara, Inc.

Printed and bound in the United States of America
10 9 8 7 6 5 4 3 2

CHAPTER ONE

Cheryl Cooper drove her dark blue Ford Focus down the quiet country road, passing a horse and buggy. The holidays were approaching, and she looked forward to experiencing them in this quaint town of Sugarcreek. Her heart ached a bit as she realized this might be the first time in five years she wouldn't be spending the holidays with family or a fiancé. Even though she knew now that her move to Sugarcreek after her breakup with Lance had been the right decision, the familiarity of their holiday routines created a hole inside that she hadn't expected.

Still, with managing the Swiss Miss and getting to know all the new friends God had placed in her life, she could look forward to a season filled with quietness and friendship. It was a nice change from her harried and busy life in Columbus. Maybe that's something she'd been wanting for a while but just didn't know it until she got to Sugarcreek: *peace*.

She ran her fingers through her short red hair. *Oh, bother.* November had brought misty, cold rain to Sugarcreek, providing just enough moisture to cause her hair to frizz. She almost wished she had an Amish prayer *kapp* to wear. That would be useful on days like this. Perhaps by the time Thanksgiving rolled around they'd have more snow.

She drove past the Miller Maze and Petting Zoo and along the beautiful creek toward the Millers' farm. She crossed a charming covered bridge that stretched over the babbling water.

A kissing bridge. That's what the locals called it. When slow-moving buggies traveled through it, courting couples sitting inside slipped from view, giving them a perfect opportunity to snatch a kiss.

Heat rose to Cheryl's cheeks as she considered whom she'd share a kiss with. *Levi Miller.* She'd told herself time and again that being enamored with an Amish bachelor wasn't acceptable. She patted her cheek, willing those thoughts to leave or she'd make a fool of herself at the Millers' farm.

When she reached the other side of the bridge, there sat the familiar huge white farmhouse with a wrap-around porch. There were no buggies in the yard today, and it appeared the horses remained in the barn. She glanced around and didn't see Levi, but that didn't mean he wasn't nearby. Cheryl patted her hair again.

"Maybe I should ask Naomi to borrow a kapp," she mumbled with a sigh as she parked on the Millers' dirt and gravel driveway. Before exiting her car, Cheryl grabbed the handles of the paper sack on the passenger seat, feeling its weight. Since hearing that Naomi was under the weather, she'd promised her friend two things. First, that she'd come pick up the newest batch of home-made candles and preserves Naomi made for the store. Second, that she'd bring some chicken noodle soup. It was Cheryl's mother's recipe and something she always enjoyed when she was not feeling well. The bag held a large Tupperware container of the soup, still warm.

The Millers' dog must have heard the car because a friendly bark greeted her. She stepped out of the car, shut the door, and then glanced to the field past the barn. The pup's head bobbed as he ran through the stubble of hayfields.

Cheryl's shoes crunched on the gravel, and the misty rain brushed her cheeks. She stopped on the path to give the pup time to catch up and soak in the sight of...peacefulness. She needed this. Needed to remember that even though she'd left behind a lot in Columbus that God had brought her to the perfect place where her soul—her heart—could heal.

The wide gray sky stretched over the fields. This spot would provide a perfect star-gazing view on a cold winter's night. In addition to passing down the delicious soup recipe, her mother had taught her to spot Orion, Jupiter, and other winter-sky wonders in the eastern sky. How fun it would be to sit on the front porch, wrapped up in blankets, and watch for shooting stars, especially with Levi—Naomi's oldest stepson. He always brought a smile to her face.

Cheryl sucked in a deep breath, enjoying the moment, and then she decided to take a quick picture with her phone. She aimed the camera at the silos that stuck up in the horizon between the cornfields and stretches of woods beyond the farm.

Sometimes she wanted to pinch herself for the blessing of living in Sugarcreek. It was so different from Columbus. Her life was so different. It was like being inside a stuffy building all day and then stepping outside to clean, fresh air. She hadn't realized how stuffy her life had been for years until now. Until the fresh air had soaked into every part of her.

The dog finally reached her, bouncing with excitement. He didn't look quite a year old and had lots of energy. Forgetting his manners, his front paws tapped her tan slacks, leaving a smudge of dirt.

"Rover, down!" A man's voice split the air, and Cheryl jumped. Levi strode from the barn. A large bag of mulch was slung over his shoulder, yet he walked with ease as if he carried a feather pillow. His blond hair stuck out from under his brimmed hat.

Levi scowled at the dog. A muscle tightened in his jaw. "Sorry to startle you. My little brother, Eli, is supposed to be training this guy, but the pup still needs work on his manners."

She brushed the dirt from her slacks. "No problem. My work apron will cover it."

Levi approached and paused, then he sniffed the air and smiled. "Something smells *goot*. Got something tasty in the bag?" He looked down with those dark blue eyes, the color of the night sky, and her stomach did a small flip.

"Soup for your *maam*." She smiled back. "Esther said she has a nasty cold. I do hope your mom is staying off her feet."

Levi shook his head. "You know my mother. I would need to tie her down to get her to stay off her feet." He looked toward the house. "But Maam did say you were coming. I am thankful she did not go into town today. I will put this mulch by the flower beds and then get your things. Maam asked me to pull out a few dozen jars of preserves and set some cheese aside for you in the root cellar. I will also grab the candles and other items for your store."

It wasn't her store—she was just running it for Mitzi while her aunt was in Papua New Guinea—but she didn't want to argue. Cheryl also thought about reminding Levi that the distance wasn't that far, and even quicker when one was driving in a car, but she changed her mind. Instead she smiled up at him. "That's kind, Levi, thank you."

Levi moved toward the flower beds with Rover following, and Cheryl continued to the front door. Her heartbeat had quickened more than normal, and she told herself to take a deep breath and forget about Levi. Or at least forget about allowing any feelings to grow for him. He was Amish, she was *Englisch*, and that was that.

Cheryl knocked twice and then opened the door and walked in. The Amish way was not to knock at all, but she still couldn't get used to that.

The large living room was warm and cozy. Heat radiated from the wood-burning stove. The oak floors gleamed, making a path to the kitchen.

Cheryl heard a loud sniffle as she walked tentatively toward the open space. Naomi sat at the long dining room table with her Bible open before her. She wore a dark blue dress covered with an apron, her graying hair perfectly tucked in her prayer kapp.

"Why are you just standing there?" Naomi scooted back her chair and rose. "Cheryl, come in. Come in!"

Cheryl hustled in, waving her free hand in Naomi's direction. "Don't you dare get up. I brought you some soup like I promised." She placed the paper bag on the table near Naomi.

The kitchen smelled of wood, kerosene oil, and baking bread. Sure enough, three loaves of wheat bread cooled on the counter. Leave it to Naomi to have time to bake this morning, even when feeling under the weather.

Naomi settled back down into the chair. "*Wunderbar*. A bowl of soup is just what I need. It is so good to see you. A bit of sunshine. Do you have time to stay for a cup of tea? Water's hot." She pointed to the teakettle on the stove.

"I'd love a cup. Since the store doesn't open for an hour, I have time." Cheryl removed her jacket and placed it over the back of the dining room chair at the head of the table. "I just hope Ben and Rueben aren't too disappointed that the front door won't be unlocked early today."

Cheryl smiled thinking of the two brothers who loved to play checkers at the table set up in her store. Their relationship had been strained over the years since Ben left the Amish, but Cheryl was glad to see that time was beginning to heal old wounds.

"Oh, I am sure the brothers will survive." Naomi closed her Bible, but not before Cheryl saw the words *Prayer List* on a sheet of paper tucked inside and the first few names. Sarah, Naomi's stepdaughter, was at the top of the list. Cheryl knew it must be so hard for Amish parents to see their children leading an Englisch lifestyle. Would reconciliation also come to the Miller family, just as it had started with Ben and Rueben?

The second name on the list was Mitzi. Thankfully, many people were praying for Cheryl's aunt. Some thought she was far too old to run off on a missionary adventure in Papua New Guinea, of all places. Cheryl prayed too. And worried.

Cheryl also wondered if her name had made that list. Did Naomi pray for her? Warmth filled her chest at the idea.

She moved to the open cupboard and removed a plain brown mug. A small basket of tea bags sat on the counter. She took a tea bag, placed it in the mug, and then withdrew the teakettle off the stovetop. She tipped the kettle, preparing to pour, when the front door banged open. The loud noise caused Cheryl to jump. She gasped and her hand holding the teakettle jerked. Hot water splashed on the counter.

"Oh no!" She returned the kettle to the stove.

Naomi rose. Levi rushed in, and Naomi's gaze moved from Cheryl to Levi and back to Cheryl. "You did not burn yourself, did you?"

"No, nothing like that." Cheryl wiped up the spilled water with a flour sack dish towel. "I'm fine, but..." Her eyes widened as she looked to Levi. His left hand held his right one, and blood dripped from his fingers. "Are you all right?"

She grabbed the damp dish towel and hurried to him. He took two steps toward her and held out his hand. "I should have known better," he mumbled. "But the root cellar..."

"Here, let's get that to the water tap," Cheryl interrupted. She dabbed at the dripping blood with the towel. He followed her to the kitchen sink. He held his hand under the water, and she saw a pretty deep gash on his palm. He wore a puzzled expression.

Naomi hurried over to view the damage. "Levi, what happened? How did you hurt your hand?"

He turned off the water and faced his stepmother. "It is bad, Maam." At her stricken look, he shook his head. "Not my hand, but it seems someone has gotten into the root cellar. They swiped some of the homemade candles we'd set aside for Cheryl. And a few jars of peach preserves are gone too, along with some apples."

"Someone? Who?" Naomi placed her hand over her mouth. Then she lowered her hand again, eyes wide. "Someone was in our cellar? A thief?"

Levi nodded and then pulled his hand from Cheryl's grasp. "I am afraid so." He cleared his throat. "They dropped a jar of peaches, and I was foolish enough to pick up the broken glass."

Cheryl looked from son to mother. Concern creased the older woman's forehead. Was it because of worry about Levi's hand or worry about the thief? She wasn't sure. Maybe both.

Cheryl's gaze turned to Levi's hand. It had started bleeding again. Naomi spotted it too. She reached into the drawer and pulled out a clean towel. Instead of turning to Levi she glanced over at Cheryl. "Press this into his hand while I get bandages."

She nodded, finding humor in her friend's response. It seemed Naomi was bent on mothering her oldest stepson, despite the fact he was a full foot taller than her. Still, she did as she was told. She pressed the clean towel onto Levi's cut palm as Naomi hurried from the room.

Levi shifted his weight from one foot to another. "Um, I can hold that if you would like."

"And face your mother's wrath? I know better than to disobey."
She chuckled and then dared to look up into his face. Levi squinted
in worry. She guessed what he was thinking: *Who would break into
our cellar and steal from us? And why?*

Naomi hurried back to the kitchen, and Cheryl let her take
over the doctoring. The cut looked deep, and Naomi expertly
applied antibiotic cream and bandages.

"Will you need stitches?" Cheryl asked Levi.

"Nah, it's just a paper cut." Levi forced a smile and winked.
"Or, if I have to, I have been known to sew…"

The front door swung open, slamming against the wood box.
Cheryl jumped, and their attention turned to the door. Naomi's
husband Seth strode in, moving with quickened steps through the
living room into the kitchen.

Seth was usually a quiet and serious man, but now he
seemed frazzled. He walked toward them, and his face held a puzzled expression.

"Something wrong, Seth?" Naomi asked.

"Wrong? *Ja*, I would say something is wrong." He shook his head.
"It seems to me someone has been sleeping in our winter buggy."

Naomi gasped. "Sleeping in the buggy?"

Levi rubbed his brow. "It must be the same person who got
into the root cellar."

Naomi took a step toward her husband. "I hope they did not
get too cold last night."

"Too cold?" Cheryl muttered the words under her breath. "I'd
be worried more about your safety." She knew she shouldn't

interfere. It wasn't really her place. Then again, she was from Columbus. She'd seen her share of crime. She read the papers. A shudder traveled down her spine. "What if they tried to come into your house? Do you even lock the front door at night?"

Their silence told her they didn't.

"We live in Sugarcreek, Cheryl." Naomi placed a hand on Cheryl's arm. "I know this may be hard for you to understand, coming from a big city and such, but if there is someone sleeping in our buggy and poking around in our cellar, then our concern is not so much about the taken items. But rather our biggest concern will be to help . . . to offer what we can."

Seth stroked his long beard, and then he clucked his tongue. "I am not sure that is the wisest thing to do this time, Naomi." His tone was serious. "Whoever is sleeping in our buggy has some far-fetched ideas about our town."

"What do you mean? How do you know?" Naomi's gaze searched her husband's face. He opened one of his balled fists and revealed a piece of paper folded inside. It appeared to be a piece of crumpled-up notebook paper that someone had smoothed and then refolded. Seth unfolded it and then held it out so everyone could read the words.

There was a time when communities cared for their own, but with great loss came diminished hope. And no town could live without hope. Sugarcreek was slowly dying but nobody knew it, especially not the two men who sat on Main Street playing checkers.

CHAPTER TWO

A chill raced down Cheryl's spine as she glanced from Naomi to Seth to Levi and back to Naomi again. No one spoke, as if they were all trying to figure out what this note could mean.

"Do you recognize the handwriting?" Cheryl asked.

"No, I do not," Naomi was quick to say.

Seth and Levi agreed.

"It is no one in our family." Levi pointed to the paper. "No one around here writes so... scribbly."

Cheryl read it again, and a sinking feeling came over her. Emotion tightened her throat, and she tried to swallow. "The two men sitting on Main Street playing checkers—they're talking about Ben and Rueben Vogel. They play checkers at my store." She placed a hand to her neck. "Is... is this note a threat to them? To me?" Cheryl bit her lower lip, telling herself not to overreact. Maybe she'd read too many mystery novels recently. She released a slow breath, reminding herself that this was not a novel. This was real life. The thought also hit her that she needed to return the last stack of borrowed books to the library before they were due in a few days.

"It surely does not sound like a threat." Naomi's voice was scratchy. She pulled out a handkerchief from her apron pocket and dabbed at her nose. "But I do hope whoever wrote this did not get too cold last night. The temperature really dropped."

Cheryl sighed heavily. She understood the plain ways of the Amish. She understood the way they took care of their own and those in need. She just hoped that her friends wouldn't get hurt in their effort to help... hoped no harm would come to her store or the two brothers.

A throaty cough escaped Naomi's lips.

"Maam, why don't you sit and get off your feet? *Daed* and I will go out and see if whoever left this took more from the root cellar than I first thought."

Levi took a kerosene lantern off the hook by the door. The men stalked off, and Naomi returned to her chair. Cheryl walked to the kettle and added hot water to the mug. Then she joined Naomi at the table. She needed to leave—needed to get back to open the store—but not until she talked some sense into Naomi.

Cheryl dipped her spoon in her tea and stirred it slowly. The steeping tea colored the water brown, and she glanced up into Naomi's face. Cheryl then reread the note found in the buggy.

There was a time when communities cared for their own, but with great loss came diminished hope. And no town could live without hope. Sugarcreek was slowly dying but nobody knew it, especially not the two men who sat on Main Street playing checkers.

Naomi read it too, looking even paler than when Cheryl arrived. The room was quiet. No hum of electricity filled the air. No radio. No television. There was nothing to distract Cheryl from her worried thoughts.

"I just do not understand." Naomi folded and refolded her hands on the table. Even though she was likely trying to hide them, worry lines formed around her lips and brow. "It seems as if this note was written by someone who knows our town. Or at least they know about Ben and Rueben..."

"Who play checkers in my store."

Naomi's gaze narrowed on the paper. "Ja, but what do you think it means? No hope? Slowly dying?"

Cheryl smoothed it again. "Well, I think I know what one part means." She pointed to the word *loss*. "A half-dozen shops on Main Street have had thefts in the last week or so. And both low- and high-price items have been taken."

Naomi's eyes grew wide. "A half-dozen shops? How come I had not heard?"

"Well, it was just last night when word started to get out. It took us that long to figure out what was going on. You know, when crowds from the tourist buses come in, items always find themselves in odd places. People pick up an item, change their minds, and then put it down in another part of the store. Once in a while things are stolen too, but last night at the Chamber of Commerce meeting August Yoder mentioned that one whole shelf from his rack of cookbooks had been cleared out. And then Marion

Berryhill from the Christian bookstore said that she was missing two Amish prayer books she'd just ordered. One was bought, but when she looked an hour later the other two copies were gone."

Naomi gasped. A shadow flitted over her face. "Cookbooks? And prayer books? Who would steal an Amish prayer book?"

Cheryl took a sip from her tea. "That's what I asked, and then Jeb Bakker joined the conversation. His father used to be a police officer when he was growing up, and he said that some people don't care what they steal. They just get the thrill from getting away with it."

"Well, my only consolation is that whoever stole those prayer books can open them and read them!" Naomi swallowed hard. "It just does not seem right. In Sugarcreek of all places."

Cheryl reached over and patted Naomi's hand. "Maybe you should call the police and give a report. Chief Twitchell is a nice man…"

"*Ne.*" The word spouted from Naomi's lips. "I do not wish to bring the police into this over a few jars of jam and a little mess on the floor of our cellar."

Cheryl squeezed Naomi's hand firmer, as if she could impart some sense into her. The hand seemed thin and frail today, not the strong work hands she was used to. Naomi's hand trembled under her touch, and Cheryl almost felt bad that she'd been so forward with the information. Then again, Naomi needed to know. Seth and Levi had to know too.

Someone—who had knowledge of the town and its people— was interrupting the peacefulness of Sugarcreek. And, at least for one night, that person had bedded down on the Miller farm.

Cheryl glanced at her watch as she drove back into town. She only had ten minutes to get to the store before it opened. She was on Main Street, but instead of turning into the alley behind the store to park, she continued to By His Grace Christian bookstore. She drove to the end of the block and turned on to Oak Street. The Berryhills' house was just on the other side of the alley from their bookstore. She always thought that would be convenient—especially the one-minute commute to work.

She parked in front of their house and took the cardboard box with the chicken potpie from the seat. Naomi had shared wonderful news just before Cheryl left the Millers'. A foster son, Gage, had recently been placed with the Berryhills, and Naomi asked if Cheryl could deliver a meal to the family.

"Everyone takes meals or gifts after the births of babies, so why not when a new child is added in this way?" Naomi had said. "I know they have already received many gifts for that new baby girl due to be born any day. I thought a meal would be helpful."

Cheryl had promised she would, but she also urged Naomi to get some rest. "Baking bread and making a potpie—all before 9:00 AM—isn't resting, my friend," she'd joked with a parting hug.

Now she hurried up the front steps and knocked on the door. Cheryl leaned in, expecting to hear a toddler's squeal and the patter of little feet. She hadn't asked how old Gage was, but she guessed he was young. It was sad how so many kids ended up in foster homes due to no fault of their own.

The door swung open, and a tall gangly teen stood there. Cheryl took a step back. "Uh, hello, is Marion here?"

He motioned behind him. "She just headed to the store for a minute. Do you need me to call her?" His voice was quiet, as if he were distracted.

"Oh, sugar and grits. I'm sorry I missed her. Just tell her that this potpie is from Naomi Miller. And I'm…"

"You're the lady from the Swiss Miss."

"Yes, uh, that's right." She cocked her head. "I've seen you walking around town the last week or so, haven't I?" She forced a smile not knowing what else to say or do. The young man seemed equally uncomfortable.

He took the potpie from her and shrugged. "I can't start school until tomorrow. Lots of problems getting my records transferred from…from my old school." Emotion—anger—flickered in his eyes, and he quickly looked away. "Uh, thanks for this. I'll tell…Marion you came by."

Gage took a step back into the house and waited, as if wanting her to turn away so he could shut the door. That's when she noticed his hoodie, and Cheryl's eyes widened. She recognized the dark green sweatshirt with the word *Freedom* in yellow down the sleeve, only today he wore it with the hood down.

She hadn't just seen Gage walking around town. When she'd returned from lunch yesterday, the hooded figure had intently watched Ben and Rueben playing checkers.

Why were so many people interested in those two brothers lately? Or was it simply an excuse for someone to case her store? Was the Swiss Miss being targeted next by the thieves? Cheryl squared her shoulders, and with a parting wave she hurried back to her car. She'd do her best to make sure that wouldn't happen.

On the drive back around the block, Cheryl tried to piece together what she knew. Somebody was stealing around town. Somebody had caused trouble on the Miller farm. Seth had just assumed that whoever had been in their winter carriage had slept there. But was it possible that someone like Gage could sneak out to the farm and then steal a few things in order to draw attention away from the thefts in town?

She softly bit her lower lip as she parked her car. How much had the Berryhills learned about Gage before inviting him into their home? Had they inadvertently invited trouble into their picturesque town when they let him come to stay?

CHAPTER THREE

Cheryl unlocked the door to the Swiss Miss Gifts and Sundries Shop, flipped on the lights, and looked around. Everything seemed in its place, but the store seemed empty without Beau. She was already five minutes late unlocking the front door, and she didn't have time to run home and get her cat. Maybe at lunch she'd collect him. Then again, maybe she should use her lunch hour to walk around and talk to the other storeowners. If she made a list of what items were stolen, perhaps she could see a pattern and ultimately find the thief.

As she walked through the store, the aroma of homemade candles, candy, and pungent cheese met her as it always did. Yet for some reason something ominous seemed to be about the store today. The dreary weather outside probably had something to do with that. Or maybe it was the foreboding note found at the Millers' farm.

Cheryl went to the back, flipped on all the lights, and then lit a pumpkin-scented candle by the front cash register. After putting on her work apron, she moved through the aisles, straightening merchandise and checking for missing stock. It's not that she could remember every item in her store, but in the last month she'd gotten a better handle on what the store had so she knew what should be ordered. She released a sigh when nothing obvious appeared to be missing.

She picked up a small Amish lap quilt designed in squares and diamonds in colors of blue, red, and green. She refolded it and placed it on a shelf next to checkerboard place mats. As much as she loved the large Amish quilts, smaller items sold better. They were easy for tourists to buy and take home or give away as gifts.

Cheryl made a mental note to ask Rhoda Hershberger for more of the quilted smaller items before sales picked up after Thanksgiving. She also needed to talk to Levi about more leatherwork pieces. That would also give her another excuse to visit the Miller farm and see if they'd discovered anything more about their visitor.

The bell above the door jingled a greeting, and Cheryl turned. A young man stepped inside. Reddish brown hair poked from beneath a baseball cap. He wasn't her typical customer, and he looked at the list in his hand and then glanced around. He moved with quickened steps up the aisle toward the shelf of jams and jellies.

"Can I help you?" Cheryl asked. She noticed the shopping bag in his hand. It would be easy for someone to slip items into a big bag like that, especially if the store was busy.

The man paused and glanced over his shoulder at her. "I'm looking for Katie's Fudge."

She cocked an eyebrow. "Katie's Fudge?" Cheryl shook her head. "I'm sorry, but I don't carry fudge by that name. I had some by Naomi Miller, but I'm all out right now."

The man's eyes grew wide, almost frantic. "My wife, she's due in two weeks, and for the last month all she's talked about is Katie's Fudge at the Swiss Miss."

"I'm sorry. I don't carry fudge by that name," she said again. A tinge of sadness pricked Cheryl's heart too. Would she ever experience a wedding, marriage, pregnancy? Her engagement to Lance had put her on the path to all those things, but with Lance out of her life now she couldn't help but wonder if those experiences would ever be hers. She was thirty after all. *Maybe I'll end up like Aunt Mitzi, living my life caring for this store until some adventure sweeps me away.* The only problem was while the former seemed possible, the latter didn't.

The man pulled off his hat and scratched his head. "She did say something about having to wait until right before Thanksgiving. I was hoping two weeks was close enough." His face fell. "I'm not sure I want to return home empty-handed."

More customers entered, and the two women and an older gentleman made their way over to the Amish prints hanging on the wall.

Cheryl placed her hands on her hips and looked around her shop. "Do you know if you're having a boy or a girl?"

"A girl." His face brightened. "Sophia—named after my grandmother."

Cheryl nodded, and she walked over to the display of Amish dolls. They came in all sizes and styles, but she had a favorite. She picked up a small crocheted one with a light blue dress. There were two others like it in darker shades, but the light blue dress seemed perfect for a baby.

Like all Amish dolls, it didn't have a face, but it was small and soft. "How about you return with this? I'll give you a twenty percent discount. And I'll also check my aunt's files to find out who supplied that fudge. If you give me your name and number, I can call you when I get it in."

The man's face widened into a grin. "Ma'am, you have a deal." He took the doll from her with tenderness and then reached into his back pocket for his wallet.

"Here, let me wrap that for you." She took it from him and moved behind the long wooden counter. She wrapped the small doll in pink tissue paper before putting it into one of the Swiss Miss bags.

As she rung up the man's order, the bell over the door chimed again, and she saw Ben and Rueben walk in, taking their places at the checkers table. Neither said a word as they began their game. She finished the transaction and then walked over to watch.

She wasn't interested in the game so much. What she was interested in was why they had captured the attention of whoever had written that note. They were two brothers caught up in religious differences—one choosing to live outside the Amish lifestyle. The other believing, for a time, that he had to shun his brother for doing so.

Should I warn them? Tell them about the note? She was still contemplating that when another customer walked in. She recognized the woman from church—one of Aunt Mitzi's friends—but she couldn't remember her name. She was tall with dirty blonde hair and a ponytail. Her face was long and her nose a bit too large for her face, but her green eyes were pretty. The woman strode toward Cheryl with quickened steps, pausing before her. "Cheryl, I have to apologize, but did you get a letter in your mailbox today addressed to me?" The words spilled out of her mouth.

Before Cheryl could respond or ask the woman to remind her of her name, the woman continued. "I got a letter in my PO box yesterday from Mitzi. I was so excited. I didn't think anything of it until I got halfway through reading the letter and Mitzi started talking about the store that I realized it was intended for you." The woman was talking so fast and loud that others in the store paused to turn. She waved the letter as if still trying to get Cheryl to understand. "My guess is that she wrote us both a letter, and they got put into the wrong envelopes."

"I'm not sure…"

"Laurie-Ann. Laurie-Ann Davis."

"I'm not sure, Laurie-Ann. I haven't checked the mail today. But if there is a letter there, I'll be sure to deliver it. What's your addre—"

"Right here." The woman tapped on the envelope. "Just have the man in the post office slip it into my box." She released a breath, and her voice calmed. "I'm sorry. I didn't mean to get so worked up, but I was worried. Worried about Mitzi, you know. I'm sure she reveals more about her struggles to you… but at least the ladies in our Bible study will now know how to pray."

Know how to pray… worried about Mitzi… struggles? The words spun through her mind.

"Wait. Is Mitzi okay?" Cheryl's voice rose slightly. The two men playing checkers beside her paused and tilted their heads upward, eyeing her.

"Everything okay?" Ben asked.

"Mitzi didn't get captured by natives, did she?" Rueben chimed in.

"Nothing like that." Laurie-Ann forced a smile. "She's just homesick, that's all." Then the woman covered her mouth and glanced back at Cheryl again. "Oh, it's your letter. I probably said too much."

Cheryl nodded and tucked the letter into her apron pocket. "Thank you for delivering it...and for your concern." She let out a heavy sigh. "At least we all know...all of us...to keep Aunt Mitzi in our prayers."

The store had numerous customers when Naomi's daughter Esther arrived, and Cheryl wondered if Esther had heard about the robbery and the person who'd slept in their winter buggy since she hadn't been home when Cheryl stopped by. The young woman had likely gotten a ride with some of her *rumspringa* friends with a car. Cheryl guessed if she didn't know yet, now wasn't the time to bring it up. She'd let Naomi and Seth talk to their daughter. How would they feel—Levi feel—if she told the young woman?

"Esther, I'm so glad you're here." Cheryl didn't wait for the young Amish girl to remove her coat before she pointed toward her office. "There are some things I need to do. I'll be in back if you need me."

She'd resisted the urge to pull Mitzi's letter from her apron pocket a dozen times in the last hour. Yet her worry must have been clear, for before she slipped into the office Rueben approached.

"Do not worry, Cheryl, God is watching over your aunt. I have known her many years, and He has gotten her out of a few pickles in her day."

"Yes." She let out a sigh. "I just wish her pickles weren't on the other side of the world."

She patted his arm and then moved to her office. Closing the door, Cheryl pulled the envelope from her pocket and sank into the desk chair.

"Dear Aunt Mitzi," she whispered. "God has a sense of humor, doesn't He? Before nightfall the whole town's going to be praying for you... Now let me see what they'll be praying about..."

She unfolded the letter.

My Dearest One,

Today is a day of rest, which means a day of writing letters. I've already penned a few to good friends, and I've saved yours until last. The daylight is fading, and I hope I can finish before it gets dark. Kerosene for lanterns is a precious resource, and we all try to do as much work as we can before the daylight fades.

I've been putting off writing this letter because I haven't wanted to worry you. I am still in a rural area without

electricity or plumbing. And what seemed like a wonderful camping trip has become rather tedious. Last night I
dreamt that I drew myself a bath in my large claw-foot
tub, and I woke up sorely disappointed.

Our translator became ill, but I've done the best I can.
I've picked up some words during the months I've been here,
but much less than I hoped I would. Many claimed to believe
in Jesus and accepted that He is the One and Only God, but
they've also tried to keep their old traditions, adding God to
their familiar ways. Please pray and ask others to pray too.
I know the prayers you send will touch the throne of God
and reflect downward here to our end of Earth.

I hope things are going well with you in Sugarcreek.
The holiday season is especially busy, but I know you'll do
fine. If you need extra help, Naomi might be willing to
come into the store a few days. With her warm smile she's
one of my best salespeople, although her humility would
never admit as much.

I'm clinging to a scripture found in Psalm 91, verses
nine through eleven, that I memorized in Sunday school a
few years ago:

If you make the Most High your dwelling—
even the Lord, who is my refuge—
then no harm will befall you,
no disaster will come near your tent.
For he will command his angels concerning you
to guard you in all your ways.

With a leaky tent and a virus making its way through our team members, this verse means more to me now than ever. Know that whatever is happening in your neck of the woods, with the hustle and bustle of the upcoming holidays, God will be your refuge too.

I love you very much,
Aunt Mitzi

PS Make sure you sample Katie's Fudge. It's my favorite!

Cheryl put down the letter and rubbed her temples. Mitzi was longing for a bath and a warm bed. That was to be expected, right? She'd pray for her aunt, yes, but it was nothing to get alarmed about.

Relief flooded over her, yet another question nagged her. What was this fudge that everyone was talking about?

She turned on her computer, deciding to scan the invoices from last November. That should give her some clue.

The computer hadn't even booted up completely when Esther poked her head in the doorway. "The manager of the quilt store is here to see you. Should I send her back?"

"Back? Is something wrong?"

Esther nodded, and her dark eyes widened. "She said someone robbed her store in the last few days, and she wants to talk to you about it." Esther sighed and touched her kapp. "She worries that the person who has been robbing other stores in the area has visited your store too."

Chapter Four

Cheryl looked around her messy office. Piles of papers, boxes of Christmas ornaments, and a few mugs filled with cold coffee were piled on her desk. She thought of her father's messy desk at his church office and wondered if he'd ever reformed his ways.

"*Cheryl Cooper,*" she could imagine her mother's reprimand, "*you aren't turning into your father, are you? And to think that poor Amish girl has to work on this desk too!*"

It would be better to go out front to meet the manager of the quilt store, she decided. She rose, smoothed her store apron, tucked Aunt Mitzi's letter back into the apron pocket, and then exited the back area. The unfamiliar scowl on Agnes Winslow's face met her, pausing her in her tracks.

Thick worry lines wrinkled the woman's forehead, and her lips were pressed tightly as if she'd just bit into a lemon. A rusty-gray strand of hair fell from the woman's curly ponytail, and Agnes brushed it back from her face. The ponytail looked exactly like a Brillo pad, and the realization almost made Cheryl smile. Then she remembered the seriousness of the visit.

I wonder if the robbery at the Millers' farm is tied in too? It had to be. What were the odds two thieves roamed the quiet streets and countryside near Sugarcreek?

Esther returned to the counter and began ringing up an older lady's purchase. Agnes stood to the side, eyeing the customer as if deciding if this sweet old woman was behind the recent thefts.

The hint of a smile touched Cheryl's lips. *I really doubt Granny has stuffed doilies into her cane.*

"Will that be all today?" Esther asked the elderly woman in an especially cheerful voice. Esther's smile was extra wide too—maybe because there was another business owner in the shop? "Our Thanksgiving merchandise is twenty-five percent off today."

"Oh, twenty-five percent off?" the customer chirped, returning the smile. "I had my eye on those pumpkin-spiced candles. They smell heavenly." She pointed to the display shelf, and then the woman noticed Agnes's intense gaze. "Maybe next time," the woman said quickly as she picked up her purchase and then skittered away.

Cheryl hurried to Agnes's side, knowing she had to either cheer Agnes up or move her out before she lost more business.

"Stay warm!" Esther called after the departing customer. Then she turned her attention to a Christmas display she'd been arranging. It was hard to believe Christmas was just a little over a month away. Outside, fall still tried to hold on, keeping winter at bay.

Cheryl reached Agnes's side and then motioned to the far corner near a stack of quilts. The sight of Agnes's frown unnerved her. Every time she visited Sugarcreek Sisters Quilt Shoppe, Agnes's smile was on display as well with her quilts and fabrics.

The thefts must be worse than I imagined.

Today Agnes wore dark circles under her eyes. When Cheryl sidled up, the older woman glanced around, as if making sure no one else was near enough to hear, and then she pulled out a piece of paper from her purse. Cheryl eyed it. From what she saw, the woman had already visited many of the store owners up and down the street—just like Cheryl had thought of doing. Agnes was one step ahead of her.

Agnes blinked slowly. "I've visited the local shops, and there are a number of items missing. Have you had any items disappear off your shelves?"

Cheryl's heart sank as she read over the extensive list. A half-dozen businesses were listed—all from the main shopping strip. And there wasn't just one item listed as missing from each shop, but multiple items.

"I haven't really noticed anything." She rubbed her chin, wondering if she just hadn't been paying attention. She looked to the shelves filled with candles and jars of preserves. Had she been keeping as good of records as she should?

The hard lines of Agnes's face softened. She released a sigh. "I hope you're one of the few places spared."

Cheryl stepped forward to get a better look at the page. "Is there a pattern to the type of items that are missing?" She pointed to the paper. "There seems to be *so* much." *Quilts, dolls, books* . . . none of it made sense.

"There is a lot, and I wonder if there are even more things many of us haven't noticed. I don't know about you, but with the busy holiday season upon us, my stock changes daily. But I know some things are gone for certain." Agnes sighed. "Last week a small quilted table runner went missing from my shop, and this week a whole stack of pot holders. A whole stack!" Agnes shook her head, and her Brillo pad bounced. "I thought I'd misplaced them, but I turned over the whole store. There must have been a dozen at least. Who would take a stack of pot holders?"

A messy baker? Cheryl stuffed down the thought as her throat tightened. Her mind raced through the list, totaling the dollar amounts Agnes had listed next to the items. The total leaned toward significant, but the thefts hadn't meant just a loss of income to business, they'd also meant lost trust. Did she really want to go through the holiday season suspicious of every person who walked through the gift shop door? There was no peace in that.

"Have you had thefts before?"

Agnes shook her head. "Not more than one or two small items a month. And always small items." She shook the piece of paper. "Never such audacious actions. An entire stack?" The woman huffed then deflated like a balloon that had been pricked. "It's so widespread. Look, the shops are up and down Main Street."

Cheryl nodded. What Agnes said mirrored what Aunt Mitzi had told her about thefts. There weren't many, but they did happen now and then. "Has anyone unusual come to town?"

"No. Nothing out of the ordinary." Agnes shook her head then sighed. "That we've noticed."

And that was the problem. If the store owners who'd been in Sugarcreek for lifetimes didn't know whom to suspect, how could Cheryl make sure the Swiss Miss wasn't the next target?

Surely Mitzi would have mentioned it if she should be on guard. And Agnes's reaction gave her a clear message that this was new for her too.

"Have you gone to the police yet? Hopefully the thief will be caught soon." Cheryl tried to keep her tone light, not wanting to build on Agnes's worry. Yet the idea that someone was stripping this plain and simple community of much more than just merchandise caused her heart to pound. They were losing their peace. They were losing their trust.

She also knew that these types of crimes weren't a top priority for the police department in cities like Columbus. But maybe things were different in the smaller, safer Sugarcreek. Still, she wouldn't admit that to Agnes. Cheryl was determined to keep a brave face and positive tone, lest Agnes crumble. The poor woman looked overwrought as she examined the list in her hand again.

"Could the police help?" she asked again. "I could go in and talk to Chief Twitchell..."

"The police?" Agnes pressed the piece of paper to her chest. "Yes, I called them already. Officer Ortega—the nice, young policewoman who stopped by my quilt store—is the one who suggested I go around and make the list. She said it would take time for the police to do the same thing. I'll stop by the police department later this afternoon to drop it off. Be sure to let me know if you come across anything missing."

"I will." Cheryl glanced around her store, noting the half-finished Christmas display. "Esther will be busy today setting up the Christmas displays, checking deliveries, and restocking shelves, but I'll have her walk around..."

"What about the Amish children?" Esther interrupted. She hung a red glass ornament on a display stand and then stepped toward them.

Agnes's mouth dropped open. "Do you think that *children* did this?"

"Ne." Esther giggled, and then her smile flitted away. She pointed to a whitewashed bookshelf. "Did you move the hand-carved wooden Amish children set up there? I was going to ask yesterday if you sold them. They were my favorite pieces, and I noticed right away they were gone."

Cheryl hurried to the bookshelf. There were a few candles on display, and a red carved bird was graced on either side by two tin pitchers filled with red, orange, and gold Thanksgiving bouquets. Next to them was a sign that read: Hello there. Sit and stay awhile. Welcome. Nice to see you. We're glad you're here. The sign had always brought a smile to customers' faces and so had the small wooden Amish children that she'd set up on display next to the sign. Since they were intricately hand-carved and painted, she'd put a higher price on them than most of the other items, but now they were gone.

CHAPTER FIVE

Cheryl lifted the tablecloth that covered the table beneath the shelf the carved items had sat upon. Had someone hidden the children as a joke? Her heart sank as it became clear the carved pieces were nowhere to be found. Disbelief mixed with anger and sadness. Why the Amish figurines of all things? Who would do that? Steal a collection of ten little girls and boys, a perfect school of children?

Cheryl ran her fingers across the cool wood where the items had sat. "No, I didn't sell them. You're right, Esther. They're gone. I...I can't believe it." She turned back to Agnes.

"How many figures were there?"

Cheryl rubbed her hands on her apron. "Ten. Five little girls matched with five little boys."

Agnes pulled a pen out of her purse and added the items to her list. "Such a shame. I remember them. Those carvings had such whimsical faces. I'd eyed them, considering buying a couple for myself more than once."

Cheryl turned to Esther. "Do you remember seeing anyone looking at them? Handling them?"

"No. No one. Well, not more than normal."

The characters did attract attention. Still, they'd only sold a few. And last week when she'd checked inventory, ten stood erect on the shelf.

"I didn't either...," Cheryl started. Then she stopped short. "Well, not holding them." A memory filtered into her mind, and she wished she could push it away. It was a memory of that foster boy. Gage had been leaning against the shelf, watching the checkers game. Had his hands been in his pockets or behind him? She couldn't remember. Surely he couldn't have shoved all ten in his pockets. She tried to remember if he'd been wearing a backpack that day. Something told her he had.

Agnes touched her arm. "What is it? You look as if you've remembered something."

"Maybe..."

Agnes's eyebrows arched. "Did you see someone holding the items?"

"Not holding them exactly..." Cheryl paused, wondering if she should say more.

"Think of what you're saying and who you're saying it to," her mother had often told her. A tightness grew in Cheryl's chest as if someone had wrapped her apron strings around it and pulled. She shouldn't say anything and potentially harm the young man's reputation until she had more than a vague impression to go on.

"Who was it?" Agnes prodded.

"I don't want to jump to conclusions. Maybe I should talk to his..." Cheryl started to say *his foster parents*, but stopped because that gave it away.

She wouldn't say more until she was sure. "I need to think before I say more."

Agnes's eyes had taken on a faint sheen of tears. "I just can't believe this has happened here, in our town." She turned to Esther. "Things like this shouldn't happen in Sugarcreek."

"She is right." Esther shifted next to Cheryl as if uncomfortable with the idea of someone stealing from the stores nearby—from their store. "I have always felt safe in Sugarcreek. I have lived here my whole life. You can ask Levi too, and he will tell you the same."

Hearing Levi's name, Cheryl straightened and stepped away from the barren shelf.

"Well, I have a couple more stores to check." Agnes studied Cheryl. "If you decide to tell me who you suspect, I'll listen."

Cheryl nodded but stayed quiet as the quilt store manager left. As much as she'd like to tell someone, she should probably start with Gage's foster parents. She needed to learn more about him before mentioning her suspicions to anyone.

She looked at Esther. "What do you think Levi would say to all this?"

The girl shrugged. "If you want to know, ask him. He does have a goot way of looking at things. He is like my maam, always watchful and insightful."

As much as she'd love to talk to Levi, Cheryl hoped it would be about happier things than the thefts around town and on the Miller farm. She remembered the feel of his hand in hers as she'd held the dishcloth against his cut this morning. How long had it been since she'd harbored the same butterflies in her stomach around Lance? Too long. She shook her head to clear the image of Levi's dark blue eyes. She knew better, had given herself a strong lecture just that morning about the futility of hoping for something more than the offered friendship with the handsome Amish man. Yet Naomi had urged them closer this morning...

No, that was her overactive, and lonely, imagination at work.

If Levi did offer his insight, then he'd be the knight in shining armor and she'd be the damsel in distress. Did the rescuer complex work with Amish bachelors too? Would Levi Miller rush to her aid if it were necessary? Would Naomi approve?

Even though it was possible, Cheryl didn't want to find out. Because to be rescued, one had to be in trouble. Big trouble. And so far a few missing carvings did not place her in that category.

Even if being the one in need would bring Levi to her side, Cheryl didn't want things to happen to get him there. No, she could handle this. And maybe she'd seek Naomi's advice too. Her friend was turning into a regular sleuth. Naomi was almost as good at helping her figure out the riddles behind things as she was baking, and that was saying something.

Cheryl put her arms into her thick black coat and buttoned it all the way to the top. "Esther, I'll be back in a couple of minutes. I have an errand. It shouldn't take me more than fifteen or twenty minutes."

Esther paused from her work of folding and restacking aprons and turned. "Does this have anything to do with the thefts?"

Cheryl pulled her gloves from her coat pocket and slid them on. She'd have to stay on top of her game to keep one step ahead of the Millers. "Maybe. We'll see, but I won't be gone long."

"Oh, before I forget again..." Esther stretched out a hand. "An Amish bachelor came by yesterday. He wanted to know if you had any handyman work for him to do."

There was a special light in Esther's face as she talked, and if Cheryl wasn't seeing things, it appeared that Esther was trying to hide a smile. Esther had never mentioned a boyfriend, but her body language indicated she was interested in this young man.

"An Amish bachelor?" Cheryl stepped closer and with a gloved finger brushed a strand of flyaway hair back from Esther's face. "Is it someone you've known for a while?"

"Oh no." Esther's eyelashes fluttered, and there was indeed a fresh pink tint to her cheeks. "It is no one I have met before. He said he had just moved into the area. Said he came to be closer to family. From the look of his clothes, he looked to be from Pennsylvania to me."

Cheryl nodded. As a child when she first visited Aunt Mitzi, she'd thought that all Amish people looked the same, but the older she got she noticed the difference—from the style of their dresses and pants to their kapps and straw hats, each community had a different idea of what dressing "plain" meant.

"I know there are many projects, but let me think about what needs to be done first and what I can afford." She reached for the door handle. "Did he leave a way for you to reach him?"

"Ne, but he said he would stop back in a few days." Esther's smile broke through this time.

"I have no doubt he will." Cheryl chuckled. Perhaps romance wasn't around the corner for her, but it would be fun if this young man was as interested in Esther as she seemed in him. Esther always worked hard and rarely asked for any special favors. It would be special if God granted her one during this holiday season—someone to sneak a kiss with as they drove across a covered kissing bridge?

The sound of church bells ringing greeted Cheryl as she entered By His Grace bookstore. That was followed by the voices of a children's choir flowing through the sound system. A half-dozen shoppers eyed the books on the shelves, and Marion stood behind the counter checking out a woman with a large stack of Christian novels.

Marion patted the one on top. "I just loved this one. You have some good reading here," she said. Her dark skin glowed with the joy of pregnancy. She was tall and thin, and her baby bump looked like a basketball hidden under her mauve sweater. Cheryl watched while Marion kept chatting with the customer with an occasional comment directed toward other shoppers. Although Marion smiled, there were tired lines around her eyes. Was she taking on too much—running a store, caring for a new foster son, and preparing for a baby? Not to mention the approaching holidays and the unease caused by the thefts. An unease Cheryl might add to in a moment.

After Marion bagged up the books and wished the woman good-bye, Cheryl approached the counter.

"Looks like things are busy in here. I always like to see that." Cheryl looked behind her shoulder for emphasis.

Marion eased herself onto a stool behind the counter and took a sip from the water bottle. "Just another blessing from the Lord this year, which means I'm not going to let the troubles in town get me discouraged." She rubbed her expanded stomach in a slow circle. "It's going to be a busy holiday season, that's for certain."

Cheryl nodded, and she earnestly hoped the trouble that Marion spoke of wasn't in her own home. "Did you get the potpie that Naomi sent?"

"Oh yes, I'll have to send her a thank-you note. Naomi always is thoughtful. And Gage said that you dropped it by. Well, not by name, but he said the lady from the Swiss Miss with the red hair." Marion chuckled. "I let him know your name was Sharon."

"Cheryl." She smiled, trying to remember if she and Marion had ever had a conversation beyond pleasantries at Chamber of Commerce gatherings or hellos at the grocery store. She supposed she shouldn't be too discouraged by the bookstore owner not getting her name correct.

"Oh, Cheryl. I'm so sorry." She grimaced. "Can I blame it on pregnancy brain?" Marion patted her belly.

"It's not a problem, really." She attempted to keep her tone light. "And I actually came to talk to you about Gage."

The smile faded from Marion's face, and her eyebrows narrowed. "He didn't do anything wrong, did he? I mean, he told me he likes to watch the checkers game at the Swiss Miss, but I hope he's not a bother."

"He's not a bother, and I don't think...well, I really don't know...if he's done anything wrong. It's just some things are missing and..."

Marion's kind face transformed into a scowl, pausing Cheryl's words. She knew talking to Marion would be awkward, but she hadn't expected this.

"Do you think Gage could be involved with all these thefts around town?"

"Just because Gage is from the foster system doesn't mean he's a crook." Marion crossed her arms over her chest, resting them on her belly. "He's a victim, not a criminal. And we're trying to give him help when he needs it most." Her look of anger morphed into sadness, and the slightest sheen of tears lined the woman's lower eyelids. "When we went through the foster care training, we heard stories about communities that pointed their fingers at foster kids." She picked up a tissue from a Kleenex box on the counter and blew her nose. "I...I just never thought that it would come from Sugarcreek."

"I wasn't implying that Gage has done anything wrong." Cheryl raised her hands in defense. "I was just going to ask you if you've found anything...anything out of the ordinary among his things?"

Marion jutted out her chin. "He came with a small white garbage bag—all his possessions in the world. I know everything in that bag. He hasn't brought home one thing...not one thing."

Cheryl nodded and suddenly wished the floor would open up and swallow her whole. She knew foster kids were often given a bad rap. And that's the very reason why she wanted to talk to Marion first.

"You're right. I'm so sorry. I just wanted to check with you… I didn't want any rumors going around." Cheryl offered an apologetic smile, hoping it would be well received.

The woman eyed her, and her face softened. Perhaps she believed that Cheryl was just trying to get to the bottom of things.

"Rumors? No, we wouldn't want that." Then she lowered her head. Her shoulders softened, and she reached her hand across the counter, laying it on a stack of discount flyers, palm up. "I…I appreciate you coming to talk to me. And if I notice anything out of the ordinary concerning Gage, well, I'll let you know."

Cheryl reached up and placed her hand in the woman's. "I'd appreciate that. And for the record, I think what you're doing for Gage is a good thing." She squeezed Marion's hand.

The woman nodded, accepting the praise. "Ray and I never thought we'd have children. That's why we signed up and trained to do foster care." She released Cheryl's hand and patted it. "And thank you for stopping by."

Cheryl nodded and then backed away. She wasn't sure if it solved anything. All she knew was that Marion hadn't seen anything suspicious. Or at least she wasn't admitting it.

She considered giving Marion her cell phone number, but another customer approached the checkout counter before she could. Cheryl turned, feeling foolish for coming. She moved to the store's front door and then paused.

Something caught her eye. Something out of place. A small figurine lay in the corner between the wall and the door. Something familiar.

Cheryl bent down and picked up the small, carved Amish child. The wooden painted boy looked up at her with a whimsical face. It bore the maker's mark from the custom-made set in her store.

She glanced back over her shoulder. Cheryl considered going back and talking to Marion about what she found, but she knew it would do no good. Marion would probably get defensive again.

Cheryl supposed that anyone could have dropped the figurine, but it was more likely that someone did who was in the bookshop often.

She tucked the small carving into her coat pocket. It wasn't proof Gage had done anything wrong, but she would keep an eye on him. It was clear Marion would give him the benefit of the doubt.

Maybe she'd ask Agnes to keep an eye out too. They had to get to the bottom of these thefts before they disrupted their community even more than they already had.

CHAPTER SIX

A t the end of the long day, one where she wondered if each person who entered the Swiss Miss would try to take something extra with their purchase, Cheryl kicked off her black loafers just inside the front door of her house and paused as Beau approached. He wound around her legs then stopped, looked up at her, and meowed.

"I know, I know, I'm in the dog house." She bent down and scooped him up. "I didn't mean to leave you at home all day. It's just the way things worked out."

Little about this day had gone as she'd anticipated.

She walked into the kitchen, thankful to be out of the cold. So much had happened today, and little of it made sense.

First there had been the discovery of the stolen food and goods at the Miller farm.

Then the shocking news that someone had been sleeping in the Millers' winter buggy.

Add in the note that seemed to mention the checkers-playing brothers, and the day had been off to a strange and unsettling start.

These were not the types of situations that should happen in a quiet, settled community like Sugarcreek. Not once in any of her visits or many conversations with Aunt Mitzi had there even been a hint of events like those that cascaded through her day.

But the news hadn't stopped there.

Instead, with Agnes Winslow's visit to the Swiss Miss, Cheryl's concerns had exploded. The thefts were not only happening to other merchants—an unsettling event on its own accord—but now the thief had hit her shop. And nothing good had come out of her talk with Marion Berryhill at By His Grace bookstore, unless you counted the fact that Cheryl discovered one of the little Amish children on the floor. Maybe it had fallen out of one of Gage's pockets? She couldn't be certain, but the item had gotten there somehow. She tried to think back concerning other foster kids she'd known. Was theft a common problem? If so, it was an outward result of all the inner turmoil inside. She couldn't imagine having to face being removed from one's home, no matter the reason.

After Cheryl had returned to her store, she and Esther had gone about their jobs, yet each also kept an eye out for other missing goods. So far, only the little carved Amish children were missing. Cheryl prayed that nothing else would turn up as stolen. She placed Beau back on the floor, slipped off her mittens, tucked them into the jacket pocket, and hung her coat on the coat rack by the back door.

Cheryl hadn't heard from Naomi since she'd left her home that morning, and she hoped her friend was taking time to rest. She washed her hands and then opened a can of soup. She poured it into a pan and turned on the stovetop, wishing she'd kept a serving from the large batch of the chicken noodle soup she'd taken to

Naomi. She had all the ingredients to make more, but her mind was on other things. Did the thefts around town have any connection with what had been happening on the Miller farm?

Her stomach rumbled at the thought of how good her homemade soup had smelled—the onion, celery, and chicken simmering together. And the smile grew when she thought of Levi enjoying some. Being raised Amish, he no doubt had eaten tasty meals his whole life. But today he'd enjoyed something made by *her* hands. Hadn't he said it smelled good when she saw him this morning? Maybe this would prove that Englisch girls could cook too.

She stirred the canned soup slowly and considered calling Naomi to get advice about the thefts. She also wondered if Seth or Levi had discovered anything more about the person sleeping in the buggy. Even though the Amish didn't believe in having phones in their homes, because of their businesses the Millers had a phone shack and a phone near the road. Cheryl would often call it to put in orders of things she needed from Naomi. On a quiet night you could hear the phone ringing all the way to the house and barn. Would it be too much of an interruption to their peaceful evening if she left a message?

Cheryl opened the cupboard and took out a bowl. *I could call just to check on Naomi and tell her I'd love some advice, couldn't I?* And then she remembered Katie's Fudge. Surely Naomi would know where it had come from. That's yet another bit of information that she needed from her friend.

She picked up her cell phone, hit the speed dial, and then waited for the Millers' answering machine to pick up like it always did. The phone rang once and then twice. She waited for the third time so that she could leave a message, but then someone picked up.

"Hello?" It was Esther's voice.

"Hello, Esther."

"Uh...Cheryl?"

Esther sounded startled, and it almost made Cheryl laugh. Had Esther been waiting for a call from a young man? She was a beauty, so that wouldn't come as a surprise.

Cheryl cleared her throat playfully. "I suspect I wasn't the one you imagined was calling."

"No...I was expecting a call from someone else."

"I'm sorry to disappoint you. I wanted to ask your maam about something Aunt Mitzi used to carry in her store, but I bet you'd know. Do you happen to know where my aunt ordered the fudge—Katie's Fudge—from?"

"Katie's Fudge?" Esther sounded distant and confused, unlike the bright and cheerful girl who worked her store. "I am not sure. I can check the invoices from last year if you would like. When I come to work Monday, that is. I asked for tomorrow off a few days ago because I am going on a birthday outing—it is a friend's birthday—so I will not see you till Monday. Unless you are at the farm this weekend for anything. I will not be gone all weekend, just tomorrow, Friday." The words spilled from Esther's mouth, and Cheryl wondered what had gotten the young woman so rattled.

"Thanks for reminding me. I'd forgotten, but I hope you have fun. Maybe I'll drive out there Saturday afternoon after work to check on your maam and ask about the fudge. I'll let you go so you can wait for your other call." Though she'd kept her tone light and teasing, there was an unsettled pause.

"Ja. I came out to the phone because Leon was supposed to call and let me know what time he was picking me up in the morning…" Esther trailed off, and then Cheryl heard a small gasp.

"Esther, are you all right?"

"Ja. I mean, ne. I am not sure." Her voice was lower now. "I just saw someone. In the buggy shed."

"Someone? Like one of your brothers?"

"Ne. I wish it was." The young woman's voice got even quieter.

"Did you hear? Did your parents tell you about someone stealing from your house too? Could that be the person?" Cheryl hoped she wasn't spilling the beans. She didn't want to be the one to tell Esther. It wasn't her place.

"They did not, but Levi told me, and I am certain someone is out there," she whispered. "They have come back."

Cheryl's thoughts scrambled. Did Esther need help? "Can you see who it is? Is it someone you recognize?"

"No. Not at all. Smaller than Daed and Levi, but bigger than Maam."

"You should try to run back to the house."

"I do not know. I…"

The cat's meow interrupted Esther's words. Beau jumped onto the chair closest to Cheryl.

Esther continued saying something, but her words were lost in the persistent meowing of the cat. Cheryl pressed the phone tighter to her ear and waved the cat away. "I'm sorry. What did you say?"

Beau jumped down from the chair, stood by his bowl, and continued to meow to be fed. Cheryl tried to shush him again, but he refused to quiet. With quickened steps she moved to the bathroom and shut the door.

"Did you get a look at the person?" Cheryl asked. "Was it a guy or a girl?"

"It is too dark. I could not really see much. He, she...whoever it was, left the buggy shed and headed to the road. I think if I run now I can make it to the house before they see me."

"Call me tomorr—" Cheryl's words were cut off by the click of a phone. She set her cell phone on the counter and released her breath. Her hand shook. She leaned against the bathroom door for support. Her knees shook too.

Whoever slept in the winter buggy last night must be back. Naomi seemed concerned the person was homeless or in need, but what if this invader was setting the family up for trouble? Had Esther made it back to the house?

CHAPTER SEVEN

Cheryl exited the bathroom and paced the kitchen. She considered calling Esther back or driving out to the farm, but she could already picture Naomi's serene face and gentle words. "We are fine, Cheryl. I am more concerned about whoever is trying to find warmth and shelter than I am about danger…"

Still, what if Esther hadn't made it back to the house? Then Cheryl would never forgive herself for not checking.

Beau continued his meowing, and Cheryl quickly fed him. A minute later, she gave in to her concerns and tried calling back. This time no one answered the phone.

Worry niggled at her mind. Could she sleep if she didn't know Esther was fine?

No. How long would it take for Esther's family to realize she might be in trouble? It would only take Cheryl a few minutes to drive out to the farm. Then she could rest easily knowing the young woman was okay. She might feel a little foolish, but better that than a mind filled with worries all night.

Cheryl turned off the soup and grabbed her purse and keys. A few minutes later she retraced her morning trip to the farm. The dark evening sky changed the tone of the scenery from the peacefulness of the morning to a more ominous tone. As she reached the

Millers' driveway, she eased off the main road and drove slowly toward the house. Her headlights swept the dirt and gravel area, but she didn't see Esther.

When she parked, someone opened the door to the house, standing silhouetted in the light. The size told her it was one of the men rather than Naomi or Esther.

"Cheryl?" Levi's voice reached her as she stood from her car. "Are you all right?"

"Yes. Is Esther here?"

He stepped out of the house, closing the door behind him. Then with hurried steps Levi walked toward her. His face was shadowed, but the strength of his frame was hard to hide. "Of course Esther is here. She is inside. She is already gone to bed. Where else would she be?"

Suddenly Cheryl's fears for Esther felt very silly. She looked up at him, hoping Levi would find her concern humorous rather than foolish.

"I was concerned because I called earlier, and Esther answered. But then she saw someone—out by the buggy shed. I called back, and no one picked up the second time. I wanted to check—to be sure she was okay."

He studied her a moment, and from behind him Cheryl noticed movement. Naomi stepped into the doorway behind Levi. The light from their kerosene lanterns lit her silhouette in a warm, yellow glow. If Cheryl knew how to paint, this would make a lovely scene. She just wished the tension tightening her gut would let her enjoy the quietness of the moment with her friends.

"Do not keep our friend in the yard, Levi. It is a cold night. Won't you come in?"

"I didn't mean to interrupt," Cheryl called back. She took a step back toward her car, unsure she wanted to raise her concerns again. Esther was safe, and that's what mattered.

"Is something wrong?" Naomi called, her voice scratchy. She stepped on to the front porch. "Do I need to come out there?"

Levi looked back over his shoulder. "Ne, Maam. Go back inside. It is just a miscommunication, that is all."

"Come inside, Naomi." Seth's voice filtered through the night. "You need to rest. You have been fretting all day. Everything is fine. If you stay out there, you are going to catch a chill and make things worse."

Naomi reluctantly stepped back into the house and shut the door.

Cheryl's chin trembled from the cold and worry. "Is Naomi okay? Does she need to see a doctor?"

"She *would* be fine if people did not work her up so. So would Esther for that matter." Levi looked down his nose at Cheryl. "I hear you got my sister all worked up with gibberish about a thief."

"I got her worked up?" Cheryl's voice rose an octave. "And weren't you the one who told her about the intruder? Don't tell me you're not concerned, Levi. You're the one who found the things missing from your cellar. The one who got hurt."

Cheryl crossed her arms over her chest, ignoring the cold chill that moved down her spine. The chill was partly from the cold night air, but partly from the intense look in Levi's gaze.

"I wasn't the one who told Esther about the thefts in town." Cheryl jutted out her chin. "Agnes—from the quilt shop—told us both about all the things missing around town. You're talking like I made the whole thing up. Like it's my imagination or something."

Levi crossed his arms over his chest. Cheryl wondered if he was mimicking her stance on purpose.

"You did not say one word?" he asked.

"Of course I commented, and of course I'll do all I can to find whoever's stealing from Sugarcreek's businesses. We can't have someone like that on the loose. Do you know how much revenue is being lost? More than that, everyone is on edge. We aren't going to have a happy Thanksgiving or a very merry Christmas if this continues. I even heard one business put in a security camera. Can you imagine that? Here in the quaint Swiss town of Sugarcreek? What's next, security guards around Dutch Creek Foods or an electric fence around the cuckoo clock so people can't get too close?"

Levi clucked his tongue and shook his head. "Listen to you now. See how you do things? I hope you have not shared those notions with my sister or Maam. Between your talk about the thief in town and Maam concerned about whoever is sleeping in the buggy shed, Esther has been upended all night. 'Nervous wreck,' I think is how you Englisch say it."

Another shiver ran down Cheryl's spine, and she wondered why she'd had such warm thoughts about Levi all afternoon. He certainly wasn't acting like the Levi she thought she knew. It was obvious he didn't feel the same about her. His cold stare now made that painfully clear.

"So you aren't concerned?" Cheryl asked.

He sighed. "After sitting Esther down and talking to her, she is not really certain she saw anyone. Well, other than me when I went to check once more—at Maam's insistence. She does not want the stranger out in the cold."

"So Esther's all right? And there's no one in the buggy shed?" She kicked her shoe against the gravel, wishing for a way to redeem herself but coming up empty-handed. Maybe Levi was right. Maybe her concerns only made things worse. Still, she'd seen things this sheltered family hadn't. She knew what could happen. All one had to do was open the newspaper or a search engine to see headlines of tragedies inflicted on families just like this one.

"I checked the buggy, and no one was there. Perhaps someone came back and then left—but I doubt it. If they did, they did not leave anything new behind. Anyway, Esther probably saw shadows."

A dog barked in the distance from behind the barn. It sounded like Rover. He also sounded as if he was trying to get someone's attention.

Cheryl tilted her head that direction. She opened her mouth, about to tell Levi that maybe he should go check out whatever the dog had found, but he held up his hand, halting her words.

"Do not bring your big-city fears to Sugarcreek, Cheryl." Levi swept his hand toward her car. "We are a peaceful people and town. We are even more so on our farms and in our homes."

"You are peaceful, yes, I know. But what about outside forces that you can't control? You can still say that even when someone has stolen from you and stayed in your buggy?" She placed a hand on her car knowing she should leave. It was no use arguing with this stubborn man. Why did she waste her time? His current cocky attitude and the smirk on his shadowed face infuriated her. And in a strange way it made her glad she'd come. Even though he would never admit it, maybe she was giving Levi Miller a few things to think about. Maybe it would make him keep an eye on things with more diligence. It's not like Amish farms were immune from thieves and vagrants. If anything, the abundance of stored food and easy-to-access outer buildings made Amish farms more of a target.

The sound of footsteps crunching on gravel sounded from behind Levi, and they both turned. A bundled form approached, and Cheryl knew she wasn't going to win any points from Levi.

Naomi joined them with a sniffle. "Levi, did you hear Rover? He is making quite the fuss."

"Sorry, Maam. Do not worry about it. I will check out the barking…and the buggy. But please go inside where it is warm."

"Ja. Just give me a moment." She reached out and took Cheryl's hand, compassion in her gaze.

Levi shook his head again and then stomped toward the buggy shed without a backward glance. He wasn't going to argue with his mother, but he made it clear that he didn't approve.

"Are you all right, Cheryl?" Worry laced Naomi's voice. While she might be concerned, Cheryl didn't feel up to a repeat lecture, albeit gentler, from Naomi.

"I had a question about Esther, but Levi answered it. Also, are you feeling better?"

"A bit." Kind eyes searched Cheryl's face in the glow of kitchen lights. "Esther mentioned she thought she saw someone in the yard. I wish whoever it was would just come to the house. Don't they know we would gladly help?" Before Cheryl could interject, Naomi continued. "Were you able to deliver the meal to the Berryhills?"

"Yes." She nodded, deciding not to mention her conversation with Marion about Gage. "Marion was very appreciative. I know she'd like to thank you herself."

"Goot. So glad..." The woman's voice trailed off as the dog's barks increased.

Cheryl tilted her head and turned toward the barn, curious about the barking. The dog continued to bark even though Levi had headed out to check on things. Cheryl couldn't help but wonder what had gotten Rover so worked up.

"Must be a coon," Naomi mumbled under her breath. Then she turned slightly as if she too considered shushing the dog.

Cheryl placed a hand on Naomi's arm. She guessed the last thing Levi wanted was his sick maam to follow him, traipsing around the cold night. "Levi's right. You should get inside. You're shivering." Cheryl increased her grip on Naomi's arm, trying to get her attention and unwilling to let Naomi's curiosity get the best of her.

"Ja, I suppose I will never hear the end of it if I do not." Naomi offered a weak smile and then another cough escaped. Catching her breath, she glanced up at Cheryl. "If you do not need me then I will get back inside, but I will try to make it to the store to help out next week. I know things will be busy." Naomi patted Cheryl's hand on her arm.

"Only if you're feeling well, promise?"

Naomi dabbed her nose with a handkerchief and then nodded. "Of course. But I also know you will need help."

"Yes, business is picking up with Thanksgiving so close."

"Not only with the store, but with solving the mystery too." Even in the dim light of the moon and the porch light, Cheryl could see a twinkle in the older woman's eyes.

"I'd like that very much." Cheryl had a hard time holding back a chuckle. Levi may think she was the one bringing her big-city fears to the farm, but he'd be surprised to know that his stepmother had such thoughts of her own. Naomi loved a mystery, and it looked like the Amish woman was determined to do her part of figuring out how to solve this one. No matter what anyone thought.

CHAPTER EIGHT

Back home that evening, Cheryl reheated dinner, ate it in silence, and then started a load of laundry. A heaviness hung around her shoulders—an invisible weight. More than once as she sorted clothes, tears crept into the corners of her eyes, but she quickly brushed them away. She wouldn't cry.

I was just trying to help...and if Levi Miller wants to let his family be put in harm's way, then he'll have to pay the consequences. The angry thought flashed through her mind, but it didn't help her to feel better. She didn't want to see Naomi, Esther, Eli, or anyone else in the Miller family hurt.

She wished Levi could see her heart—and that he'd stop being so stubborn. Cheryl let out a heavy sigh. She'd continue to try to find the answers in her own way, even if it had to be from afar. No matter what Levi thought. Her friends deserved nothing less from her.

Cheryl tossed the first load into the washer, and as soon as she shut the lid to the machine Beau jumped to the top of the washing machine. He curled up in a ball as if assigning himself to protect the clothes she'd just dropped in. Either that or preparing to take a nap with the tremors of the machine to lull him to sleep.

"You appreciate me, don't you, Beau?" She ran her hand down his back, all the way to the tip of his tail. It was amazing how the silly cat lightened the heaviness inside. She reached to turn on the machine. "I'm so glad that you didn't mind moving to Sugarcreek. Aunt Mitzi's place would seem so quiet..." *Aunt Mitzi.*

She pulled her hand back from the Start button as if it were going to sting her. She'd nearly forgotten the work apron inside the washing machine. Cheryl picked up Beau and plopped him to the floor. Then she fished out the letter and released a breath. *That was close.*

Apparently offended he'd been tossed off the washer, Beau jumped back up as soon as she closed the lid. She thought about writing Aunt Mitzi back, but what could she tell her? Things were going well except for the thefts all over town. And everyone was doing well except for Naomi's illness. And, oh yes, there was the person sneaking around the Miller farm who might bring harm to the family. And that Levi nearly kicked her off the farm when she was just trying to help.

No, a letter like that wouldn't help her aunt with her own struggles.

Cheryl started the washing machine, picked up the letter, and then moved to the living room.

She sank down onto the floral sofa, wishing Aunt Mitzi were around to give her advice. What would her aunt do? Would she insist Naomi use common sense when it came to the stranger? Would her aunt urge Cheryl to call Chief Twitchell herself concerning all the thefts around the businesses of Sugarcreek, instead of depending on Agnes Winslow to do it?

She blew out a heavy breath. Would Mitzi think the person sleeping in the buggy was dangerous? Cheryl couldn't shake off the feeling that Rover had been barking at *someone* not *something* when she'd been out at the Miller farm.

She smiled. Then again, Aunt Mitzi would most likely worry about the person's soul. She'd pitch a tent in the buggy shed with a kerosene lantern and stay there until the person could hear about Jesus. Aunt Mitzi's faith had always been inspiring.

Cheryl thought of the scripture Aunt Mitzi had written in her letter. Something about God's protection—words Cheryl needed to hear. Cheryl opened the envelope and found the scripture again:

If you make the Most High your dwelling—
even the Lord, who is my refuge—
then no harm will befall you,
no disaster will come near your tent.
For he will command his angels concerning you
to guard you in all your ways. *Psalm 91:9–11 (NIV)*

How did her aunt know she'd need those words? She repeated them in a whisper and then said them as a prayer. Even though she didn't know who the thief was, God did, and Cheryl had to trust that justice would be done eventually. She just hoped a lot more losses didn't happen before then. And she hoped that she wouldn't alienate Levi completely if she continued to keep her eyes and ears open and try to figure out who the intruder was, and if they were connected with the thefts on Main Street.

Her thoughts calmed further. Even if a stranger were lurking around the Miller farm, God's angels were there, protecting them. Yet that also didn't mean they should leave themselves open to unsafe situations. She'd have to remind Naomi of that.

After getting ready for bed, she sat down with her pen and writing paper. Beau, like always, curled up at her side. Cheryl leaned against a pillow on her headboard and used a book as a table on her lap.

Dear Aunt Mitzi,

I was so thankful to receive your letter. It's hard to believe that it's almost summer in Papua New Guinea. As the days are warming up for you, they are getting colder here. Some are predicting more snow by Thanksgiving.

I have to admit that your last letter made me nervous. I'm thankful that you opened up to me about your struggles, but I'm a little bit worried about you, even though I know that wasn't your intention. Will you be leaving the rural areas soon? I like the idea of you getting a bath and sleeping in a real bed.

Your letter made me remember how much I take for granted. The fact that I was able to shower tonight and turn up my electric blanket made me thankful. (Oh, and Beau who is curled by my side is thankful for the electric blanket too.)

I wish I could say that everything was perfect around here. There have been some thefts at the shops around Sugarcreek, but I'm sure the matter will soon be resolved. Naomi has also been ill, and so I took her some of Mom's chicken noodle soup. Were you or Grandma the one who gave my mom the recipe?

I reread your letter, especially the part about many of the natives claiming to believe in Jesus but keeping their old ways. It seems to me that most people aren't so different. It's easier to keep our traditions than it is to trust God. It's easier to stick to our familiar ways than try to put our faith in something new.

I'm thinking about this as I consider all the changes for me this year. I'll be missing the Columbus Turkey Trot for the first time in many years. And the Grand Illumination downtown. Remember when you came to see the lights a few years ago? It's not that I miss Columbus—not much anyway. It's just hard to break out of the traditions of things.

Of course those traditions matter little compared to the new friends that I've found here in Sugarcreek, especially the Miller family. Naomi and Esther are gifts to me. But you knew they would be, didn't you?

Sleepiness overcame her, and Cheryl put down the notebook and pen, deciding to finish the letter tomorrow. She yawned. She wanted to mention Levi too. He was becoming special to her in a way that she couldn't understand. In a way that she didn't want to admit to anyone, not even Aunt Mitzi.

While Levi was becoming special, tonight he had been harsh. Accusing her of bringing her big-city fears to Sugarcreek. She sighed as she shifted on the bed, tucking the pillow under her cheek. Maybe it was because she was from the big city and she did have different ideas.

How well did she know the Millers? How well did she know anyone in town?

Yes, Naomi and Esther were gifts, but maybe they weren't as good of friends as she liked to pretend. How well could you really know someone in just a few months?

Cheryl turned off the light and listened as the train blared its horn just outside of town. It was a lonely sound, yet it seemed familiar. It seemed like...home.

She couldn't imagine returning to Columbus. She didn't want to.

And that's why it was so important that she urge Naomi to contact the police soon. Somebody was threatening the peace of Sugarcreek, and she and Naomi needed to work together to figure out who. Could it be Gage or the mystery person on the farm? Or what about that young woman who had been lurking around the store today? She certainly seemed suspicious.

No one would truly have a peaceful holiday season until they figured out who was taking what didn't belong to them—merchandise from Main Street, a bed in a buggy, and the peace of the residents in town.

CHAPTER NINE

Friday and Saturday passed by in a blur. Cheryl had little time to think about the thefts—or the person sneaking around the Millers' farm. The Swiss Miss was busy with shipments arriving with Christmas merchandise. Customers filtered in and out, and Cheryl didn't get a chance to get off her feet either day.

On Sunday, she'd attended the Silo Church and went home to catch up on laundry and housework. She thought about driving out to the Millers' farm to check on Naomi, but she didn't want Levi to think she was nosing around. Instead, she fell asleep watching a prerecorded Hallmark movie and awoke to Beau climbing over her head—which had slipped down onto the chair's wooden armrest.

On Monday morning when Esther arrived for work earlier than expected, Cheryl couldn't have been happier to see the young Amish woman. She wasn't sure she'd make it through another day without Esther's help.

If there hadn't been customers in the store, Cheryl might have hugged her. "Did you have a good weekend? A nice birthday celebration?" She didn't mention how busy she was, but she guessed Esther could see from the weariness on her face. As Cheryl's mirror had related this morning, the bags under her eyes and the thin wrinkles on her brow were hard to hide.

"It was fine. We stayed the night in Berlin with a cousin."

Cheryl didn't prod, but she could see disappointment in Esther's face. It must be hard to be in rumspringa and not so interested in becoming wild like her friends.

"Lydia came too, and we mostly hung out together." Esther scooted closer to Cheryl's side. "We had fun coming up with stories of who is sleeping in our buggy," she whispered. "Our favorite was a secret-service man trying to protect our town from uncertain doom."

Cheryl chuckled and then placed her hands on her hips. "Yes, well, you can tell your brother Levi that I'm not the one putting all those big-city notions in your head. I have a feeling you've been either reading some interesting novels or watching too many conspiracy shows on a friend's television."

Esther nodded and smiled and then stepped forward to help a customer decide between two table runners. The smile told Cheryl the truth was Esther's own, and she wouldn't divulge any information.

The tour bus arrived on time, bringing women and couples eager to buy. As she rang up the purchases, Cheryl did her best to remember what items were chosen. First, so she could restock. Second, it helped her peace of mind knowing the numerous items were actual purchases and they hadn't found their way into a thief's pocket.

Nearby, Esther fussed with an arrangement of Christmas tree bulbs. She'd gotten Levi to cut a few pine branches and mount them on wooden stands so they looked like miniature trees. For the last hour, the young woman had added glass bulbs to the branches. Cheryl had liked the idea of decorating with a few Christmas decorations here and there over the last few weeks since some customers liked to shop early. Esther had a creative streak to her that Cheryl knew her Amish upbringing didn't always appreciate.

Toward lunchtime, Cheryl noticed a young woman hovering near two middle-aged women who were busily shopping. Cheryl helped Esther wrap up a large purchase, and then she watched as the young blonde moved from the cheese to the candles then shadowed the women to the jellies. The blonde didn't approach the other two women, but stayed a few steps back.

She seemed to be listening to the women intently. Then, without them noticing, she looked at her phone and typed in a text with her thumbs. The chatting women moved toward a display of Thanksgiving platters, and the young woman followed closely behind. The women moved on and continued to talk as they chose a few Amish dolls, oblivious to the fact they were being followed.

Cheryl leaned close to Esther. "I'm going to see if she needs help."

Esther patted her kapp. "Goot idea."

Cheryl approached the young woman, whose long, straight blonde hair was braided with a hot pink hair tie. Her braid hung over her shoulder, and her head was topped with a pink stocking cap. She wore jeans, a pea-green army jacket, and hiking boots. Her backpack was also pink, as was the cell phone she held in her right hand.

"Can I help you?"

The young woman, who looked to be no older than twenty, jumped and glanced up. Then she paused and looked around, as if she had just realized where she was.

"Oh no, I'm uh…" She picked up a peppermint candle, sniffed it, and then looked around again. The two women she'd followed moved over to the display of Amish wall hangings, and the young woman seemed confused. She sniffed the candle again then looked at it. Finally, she glanced up at Cheryl sheepishly.

Her cheeks turned pink, and she set down the candle. "The truth is I wanted to hear the rest of their story."

"Their story?"

"I was behind them on the sidewalk when I heard them talking." The woman pointed discretely. "The one in the purple jacket said her father is a World War Two veteran. He was flying to Arizona recently, and someone gave her father his first-class seat. She was telling the other woman they later found the kind stranger." The young woman's gaze met Cheryl's. "I shouldn't have eavesdropped, but I wanted to hear how it ended. I wanted to hear how they found the kind stranger. I, well, I just love stories like that."

Cheryl eyed the young woman. It seemed she was telling the truth, but that didn't explain her texting.

As if reading her thoughts, a buzz sounded from the young woman's pocket, and she pulled her cell phone out, glancing down at it. She smiled.

"It's a text from my grandpa." She held up the phone for Cheryl to see. "He's a former Marine, and I haven't texted him in a few days. I'm here on a, uh, work trip." She paused. "He wanted me to keep him up-to-date on how I'm doing. He worries about me." She smiled.

"A work trip? Oh, really? What type of work do you do?"

"Journalism." The word shot out of the woman's mouth, and then she quickly smiled as if hoping Cheryl would believe her.

"Do you write for a paper in state or out of state?" Cheryl asked.

"Oh, I write for a small publisher, I mean paper. You probably wouldn't know it."

"Does it have a name?"

The blonde looked up at the ceiling, as if trying to come up with a name. "Oh, the *Little Rock Times*, sort of like the *LA Times*, but in Little Rock. That's where my grandpa lives—the grandfather who always wants me to check in. It doesn't seem to matter how old I get, he still sees me as a little girl with pigtails."

Cheryl nodded, even though she was pretty certain there was no *Little Rock Times*.

The young woman tucked the cell phone back in her pocket. The motion interrupted Cheryl's thoughts. "The woman's story reminded me to tell my grandpa I was all right and thank him for his service." She smiled. "I'm going to surprise him by making it home to visit in a couple of weeks—right after Thanksgiving—but I didn't text that." Her smile was impish.

"That's kind of you, texting your grandpa," Cheryl finally said, even though she could clearly tell that the blonde was hiding something. "And thanks for explaining. All the storeowners have been on edge lately." Cheryl stopped short, catching herself from explaining the thefts.

"Oh, the holidays. It gets so busy." The young woman cast one last look at the two women then turned and moved to the door, opening it. A brisk breeze blew inside. "Thanks so much for listening."

Seconds later the woman walked down the sidewalk and out of sight, and if it wasn't for the jingle bell on the door that softly chimed, Cheryl would have wondered if she'd really just had a conversation with the young woman. Should she have learned her name?

Cheryl moved to her office and typed her password into her computer. She typed in *Little Rock Times*.

There was an *Arkansas Times* and the *Times of North Little Rock*, but no *Little Rock Times*. Surely a reporter wouldn't get the name of the publication she wrote for wrong.

Cheryl returned to the front counter and noticed the same curious look on Esther's face. The stranger had answered all her questions—and at least one of her answers was a lie. There was also a mysterious quality about her Cheryl couldn't put her finger on. Had the young woman also lied about why she'd followed the women? And were her texts as innocent as she made them seem?

Or maybe she had a partner on the other side of that phone...someone she stayed connected with as they found the weakest stores to hit.

CHAPTER TEN

Naomi's smiling face greeted Cheryl when she arrived at the shop on Tuesday. Esther was already behind the counter, sifting through a few more boxes of Aunt Mitzi's Christmas decorations, and Naomi had donned an apron too. She was rearranging small white boxes on a front table.

"Naomi!" Cheryl set down Beau and then gave her friend a quick hug. "It looks like you're feeling better, but you shouldn't overdo it."

Naomi chuckled. "Overdo? I am setting up fudge, that is all. I know what a busy time of year this is for the Swiss Miss. I always come help Mitzi. I guessed you could use some help too."

"The fudge?" Cheryl's mouth dropped open. "I've been wondering."

"I know, Esther told me. I should have mentioned it before. Mitzi has a standing order from Heini's Cheese Chalet in Berlin—fifteen minutes down the road. An Amish lady there, Katie, makes it all. Seth claims it is almost as good as mine." Naomi winked. "But I would never keep up with holiday demand, so Mitzi orders it in. We are the only place in Sugarcreek that carries Katie's Buttercream Fudge. We will get a delivery now and another large shipment in December." Naomi laughed. "It brings business too. Mitzi loved it because customers pick up other gifts while they are in the store."

"That's wonderful, and I know a young man I owe a call. His wife is expecting a baby and some fudge."

Naomi chuckled as Cheryl picked up a box. A memory filtered in—a time when Aunt Mitzi had taken her to Heini's when she was just a small girl. She remembered the fun she had tasting all the cheese samples, but she didn't remember fudge.

Cheryl picked up a second box of chocolate fudge and tucked it under her arm. "I better try this out." She grinned. "I can't sell what I'm not familiar with, right?" Then she brushed her hair back from her face for dramatic effect.

Naomi laughed and finished her display. Cheryl was about to ask Naomi if they ever discovered who'd slept in the buggy—and if they'd come back after Esther's scare—but the morning bus from Annie's Amish Tours arrived, and the store soon overflowed with customers.

Forty-five minutes later, after the last tourist exited, Cheryl was certain she knew why Aunt Mitzi had asked Naomi to come in as often as she could around the holidays. The tourists from the tour bus had always been good customers, but today they'd bought double the normal amount. They were in the buying spirit, and not one of them could say no to Naomi when she showed them additional items she thought they would like.

It wasn't even noon yet, and Cheryl's feet were already sore. She combed her fingers through her short hair as she sat on the stool behind the counter. She'd do well if she could keep the store stocked during the holidays—and that was only if there weren't more thefts. She hadn't heard from the police or Agnes, and she wondered why. Then again, she hadn't seen Gage around either. He'd most likely started school, which made her even more certain he'd been the thief—no matter what Marion thought.

"So did you discover who was sleeping in the buggy?" Cheryl asked as she sniffed the Snickerdoodle candle displayed by the cash register.

"No, we still do not know." Naomi's voice held a hint of concern. "Whoever it was returned last night." Naomi sighed. "I do worry if he or she is warm enough."

The candle nearly slipped through Cheryl's fingers. "He came back? Or she…she is *still* sleeping there?" Her throat tightened, and she glanced to Esther. The young woman's cheeks had lost their color, but she refused to meet her mother's gaze. "And you're letting them? Or him or her…or whoever it is?"

Naomi paused and turned. "We are not really happy about it, but what can we do? I left a note telling whoever it was to come to the house. We would be happy to offer a meal, maybe a bed."

Cheryl's mouth gaped open. "You left a note?"

"Ja, what would you do?"

"Um, put a lock on the door to the buggy shed. Or confront him." Cheryl pursed her lips. "Hasn't Seth or Levi tried staying up to see if they could find the person?"

Naomi offered a humorous smile. "Oh, if you knew them better you would not have asked that. They are early to bed and early to rise. Even a tornado could not stir them. It would be a big feat if Levi managed to stay up. But I am really not too worried. It seems that whoever is there wants a place to sleep and something to fill his or her stomach occasionally." She smiled. "They even left a ten-dollar bill on a shelf by the peaches. They surely would not harm us if they were thoughtful enough to do that."

"But you don't know for certain. It's not safe having a stranger hanging about your place with your children there." Cheryl fixed her eyes on Esther. "Do you feel safe?"

Esther lowered her gaze and then looked away. "Whoever it is comes in after dark and leaves before dawn. Levi says he will try tonight to stay up and talk to the person." Esther shrugged. "I just make sure not to head to the phone shack too late…"

The front shop door opened and three school-aged girls entered, interrupting the conversation. Cheryl blew out a frustrated breath, and then she turned to them with a smile. "How can I help you?"

"We're having a silent auction for our Girl Scout troop. Would you donate some items?"

Cheryl felt Naomi's gaze on her and knew her friend expected her to be generous, but it was the third cause who'd asked in the last week. The first was a framed print for an auction at the food bank. The second was Amish dolls for the Haiti Christian Union Missions fund-raiser. And, of course, she couldn't say no to a donation for the Ohio Crippled Children's Fund. It seemed everyone wanted to finish the year strong with donations.

"Uh, sure." Cheryl moved to the shelf with jams and jellies. "How about two jars of strawberry jam?"

The girls nodded excitedly.

"Make that four jars!" Naomi called from where she reorganized the quilts. "Levi is coming into town tomorrow. I will make sure he replenishes your stock—the two extra jars are a gift from us."

A few minutes later the girls exited with their bounty, and Cheryl made the note in her ledger. Naomi's gesture was kind, but would it set a precedent? How many more nonprofits would ask before the holiday season was over?

In addition to those who'd come in her shop, there was still a stack of donation request letters from other local organizations waiting for her response. Each letter was addressed to Aunt Mitzi and mentioned her generous past donations. That was yet another thing she wished her aunt had done a better job explaining before she'd left. Setting up and staffing the store was one thing, but there were so many other details that were hard to keep track of.

It also bothered her that the letters were still addressed to her aunt. It was a small town. Most people knew Aunt Mitzi was traipsing through the jungle on the other side of the world. Even though Cheryl was pouring everything into the store, did they still consider her just "filling in"? Would they ever accept her like they did her aunt?

The brightness she felt when she first arrived and saw Naomi's smile faded, and the cheerful music she heard playing from the shop's CD player now grated at her nerves. While she appreciated Naomi's help, it bothered her the Millers brushed off her concerns. How could she make them understand that allowing some unknown person to sleep in your winter buggy wasn't safe?

Cheryl excused herself and made her way to the office. At the top of her messy desk was the stack of donation requests. Cheryl drew a huge breath and let her cheeks puff out. She had nearly made up her mind to refold all of them and tuck them into the desk drawer when Esther sauntered in.

"I have the mail here. Looks like you have another letter from your aunt Mitzi. Maam is hoping she has one waiting at home too."

Cheryl took the mail from the young woman's hand. "Thank you."

Esther turned and then paused. "Oh, and Maam and I are running next door to get sandwiches from the Honey Bee, do you want us to get you a chicken salad sandwich?"

Cheryl forced a smile. "No, that was Aunt Mitzi's favorite. I'll take a club sandwich." Cheryl reached for her purse.

"No worries." Esther waved her hand. "You can pay when we return."

"Thanks. Are there any customers up front?"

"Ne. And I locked the door and put up the Be Back in Fifteen Minutes sign. Something tells me you need a few minutes—the busyness of the season wears on me too."

Cheryl studied the young woman's face, and she wondered how someone so young could be so insightful. "Thank you."

Esther hurried out, and Cheryl took the letter with the airmail markings from the stack. Two letters in less than a week. This couldn't be a good sign. Cheryl ripped open the envelope, almost afraid to read Mitzi's words.

My Dearest One,

I received your letter that you wrote back at the beginning of October. It came just yesterday. Our letters must have crossed in the mail, and I wonder how many you sent. It takes a while for mail to get to me out in these rural areas, as you can imagine, but your description of the changing fall colors was delightful. You're right that the drive out to the Miller farm is as pretty as any you'll find on the planet. And your description of Naomi's pumpkin pies cooling on the counter caused my mouth to water. I guarantee if I had access to a jet plane I'd put up with the two-day journey to get home just to taste one of those pies.

I'd been planning my trip to Papua New Guinea for so long—and praying about it—that I never expected I'd get homesick the way I have. It's not just the changing fall leaves or the pumpkin pie that I'm longing for, but all of it. All of Sugarcreek. It makes me realize that no destination— no matter how much it is anticipated—can take the place of home. I wonder if you've ever felt the same?

The days are getting hotter here, and I've never seen so many insects. Everyone laughs, even so I can't help but check my hair numerous times a day for a hitchhiker— and half the time I find one.

I have to force myself to not let my mind wander back to Ohio so much and instead just enjoy the fruits of my work here—both sweet and sour. In a way these mixed emotions help me to relate to many of the tribespeople who I'm working with. I can't remember if I told you, but around eight hundred languages are spoken in Papua New Guinea, and this isolates many of the tribes. There is lots of poverty, and it's hard for young people to go to school or find decent work. So whenever I start having a pity party about missing home, I compare my challenges with theirs. My challenges of missing all that's familiar pales with what the people experience here, such as the wife who is divorced and turned out of the village because she is unable to conceive a child. Or an eighteen-year-old forced to provide for five siblings after a mother's death.

I don't know why I'm writing all this except to say your letter made me dream about Sugarcreek. Mostly good dreams, of course! The good news is my longing for home makes me trust in God more—which is exactly where a missionary should be.

Oh, and don't forget to find someone to fix the awning out front. It's sagging from the heavy snowfall last year, and I'm afraid the first snow will bring it down. (Hopefully not on a customer's head!)

Write to me and tell me how everything is and how you are. Missing Columbus?

Love,

Aunt Mitzi

Cheryl folded the letter, and a strange uneasiness settled upon her. For the first months she'd been away, Aunt Mitzi's letters had been filled with excitement, adventure, and spiritual truth. She'd encouraged Cheryl. Mitzi's letters had been a bright spot. But Aunt Mitzi's notes had changed. And it made her wonder if Aunt Mitzi's plans to stay in Papua New Guinea had changed too?

Worries flashed in Cheryl's mind like warning signals, and the emotional drain of the busy week and the numerous questions about the thefts mixed with new worries about Aunt Mitzi. Maybe her aunt was discovering after all that she was too old for the mission field. Could that be possible?

What if she wanted to return to Sugarcreek? The community would welcome her with open arms—Cheryl had no doubt. And then what? Cheryl pressed a hand to her forehead. What would she do? Where would she go?

She couldn't share a house with her aunt. She would no longer be needed at the Swiss Miss. And she couldn't return to Columbus. She'd successfully dismantled her life there. Maybe too well.

Cheryl placed the letter on the stack of papers in front of her and then folded her hands and placed them on top. She heard the sound of the front door bell's jingle followed by Naomi's and Esther's laughter. Cheryl rose, crossed the small office, and closed the door, needing just a few more minutes.

"Oh, Aunt Mitzi...what am I going to do if you return and I don't have a place to go?"

Looking around the office, she studied the calendar still pinned to October and the stack of bills she needed to pay. But other things drew her attention.

On a bulletin board above the file cabinet, Aunt Mitzi had pinned her favorite things. There were a few quotes, but there was something else too. There were family photos from when Cheryl and her brother Matt were young. Her favorite was one when Matt was just four or five years old. He had a big gap-toothed smile with a new front tooth coming in. Cheryl was a little older, and her hair was in two pigtails. Her bangs were too long and brushed her lashes. If she remembered right, her mother had taken her to the salon the day after the photo for a trim.

There was also Cheryl's college graduation photo. Aunt Mitzi stood by her side, smiling even broader than she was, as if she'd earned the degree. What an encouragement her aunt had been all those years—sending care packages to college, driving hours and hours to take photos at homecoming, always being available to talk on the phone.

And Aunt Mitzi hadn't cut back on her love after Cheryl graduated. In fact, allowing Cheryl to take over the Swiss Miss—trusting her—was her aunt's biggest encouragement yet. Aunt Mitzi believed she could do it. And Cheryl knew what that meant, despite the challenges.

First, she couldn't disappoint her aunt. She had to do her best to care for the store and the community as Mitzi would, for whatever amount of time Cheryl was needed here. It also meant that Cheryl needed to give Mitzi what she'd received—encouragement and support, even from far away. Aunt Mitzi sounded like she doubted herself and her choice, and Cheryl needed to let her aunt know she believed in her dream.

A soft knock sounded on the office door. "Cheryl, I have your sandwich." It was Naomi's voice.

Cheryl stood, tucking the chair back under the desk, appreciative that her aunt trusted her with her friends too. She wouldn't let Mitzi down. Instead, she'd help figure out who was sleeping in that buggy shed, even if the Millers weren't concerned. There were more than broken jars of preserves at stake.

CHAPTER ELEVEN

Cheryl's thoughts tumbled around as she returned to her work. Naomi was manning the counter, and it looked as if Esther was out running an errand. Cheryl wondered where to start first. There were always shelves to be straightened, merchandise to be returned to its correct spot, and new inventory to be ordered. She'd thought her energy would be focused on ordering more of the right items to sell during the important Christmas season. Instead, her attention kept returning to the missing merchandise. With each pass down an aisle, she wondered if she'd notice something else missing…something other than the carved children.

Her hand traveled to her apron pocket, and she felt Aunt Mitzi's second letter, now resting there.

The shop door opened, and a customer came in. Right behind her was Agnes.

Agnes approached. She paused and then pulled the sheet of paper from her purse. "Cheryl, I came to talk to you. I need to know about the person you suspected. Look at this." Agnes stretched out the page. "It's growing. I had to take a second sheet to Officer Ortega."

"There have been more thefts?"

The last customer left, and Cheryl waved Naomi closer.

"Yes, in the last few days a number of store owners have found more items missing. This can't go on. I need you to tell me who you suspect."

"But I don't want to start rumors..." Cheryl didn't know what to do. Marion believed Gage was innocent, and Cheryl hadn't noticed him around much during this week. Or rather, he hadn't been around her shop much. Maybe he'd somehow found out she'd talked to his foster mom and hadn't come to her store on purpose?

"You're not spreading rumors, Cheryl." Agnes forced a smile. "You're helping with the investigation." Agnes pushed her glasses up on the bridge of her nose. "It's a *him*. You said 'his' the last time we talked."

"I shouldn't have said that much." Cheryl swallowed hard as two sets of eyes studied her. She again tried to remember if she noticed Gage acting suspicious. As far as she could recall, he'd stood there watching the checkers game as intently as other teens focused on computer games. Maybe because he hadn't been able to start school yet, even checkers was more interesting than staying at home.

"He—this person—doesn't seem like someone who would steal. No, it couldn't be him..." She shook her head. "I mean it seems like a particular type of person would want hand-carved figures of children, right? Or potholders. Or the other items on the list."

Agnes's eyes grew wide and round behind her glasses. They were a pale blue, the color of a light summer sky. "I went to a retailers' conference once, and a speaker said most people don't steal because they can't afford the items. Sometimes they can't help it. Sometimes they're depressed and it makes them feel better. Or other times because it gives them a 'high.'"

Cheryl nodded. "I've heard that before, but still..." The frustration and anger she'd felt days ago when she discovered the carvings were gone had dissipated. The monetary amount wasn't that great, not enough to risk ruining a young man's life. Instead, the emotions were replaced with sadness. Lance's parents had taken in foster kids for a short time, and they'd come with so much baggage. They'd been young, but from the stories she'd heard they'd seen and heard things well beyond their years.

Could the same be true about Gage? Had he been taught to steal? Was he depressed? Would he steal items—lots of items—to try to feel better? The best way to help Gage, she knew, would be to bring his problem out into the open. But how?

"Cheryl, maybe it would help if you told," Naomi said. "Then everyone could keep their eyes out."

The bell on the door jingled, and Cheryl turned to greet her customers. Two middle-aged women with their hands full of shopping bags entered. They were chatting away, like two girl-friends on a shopping trip. Cheryl's favorite type of customers.

Cheryl turned to Naomi then back to Agnes. They waited for her to spill who she thought the thief was. If she kept her beliefs to herself then it would be impossible to catch Gage in the act, but with a few people aware maybe they'd have a better chance of seeing something. Was it gossiping? Or was it helping solve these crimes? Naomi must think it was the latter since she was encouraging Cheryl to share.

She sighed. "I'm only going to tell you my suspicions because I'm afraid that if we don't do something about this problem now, it could get worse. Who knows if the thief will start moving on to bigger items? Or even move beyond this main shopping district?" She didn't tell them about the robbery and uninvited guests on the Millers' farm. She'd leave that to Naomi to inform Agnes—to make the connection.

"I saw the Berryhills' new foster son standing over there." Cheryl pointed to the empty bookshelf. "I didn't see him take any-thing but…" She paused. "But my eyes weren't glued to him every minute. I can't be certain he took the items, but if it was…well, maybe the best way to help Gage is to catch him. So maybe you two should keep your eyes out for him too."

Naomi crossed her arms over her chest, as if not wanting to believe what Cheryl was saying. "But he has not been in town for very long."

Agnes nodded. "And it's just recently that things started disap-pearing." She sighed. "He's been in my store too. It just makes sense."

Cheryl sighed. "I hate to admit it, but I agree."

Agnes scratched her head. "Should we go over there and ask him outright?"

Cheryl felt her throat tightening just thinking of approaching him or Marion again. "We don't have proof. Why don't we watch him?"

Agnes folded up her paper and tucked it back in her purse. "I think that's a good idea."

"And what if he does not have anything to do with it?" Naomi asked. "The poor child must be having a hard enough time fitting in. I cannot imagine all that he has lost, and then to know that everyone is thinking unkindly of him. I agree with Cheryl. Let's just keep an eye out."

"Well, I wouldn't want to make him feel bad." Agnes said it in a way that Cheryl could tell the quilt store manager still thought it was him but wasn't going to push.

Then Agnes glanced at her watch and startled. "Oh, I must get back. Sandy has to leave early today for a doctor's appointment. Good thing I only have to walk next door!" Agnes offered a quick wave and the slightest smile as she walked away.

Naomi leaned close. "I think watching young Gage is a good idea..." Naomi cleared her throat. "But is he the only one we should watch?" she whispered. "Is there anyone else, Cheryl? Anyone at all?"

It seemed funny Naomi was so interested in the thefts around town, but the woman wasn't concerned about the person invading their own property.

Cheryl was about to mention this when the ringing of the telephone interrupted. She hurried to the back office and picked up the phone. "Hello, Swiss Miss."

"Cheryl? This is Pam."

She recognized the voice, but she couldn't remember where she remembered it from. And she couldn't remember the name Pam. Was it someone from Columbus? Someone from here?

"Oh yes. Hi, Pam. Good to hear from you." She hoped her voice sounded convincing.

"Now I don't usually do this, but I'm calling to tell you the books you checked out are late. I know you just moved here, and you may not be familiar..."

Cheryl placed her palm on her forehead. "Oh yes, my library books. You're right. They're sitting on my bedside table. I'm so sorry. I can bring them in..."

"That's good. That's good." Cheryl could hear the smile in Pam's voice and could picture her nod. "And when you come in, make sure to ask for me." Pam lowered her voice. "Don't tell anyone, but I'll take off the fines. Just consider it a welcome to town present."

"Well, thank you, Pam. I appreciate it..."

"Okay then, I'll see you soon! Happy reading!" Pam's voice grew louder. So loud that Cheryl had to pull the receiver back from her ear. The phone clicked as Pam hung up, and Cheryl looked down at the receiver. She'd never had a librarian call her before. Another benefit of living in a small town.

Cheryl couldn't hide the smile on her face as she hung up the phone. She stopped short when she saw a man standing just inside the front door. Naomi was talking to him, but she kneaded her hands as if she were nervous. The man was tall with dress pants and a Carhartt jacket that was more gray than golden brown. In his hands he held a box, and in it Cheryl could see all types of things—old books, a shiny new lantern, a brass globe. Cheryl's mind raced trying to remember if any of those were on Agnes's list.

But surely if this man was the thief he wouldn't walk around so boldly, unless that was the whole point. Maybe the best way not to be suspicious is to act as if you aren't hiding anything.

Naomi looked back over her shoulder and offered what appeared to be a forced smile. "Cheryl, there is someone who wants to talk to you. He says he was here a few days ago."

There was an uneasy look on Naomi's face. "His name is Mr. Johnson. He wants to know if you would make a donation."

"A donation?" Cheryl walked forward. "Well...I have given out quite a few things already."

"Yes, as I was telling this young lady, I'm helping out Every Woman's House in Millersburg. They're a shelter for, uh, women and children."

"Like a homeless shelter?"

"That and...what is that called...yes, domestic violence." Mr. Johnson lowered his head as he talked, looking at his scuffed-up boots. He didn't seem very confident in his pitch.

"And what type of things does the shelter need?" She eyed his box again. "It seems like you have a wide variety of things in there."

"I was thinking of gifts for Christmas—just stuff they could have on hand. I can't imagine a mama having to flee with her little boys and girls knowing they won't get a Christmas if they do. I wasn't thinking of anything very expensive." He pointed to a child's wooden rocking chair in the corner near the front window.

It was a worthy cause, indeed, if she could be certain Mr. Johnson was connected to such a shelter. Had he just made up this story to get access to free merchandise and storeowners' trust? By his own confession he'd been to her store before when she hadn't been there. Was it possible that he'd just helped himself and was now coming back for more?

Cheryl cleared her throat, telling herself not to jump to conclusions too soon. "Oh, it is a lovely chair, and I'm sure it was valuable at one time, but unfortunately it's broken."

Cheryl stepped forward and held it up. Then she turned it over. "See, one of the rockers is broken. It's been that way since I've taken over the store. I just keep it here to display items on."

"I can fix it." The man jutted out his chin.

"You can? But..."

"What if we talk about it and you come back?" Naomi smiled. "We have a few things to unpack. Our stock was getting low and merchandise just came in. Do you think you can come back in an hour? I would like to talk to Cheryl about this. Maybe we would even consider delivering the items ourselves."

He shifted slightly on his feet. "You take them down? Oh, I don't know. They don't often let outsiders in... being a shelter and all."

Cheryl glanced at Naomi. "Yes, we'd like to talk about it. Like Naomi said, there is work we need to do." She wasn't lying to Mr. Johnson, but it wasn't crucial they stock the shelves at this moment. Yet there was a curious but also fearful gaze to Naomi's eyes too. And if Naomi said they needed to talk, then she needed to see what was bothering her friend.

Unsure of what she was up to, Cheryl added, "Yes, an hour would be good."

"Just look at all you have already," Naomi said. "Everything from books to preserves." Naomi picked up a jar of canned peaches and glanced to Cheryl. "These look especially good. Canning peaches is one of my favorite things to do."

Cheryl's eyes widened, and then she understood. Those weren't just any peaches. They were Naomi's peaches. Maybe she recognized them from the writing on the lid? And from the look in Naomi's eyes, Cheryl guessed Mr. Johnson was sleeping in her buggy too.

And for the first time since they discovered what was happening, Naomi's gaze had a hint of worry.

Chapter Twelve

Mr. Johnson left the store with his box in hand, slumping under its weight. Cheryl waited by the front window and watched until he was out of sight, and then she turned to Naomi. What had that been about?

Naomi moved to the boxes of fudge and straightened them as if nothing had happened. As if she hadn't just seen a man carting around her stolen peach preserves!

"I think you are working too hard, Cheryl," Naomi finally said, her voice as smooth as butter. Cheryl bit her lower lip, certain she saw worry in Naomi's gaze. "I think we both are."

Naomi would tell her what was going on, Cheryl knew it, but for some reason she wasn't coming straight out with it.

Cheryl walked back to the counter, deciding to sort through the important stock Naomi had told the man they must get on the shelves. "Things are busy because of the season. Things will be better after the holidays."

"I am not talking only about being busy with the store. I am talking about being busy with figuring out the thefts too. And with your concerns about the guest in our winter buggy. I appreciate it even though Levi does not. To tell you the truth, I would like to figure out the mystery too." Her eyebrows folded inward, and she looked at the shelf in front of her, but wasn't really looking at it.

Maybe Naomi had pictured a homeless teen camped out or a young woman who'd run away from home. Maybe the idea that it could be someone like Mr. Johnson, unkempt and built like an ox, was more worrisome.

"I am going to propose we head down to that shelter in Millersburg, drop off some donations, and ask them about Mr. Johnson..."

"Do you think we'll find out anything?" Cheryl asked.

"We will not know until we try, will we? If he's really connected with them, then our minds will be at ease. And if not, well, we have yet another clue. A more substantial one." A bit of a twinkle lit Naomi's eyes at those words, curiosity too.

Cheryl placed a hand on her hip, chuckling. "I see what this is about. You're ready for some adventure. Why, Naomi Miller, you're turning into a regular sleuth."

Naomi wagged her finger. "Ja, but I want you to know that while I enjoy solving mysteries, I enjoy it most because I am doing it with you. I have fun with you, Cheryl. We in the Amish community are known to be hard workers. Without modern conveniences, it takes more time to do just about everything, but we do it *together*. So I would like to help you figure out who is robbing the stores, and I I would like you to help us figure out who is sleeping in the buggy."

"Thank you, Naomi. I needed to hear that. You know, there are days where I wonder if I fit in... with my 'big-city ways.'" She didn't tell Naomi who'd accused her of that. She didn't need to. From the look in the Amish woman's eyes, she knew.

Naomi tilted her head to the side, compassion softening her features. "Do you miss Columbus much?"

"There are some things I miss."

Naomi glanced out the window again, watching a couple stride by hand-in-hand. "Just like Mitzi is missing some things about Sugarcreek. First she lost her husband and then she left her home. Even though it's a noble cause, it must be hard, ja?"

"Did she write to you too?"

Naomi finished straightening the boxes of fudge, and she turned to the candle display, arranging them so that all the labels faced outward. "Ne. I heard it at Yoder's. One of the waitresses told me. She heard two women talking about how Mitzi needed prayer because she wanted to come home. Sharing a prayer request is what they called it. Do they really pray?"

Cheryl shrugged. "Sometimes. Usually it's an easy way to spread news that doesn't sound like gossiping. One person knows this, and one person knows that. They get together and think they have the whole story, but…" Cheryl paused and stood straighter. "That's it!"

"What is it?"

"Well, I know Agnes has gone around to find out what items were taken, but maybe we need to talk to the shop owners and ask if there's anything else they've noticed. Have they found anything peculiar? Have they noticed anyone suspicious? For example, I found one of my little Amish carvings at the bookstore. That must mean something, right?"

"Like clues?" Naomi asked.

"Exactly."

"Well, since you already have one clue with your Amish carving, I will add another one."

Naomi handed Cheryl a piece of paper. It was a sheet of notebook paper crumbled up.

"Seth found this in the winter buggy, same as last time."

Cheryl began to unfold the paper, but Naomi put her hand over Cheryl's, pausing her efforts. Again Cheryl didn't understand why Naomi would delay, but she knew in order to get Naomi's cooperation she needed to play along.

Cheryl smoothed out the crumpled piece of paper, refolded it, and then put in her apron, next to Mitzi's letter. That seemed to satisfy Naomi.

"The thing I don't understand is why your place?" Cheryl asked. "There are a dozen Amish farms between town and your farm. Why would someone walk all that way?"

"Maybe the Lord is sending this person to us. Maybe we have something to give. Maybe we have not done enough to try to help." Naomi glanced to the door where Mr. Johnson had just exited. "Maybe the person is in greater need than we thought."

Cheryl stepped closer to her friend. "What do you mean?"

"Whoever this person is, they are no longer limiting themselves to the buggy shed and the cellar. We discovered someone had made himself a bed in the clean hay of the barn, using horse blankets. We never would have figured it out, but Seth is peculiar on how he folds his blankets. Seth must have them a certain way. He could tell as soon as he saw the pile."

"Or maybe your 'guest' invited a friend?" Cheryl leaned forward, resting her arms on the counter. She offered a playful grin. "Maybe Seth needs to add another sign, Welcome to the Miller Inn. It sounds warm and goes perfectly with Miller Maze and Petting Zoo."

Naomi smiled and winked. "And since Levi falls asleep every time he tries to stay up to find the person, we can put 'peaceful and highly recommended for a good night's sleep' on the brochures."

Cheryl was amazed at Naomi's attitude. She supposed if one was a maam of all those children that teasing would be a perk to go with her job.

"Have you thought about setting a trap?"

"Oh, we tried that too," Naomi admitted. "At least Eli did. He set up an alarm of sorts made up of twine and bells."

"That's a good idea."

"It was a good idea. The person figured it out." Naomi rubbed her chin. "Not only figured it out, but rolled up the twine into a nice little ball. The bells were set next to it in a small pile."

Cheryl tried to picture that. The intruder finding the twine and bells and cutting it, taking off the bells, rolling up the string.

Naomi shook her head and chuckled again, apparently struck by the humor of it.

"And you think it's funny?" Cheryl asked.

"Cheryl, when I was younger I used to be so uptight. I believed I had to have my house perfect—my life perfect. I would be rattled when anything happened that was not in my plans, and I was not any fun to be with."

"Really, Naomi? I can't picture you like that."

Naomi walked over and patted Cheryl's hand. "And it is a goot thing you cannot. A miracle if I were to say so myself. Falling in love with Seth, marrying him, and becoming an instant maam changed things quick. I remember how hard it was. Moving to a new community and leaving all my friends was harder than I thought. I had been part of the same district and attended the same church my whole life, and then I got married and moved from Dalton. Overnight I was living on an unfamiliar farm, trying to learn to be a wife, and caring for children who were still mourning the loss of their mother."

"How did you learn to make this new place home?"

"It started right here." Naomi used her pointer finger to tap her temple. "I had to think and choose differently."

"What do you mean?"

"It all started with Levi. He was just a little guy with floppy blond hair and wide, round eyes when I became his new maam. Seth and I had been married less than a month when he woke up and came out of his bedroom eyeing me. 'Are you going to be the grumpy maam or the laughing maam today?' he asked. 'Because I like the laughing maam better.'"

"He said that?" Cheryl's jaw dropped, and her heart warmed even as Naomi revealed this part of herself that Cheryl couldn't imagine. Naomi was cracking open her heart and inviting Cheryl in—like a true friend. It was intimate and powerful.

"I decided then I was going to be the laughing maam—for Levi, my husband Seth, and the other children."

Naomi's words penetrated Cheryl's heart, pushing out the gloomy dread that had been there earlier. The dread that maybe her aunt Mitzi would decide being a missionary in Papua New Guinea was too hard and would want to return, uprooting Cheryl from the home and community she was establishing. Also fears that something more serious would happen on the Millers' farm—something far more serious than stolen preserves. And fears the thief would manage to upturn the business district and rob the peace from the holiday season when they should be focused on discovering the true peace God offered through His Son.

The door opened and a small group of customers entered. Cheryl greeted them and then turned back to her friend.

Naomi's voice lowered. "You see, in light of all the hard things of this world, Cheryl—hunger and hardship, cancer and catastrophe—what we are facing is such a minor thing. I want to help you solve both mysteries, you can be sure of that. But we do not need to let it rob our joy."

On the sound system overhead, Nat King Cole crooned, "Chestnuts roasting on an open fire." Around them, softly murmured voices of her customers reminded Cheryl that people were enjoying the season's shopping, and they had no idea what was happening behind the scenes. Cheryl lifted up the evergreen scented candle, and she took in the peace in Naomi's gaze. Not the peace that came and went with the weather or with life's situations, but the one that was settled and deeply rooted like the giant maple trees on the Miller farm.

"I forgot to thank you the other night for coming by the farm to check on Esther. That was nice of you."

"Well, Levi didn't think so. He accused me of trying to stir up trouble, of bringing my big-city fears to the farm."

Naomi laughed, surprising her. "Oh, I think there is enough trouble around that we do not need to worry about stirring up any extra. Seems to me we cannot go through life without one problem or another to work through, and I think there is a reason for that."

"How so?"

"Well, if there were not any problems and we could figure everything out on our own, we would not need God, would we?"

"I haven't thought of it that way before."

"Just like Mitzi…your aunt knew she'd face hardship. She has faced it before. Losing your uncle Ralph was very hard on her. As we grow older, we are schooled—through life's hardships and trials—on how to follow God. Following our calling is never easy, whether it is in Sugarcreek or Papua New Guinea. Mitzi and I prayed together before she left, and she did not pray for an easy time."

"She didn't?"

"Ne. She prayed that she would be strong in the middle of the hardships."

The front door opened again, and Mr. Johnson entered once more. He no longer had the box he'd carried earlier, and the worry in Naomi's gaze was replaced with genuine concern.

With a quick glance at Naomi, Cheryl walked around the counter and approached Mr. Johnson. "I've been talking with my friend, and I'm sure it's very hard for those women and children. I'd love to make some donations, but we'll drive them over ourselves."

The man's head bobbed in a nod. He pulled a cell phone out of his pocket and held it up. "When you mentioned that that's what you'd like to do, I called and asked about that. Because of the families they help, they don't let folks just come in and out. Worried about safety and all. But I told them you seem like real nice ladies, and they said you can come." He pulled out a slip of paper and handed it to Cheryl. A phone number and address were scribbled on the note. "Here's the number. Just call ahead before you head there."

Cheryl tried to tell if it was the same handwriting as on the papers that Seth had found in the winter buggy, but she'd have to compare them later.

Naomi stepped forward, tilting her head to gaze into the man's face.

"And will you be there?"

"Oh no." The words blurted out of Mr. Johnson's mouth. "I don't hang around there. Just like to help, that's all."

From the corner of her eye, Cheryl caught Naomi looking at her, waiting for a response.

"I'll get some things together, and we can head out there tomorrow."

Mr. Johnson eyed the small rocking chair longingly and nodded. "Don't know why you'd want to waste a trip when I can go," he mumbled as he exited. "But thank you anyway," he said with a wave just before the door of the shop clicked shut.

CHAPTER THIRTEEN

The next day dawned bitter cold and windy. Cheryl put on her thickest sweater and pulled on her UGG boots. Yesterday she and Naomi decided that Naomi and Esther would ride into town with Levi in the buggy. Esther would then stay to watch the store while Cheryl and Naomi drove to Millersburg.

Knowing she might see Levi, Cheryl spent extra time on her hair. *Why do I bother?* she thought as she climbed from the car and tucked Beau into her coat for the walk up the sidewalk to the store. Levi had made it clear the last time he saw her he considered her a foolish city girl who made a big deal out of little problems. Since Naomi admitted their visitor was still around, did the Amish woman worry it might be Mr. Johnson? And if so, had she told Levi?

Even if she didn't expect to be anything more than a friend with Levi Miller, Cheryl still looked forward to seeing a light in his eyes when he saw her. He was the type of man Cheryl could see herself marrying: hardworking, kind, with a love of family.

Of course the problem was he was Amish. Naomi and Seth had already lost one child to the "world." Having a second child leave the community would break their hearts. Then again, Cheryl couldn't see herself becoming Amish, even if there were wonderful qualities to the lifestyle.

She pictured the view from the buggy ride that morning: rolling hills, fields, and naked trees stretching into the air, frozen streams, all gray, unlike the bright colors from inside the Swiss Miss's front window—the gold and red decorations for Thanksgiving mixing with the red, green, and silver decorations for Christmas. And with a buggy ride one actually had time to enjoy it. Who else really took the time to take in the world around them these days?

The wind tugged at a strip of red and white fabric overhead. Cheryl paused just outside the door to the Swiss Miss and gazed up at the striped awning. The wooden supports that held it up were rotted with age. She'd known that for months, but today the awning swooped more than usual and a piece of it flapped in the breeze. It reminded her of Mitzi's reminder to hire a handyman for the job. In its present condition, the awning wouldn't last the winter.

A cold wind picked up again, and Cheryl hurried inside. Esther was already there, and candles around the shop had been lit. A pleasant, sweet scent filled the air.

"Esther, last week you mentioned an Amish handyman. Have you figured out how to find him?"

"Ja!" A smile filled Esther's face. "I saw him this morning when Levi offered him a ride. He accepted, and Levi dropped him off when we parked. I told him you might have some work for him. LeRoy said he will stop by later today."

"LeRoy, is it? That's good news. And I can use good news right now. I didn't sleep at all last night. My mind just won't take a break. Every five minutes I start replaying our clues or searching my mind for something I've missed." Cheryl placed Beau on the floor and then stood, brushing off her coat. Then she paused. Esther had opened the shop, but where were the others? She looked around, not seeing Levi and Naomi.

Cheryl glanced out front. Levi's buggy was parked across the street. "Didn't your brother bring you?"

"Ja, he is already at the Honey Bee. He and a few others are meeting with some marketing person. They are making plans for drawing in summer tourists. Levi is considering adding hands-on activities to the petting farm—you know, Amish chores that Englischers can try to give them a firsthand experience of what it means to be Amish."

"What type of activities? Not birthing calves, I hope." Cheryl snickered.

"Ne." Esther giggled. "Things like churning butter, rolling out pie crusts…" She shrugged. "The marketing firm even said hanging laundry on the line would be of interest, but it sounds like foolishness to me. Why would people pay to do chores?"

"Some would. It's a chance to try something that's new to them." Cheryl tried to hide her disappointment in not seeing Levi. Then again, Levi hadn't been in a happy mood last time she'd seen him. "Where is your maam?"

"She is at the quilting shop. This morning she loaded up some old quilts she had, hoping the women's shelter can use them. On the way she noticed one of the quilts was tattered on a corner. She is getting a needle and thread so she can mend it on the drive to the shelter."

Cheryl buttoned her coat to the top, preparing to return to the cold. "We're going in my car. It's much quicker to Millersburg than going by buggy."

"Maam sews quick. She will probably have it done before you reach Berlin."

Cheryl glanced at the time on her phone. "I'd better go get her. I want to return before the first tour bus arrives. Watch Beau for me?"

Esther smiled. "Of course."

Cheryl hurried next door and found Naomi chatting with Agnes. They were in deep conversation near the cutting tables. They glanced at her as she approached, but then Agnes continued as if she hadn't arrived.

"You know, Mr. Johnson has been around a number of times. Once or twice he hauled around that box. I gave him a few things for the shelter, and I just assumed everything else he carried had been donated too." Agnes's brows furrowed into a V. "Now I'm not so sure. I mean, he did seem like a rather odd fellow, and anyone can claim anything. I imagine no one checked his story for accuracy. I know I didn't."

"We are checking." Naomi smiled. "That is why I suggested we deliver the items ourselves. I would hate to see anyone in town caught up in this business if the man is not who he said he is."

Cheryl noticed Naomi didn't mention the jars of preserves from her basement, or even the intruder on their farm. One word of it mentioned to Agnes, and they'd have more than enough volunteers to camp out to catch their intruder.

"You make sure you let us know what you find out…" Agnes's words were cut off by the opening of her front door and the cold burst of wind that rushed inside.

An Amish man sauntered in, holding his hat on his head. He wore a pair of homemade pants and a white shirt with a thin sweatshirt jacket halfway zipped. His boots looked worn, as if they'd seen better days, but he had a handsome face and a wide smile. All the women in the store—Amish and Englisch alike—glanced at each other with approval as he entered. And Cheryl guessed this was the Amish bachelor Esther had mentioned. LeRoy, was it?

He walked to the back—nearly strutted actually—toward a tall cabinet.

"Did he make that?" Cheryl asked, pointing to the cabinet.

"Oh yes. LeRoy took a couple of my old pieces and redesigned them. I was quite impressed. It'll be perfect for displaying spools and notions. I'm so glad I gave him a chance when he came by the shop seeking work."

"Can you excuse me a minute?" Cheryl approached the young man.

He whistled while he worked, which was odd for an Amish man, but not completely unusual. Sometimes the Amish in the area took jobs in nearby factories where they worked with Englischers, used power tools, and listened to the radio. The man paused his whistling as she approached.

Cheryl eyed the cabinet, taking in the shelves with slots for displaying spools and the two drawers, one labeled Needles and the other Buttons. "Wonderful job on the cabinet."

"Thank you." He shrugged. "I just like happy customers. Are you from the Swiss Miss?"

"Yes." Cheryl tilted her head. "I haven't seen you in there, have I? Sometimes the place is so full of customers."

"Oh, I've been in a few times, talking to Esther." His eyebrows rose slightly as he said the girl's name. "But I could tell because of how you smell." He sniffed deeply through his nostrils. "You smell like cookies...like that candle you burn there."

"Ah, the Snickerdoodle candle, one of my favorites." She lifted her jacket and sniffed, getting just a hint of the sweet aroma. "Did Esther tell you I was interested in a bid for some work?"

"She mentioned you wanted to see me." He paused and zipped down his jacket, and then he rubbed the back of his neck, as if waiting for more information.

"I'd like to start on the awning above the front door. It won't last the winter in its current state."

"Ja, I saw it was sagging quite a bit. I can redo the frame and reattach the fabric you already have. It might be a bit pricey for the new wood, but I can come in a few hours before you open tomorrow morning. It'll give me a head start so I'm not scaring off customers from the tour buses."

He quoted a price, and Cheryl was pleased. It was much less than she'd expected for the repairs.

"That would be wonderful, but are you sure you want to start so early? It's quite chilly in the mornings."

He didn't seem fazed. "I grew up on an Amish farm. We were sometimes out at three o'clock in the morning in snowstorms doing chores. I'd be happy to do it if it helps you."

"Yes, I'd appreciate it. But make sure you come inside to warm up now and then. Esther's there most mornings because of all the holiday business, and I'm sure she'd enjoy the company."

"I like Esther." He nodded enthusiastically and then turned back to the cabinet, picking up his screwdriver and some cabinet knobs. "She's nice."

Cheryl felt the urge to gush about what a wonderful young woman Esther was, but instead she stepped back. "I see that you have work to finish. I won't keep you, but thank you for your willingness to do the awning."

"No problem," he said and then added, "*Danki*, for the opportunity."

The way he said danki seemed different than the way Esther and Naomi said it, maybe because he was from out of town. She'd ask tomorrow. If he was new to Sugarcreek, perhaps it might help to talk to someone going through the same transition. It had to be hard to move in and try to make new friends whether Amish or Englisch.

With a final wave, she returned to Naomi who was now holding a small paper sack, which she assumed held a needle and thread. "Ready to go?"

"Ja, we do not have much time to waste. The first tour bus will be here before you know it." Then Naomi turned back to Agnes. "And we will let you know what we discover about Mr. Johnson.

I would hate to think someone would use the good name of a real place for their own gain."

"Mr. Johnson? The man collecting items?" The voice of the Amish man called out.

"Ja." Naomi turned. She approached, probably so she didn't have to shout across the store, and Cheryl joined her. Naomi tilted her head in curiosity. "Do you know him?"

LeRoy shrugged. "I've seen him around town. Seems to visit every shop. He always has a full box...too full, maybe?"

"What do you mean too full?" Cheryl asked.

Some of the customers in the store paused from their shopping and seemed to pay attention. Cheryl took a step closer and tilted her head toward the customers, trying to alert LeRoy others were listening.

"It isn't my place to say anything," he spoke in a lowered voice, getting the hint. "A man's deeds will eventually come out. If'n he's taking what he wasn't given, he won't be able to hide it for long. Isn't that what the Good Book says, that if you've sinned against the Lord, be sure your sins will find you out?" Then he turned, picked up the screwdriver again, and resumed his work as if his words hadn't caused Cheryl's uneasiness.

Naomi sighed. "Ja. Whoever it is will slip up. I am not too worried about *if* we find the person. I am not even worried *when*. We just have to pay attention. Like my own maam used to say, 'You can tell when you are on the right track, it is usually uphill.'"

Cheryl nodded, hoping that was true in this case.

Naomi eyed LeRoy for a few seconds, her eyes narrowing as she studied him. Then she shook her head slightly and turned to Cheryl. "Ready?"

"Are you going somewhere?" the man seemed surprised.

"Oh, just for a drive."

LeRoy nodded and then looked away. She noted something in his gaze before he did. Concern maybe? He needn't worry. Cheryl had promised herself this morning that she'd trust her gut. She wouldn't put herself or Naomi in any situation that seemed unsafe.

With determined steps, Naomi made her way to Cheryl's car, and Cheryl followed her friend.

It didn't surprise her that LeRoy had heard about the recent thefts since he was in and out of different stores all day working. Did he suspect Mr. Johnson too? It sounded like it.

She considered going back and asking the Amish man his thoughts on Gage, but was it necessary? No, depending on what they found in Millersburg, they'd have a clearer knowledge of just who this Mr. Johnson was—and what he was up to.

They approached Cheryl's blue Ford Focus, and Naomi opened the passenger door. "I hope you do not mind Levi putting the quilts inside. We saw your car was unlocked."

"A habit I started after moving to Sugarcreek, but maybe one I should reconsider." Cheryl climbed into the car. "Let's hope we're just letting our imaginations get the best of us, and Mr. Johnson really is who he says." Yet from the look on Naomi's face, her friend had already decided their trip would confirm her suspicions.

It took a few minutes for Cheryl's car's heater to blow warm air. It finally warmed up and Naomi pulled off her gloves, leaned back in the passenger seat, and got comfortable. She arranged a quilt on her lap and then began sewing with a needle and thread in the same relaxed motions as when she sat before her wood-burning stove back home. Cheryl smiled to see Naomi moving in the slightest rocking motion, as if she were rocking in a chair.

"Did you have a chance to read the paper I gave you yesterday?" Naomi asked.

"The paper? Like a newspaper?"

"Ne. The crumpled piece of notebook paper I handed you. Do you remember? I gave it to you right after Mr. Johnson came in. It is a story of sorts, and it also mentions the Swiss Miss, or at least someplace very similar to it."

"A...a story?"

"Ja, and I knew you would want to decipher it, and my mind was so out-of-sorts from seeing that jar of preserves... *my* jar of preserves in that man's box."

"The paper must still be in my apron pocket." Cheryl tapped her forehead with her fingertips. "I can't believe I forgot to read it, but I'll read it when I return. Do you remember what it said?"

"Oh, I will never do it justice." Naomi's hand tucked and pulled the needle and thread as she spoke. "A lot of fancy words, but there was something about a woman named Meryl who worked at a gift shop and she found a homeless man on her front steps and brought him inside."

"Meryl? Not Cheryl? Maybe someone didn't hear my name right."

"No, from the setting it seemed like someone was trying to place the Swiss Miss back in time. From the way whoever described the woman's clothes..."

"Meryl's clothes."

"Ja, Meryl's clothes, and the businesses on Main Street, it just seemed like it was talking about long ago, not today."

"Like someone is writing a fictional story?"

"It was not present day, that is certain. And I do not know any Meryls with a gift shop in Sugarcreek."

"That makes me feel better about the first note." Cheryl chuckled. "Especially that part about the people of Sugarcreek not knowing the town was dying. Maybe that was a fictional story too instead of a threat."

Naomi pushed the needle into the fabric. "I never saw it as a threat, Cheryl. If someone was going to write a threat, they would be more clear."

"That's true." Her thoughts turned to Gage. "If Gage is back in high school, he might have a writing assignment, and..."

"And he would sneak out to come all the way to the farm? That does not make sense."

"Maybe it reminds him of someplace he once knew," Cheryl said. "Maybe it makes him feel a connection to the family he'd lost." Moisture filled her eyes thinking about that, but she quickly blinked it away.

"I suppose that could be an option," Naomi said, although she didn't seem convinced. "Just find the paper and read it when you get home—or to the store—or wherever it is. Then tell me what you think."

"I think your intruder may be more civilized than we thought. Or more educated at least."

Cheryl's GPS guided her in a robotic voice, and she turned down a street in Millersburg that she'd never seen before. It was an older neighborhood filled with family homes. Tall oaks stretched their bare arms into the sky. A woman walked her golden retriever by a house that already had Christmas decorations on display. Nothing about this neighborhood seemed dangerous, but that didn't ease the quickening of Cheryl's heartbeat.

"Maybe our guest plans to stay until spring." Naomi studied her mending. Satisfied, she cut the thread with her teeth and tucked the needle into the spool. Then she put the spool back into the bag. "Whoever is staying in the cellar has no plans of leaving."

"What do you mean?"

"In one corner of the cellar we found some plastic forks and paper towels tucked behind a bin of potatoes. We also found a flashlight and blanket."

"That does sound strange. This person is obviously homeless."

"Levi plans to sleep out there tonight—in the buggy shed. There is supposed to be a warm spell, and Seth talked him into it."

"Seth talked him into it?" Maybe the Millers were starting to become more concerned after all.

"Well, after I mentioned the jar of peaches in Mr. Johnson's box, Seth became worried. If Mr. Johnson is bold enough to carry around a jar of preserves, then he is not trying too hard to hide himself. And like you said before, why our house out of everyone's? There are dozens of barns and buggy sheds between us and town. What makes our place so appealing?"

CHAPTER FOURTEEN

Cheryl's GPS led them to a small, unassuming house. It was painted golden brown with a brick chimney and a small front porch. There were a few naked shrubs on either side of the porch, and a sedan was parked in front of the two-car garage. She checked the address again, wondering if the GPS had led her to the right place. Or worse, if Mr. Johnson was playing a game. She turned off the engine and turned to Naomi. "There is no sign. This sure doesn't look like the right place to me."

"It is a women's shelter. Maybe they keep it that way for safety reasons."

"This looks more like a regular house than a shelter. I pictured a large building with, I don't know, small apartments or something," Cheryl said. "I should have Googled it. What if this is just someone's house? What if it's a rabbit trail?" She blew out a frustrated breath, thinking about all the things she needed to do. She didn't have time for games. Why had she even listened?

Naomi opened the car door. "I suppose we will not know unless we try." She climbed out and grabbed her pile of quilts from the backseat.

Cheryl was going to suggest that she at least call the number first, but Naomi had already mounted the steps of the small porch.

She knocked at the front door without a glance back. Cheryl got out of the car and hurried after her. She'd get the donations later, if this was the right place. She had just gotten to Naomi's side when the front door creaked open.

A petite woman with short brown hair peeked out. A child's laughter echoed from somewhere inside.

The woman looked to Cheryl first. "I'm sorry, no soliciting..." Then she paused when she saw Naomi and the pile of quilts in her hands. The woman's eyes widened in surprise, and her face softened. In fact, she almost smiled. It was amazing how Naomi's kapp and warm smile put folks at ease.

"Is this the shelter?" Naomi asked. "I am sorry, I do not remember the name."

"Every Woman's House," Cheryl added. "We were told this was the address, and we had some donations, but if we've come to the wrong place we can leave."

If it's even a real place, she wanted to add. Why had she trusted Mr. Johnson?

"Who told you?" The woman opened the door a bit wider and leaned out. "Maybe one of the board members?" Her light blue eyes widened, and the worry from a moment before was gone.

"It was a man. Mr. Johnson." Naomi looked to Cheryl. "He came by my friend's shop."

The woman's brow furrowed. She twisted her lips as if trying to remember someone with that name.

"You do not know a Mr. Johnson, do you?" Naomi didn't seem surprised.

Cheryl lifted her hand above her head, marking off what she guessed was six feet. "He's a tall man. His, uh, clothes were… Well, he wasn't wearing newer garments. But he gave me the phone number and address to this place. He said he was concerned about the women and children having gifts—nice things here for Christmas. He was going around asking local businesses in Sugarcreek about donations." Cheryl pointed a thumb behind her toward her car. "I have a small rocking chair in the car. Mr. Johnson said he would fix it. I gathered up some other things too."

"Mr. Johnson? I really don't know a Mr. Johnson, but we do have a few needs…" The woman opened the door a bit more. "Are you sure he said *mister*?"

"I believe so…" Cheryl's words were interrupted by the rumbling of a truck's engine. An old Chevy chugged down the road, and surprisingly it pulled in and parked next to her compact car. The door opened, and a tall man stepped out of the truck. Cheryl recognized him immediately. He was wearing the same worn coat that he was wearing yesterday.

"That's him." The words escaped Cheryl's lips. She pointed, and her eyes widened. *So Mr. Johnson told us the truth after all?*

A smile on the woman's face caused her cheeks to lift. She chuckled. "That's not Mr. Johnson. We call him John-John, but his given name is Johnson Williamson." The man walked to the back of his truck and retrieved the familiar box. He set it on the ground, and then he climbed into the truck bed to reach a few more things. "My husband Brad likes to tease John-John, referring to him as the man with two last names."

"So he's with you? Uh, John-John? I mean he's helping you?"

"Yes, we see him a few times a year, usually around Christmas and Easter. He brings donations. He just came by last week with a few boxes of nice things. We've already wrapped them." She clasped her hands together. "We were so thankful to have gifts to put under the tree."

The woman stepped out, pulling the door closed behind her, then she moved closer to Cheryl. "His sister..." She pursed her lips. The woman lowered her voice. "His sister came here one Christmas, but before we could help her find her own place she decided to...return home...to her husband." Tears filled the corners of the woman's eyes, and she quickly brushed them away. Then she looked again over Cheryl's shoulder, and a soft smile touched her lips as she watched John-John set another box next to the first.

"John-John has always been grateful we helped his sister have a good Christmas that year." She shrugged. "I think he tries to help so other women will feel loved here. Then maybe they won't return to those situations. Maybe he's trying to save other women who face similar threats. In a few months, it'll be the fifth anniversary of her death." A sad smile rose on the woman's lips. "And I think he's right. Small gifts really make our women feel loved and valued."

"I am glad we could help with that." Naomi hugged the quilts tighter. "Cheryl oversees the Swiss Miss, and she brought some things. And I have quilts. They are not new but..."

A soft gasp escaped the woman's lips. "Oh, these are lovely! That is so kind. They'll make perfect gifts." She glanced behind her briefly into the house, and then she lowered her voice. "Some women have to leave everything, including family heirlooms. In our center it's not the new, fancy things that get the women excited, but things with history. I suppose it reminds them of good memories from their past."

She turned and pushed the door wider. "I'm Violet. Welcome to Every Woman's House. Would you like to come inside and meet some of our gals and kids? We don't allow a lot of visitors, but any friends of John-John are friends of ours."

"Do you think the women will mind?" Cheryl asked.

"No, not at all." She offered a sad smile. "They feel safe here. They trust us to protect them, but they also appreciate friendly faces."

"Let me get the things I brought…" As Cheryl walked back to the car, she wished she'd brought more. Seeing the tenderness in Violet's face and hearing the children's laughter caused a warmth in her heart that spread through her chest. How wonderful it was that these women had a place to come.

Cheryl used her key fob to open her trunk and then sighed, realizing the trunk was mostly empty. How puny her offerings seemed—a broken rocking chair, a few aprons, and two Amish dolls. Of course she hadn't trusted Mr. Johnson, or John-John, or whatever his name was. Now she wished she had.

She grabbed the items and then entered through the open front door. John-John waited inside too. He placed one box on the simple dining room table and then turned to her. "I'm glad you came." He chuckled. "I'm also glad Violet let you in. She's small, but she's protective of her ladies. I called and talked to another volunteer yesterday, but she must have forgotten to pass the word."

He reached out to take the rocking chair, and Cheryl handed it to him. John-John eyed it and then set it on the floor. "Come with me. I'd like you to meet a special little girl. I had her in mind when I saw this chair."

Cheryl followed him into a living room. Naomi already sat on the couch next to a young woman. They were chatting about gardening as if they'd been friends all their lives. Another woman sat on a love seat with a little girl on her lap. The girl looked to be about two or three years old, and she was fiddling with her mother's necklace. Hearing them approach, the girl glanced up and smiled. It was then Cheryl noticed the young girl had Down's syndrome. Straight black bangs framed a round face. The girl giggled when she noticed the guests looking at her and then snuggled into her mother's chest.

"Why are you being shy?" her young mother coaxed. "Is it too close to your naptime?"

The girl didn't say anything, but she smiled and poked her thumb into her mouth. Her eyes fluttered softly, almost closing, and then they popped open wide once again.

Cheryl sat down in an empty chair. "I know how I get when I need a nap." She wrinkled her nose and grinned back at the girl. Then she glanced at her mother. "What's her name?"

"Grace," the woman said with tenderness. She leaned back in her chair, and Grace snuggled in closer. The mother was pretty with blonde hair and creamy white skin, opposite of her daughter's coloring. Yet dark circles under her eyes and a forlorn look in her gaze gave her an appearance that the weight of the world rested on her shoulders. Thick makeup covered her cheeks and chin, but it didn't hide a purplish bruise. Cheryl sent up a silent prayer for the women and then looked away, but not soon enough. The woman lowered her gaze, aware of Cheryl's realization of her abuse.

Oh, Lord, and her emotional wounds must go even deeper…

"I brought a gift for Grace," Cheryl said, trying to lighten the mood. Then she turned to John-John. "Well, it's a gift from both of us…after Mr. John—I mean John-John fixes it."

"That's nice. She enjoys gifts." The woman didn't ask any questions. It was almost as if her mind was so full of worries it had room for little else.

"Is Grace sleeping any better?" John-John's voice was tender as he asked. He stood to the side almost as an observer, but Cheryl could tell he was glad to be there.

"Neither of us are, but that's to be expected."

John-John nodded, and Cheryl did too. She didn't need to hear the woman's story to know it was filled with pain and loss. *Lord, remind me to be grateful…*

Across the room, Naomi continued to share about last year's harvest and her canning, and a growing ache filled Cheryl's chest. Her own worries and concerns paled in comparison to those of these women.

Yes, she worried about being displaced if Mitzi returned, and she struggled with fitting in to this new place, but she'd never been abused. She'd never been displaced for reasons beyond her control.

Had these young moms left everything in order to be safe? Cheryl sighed. What would it take before they finally found "home" again?

Together, they talked about Thanksgiving the following week, and their guesses about whether or not they'd have a white Christmas. Cheryl realized it had been too long since she'd just relaxed and enjoyed good conversation, but then she glanced at her watch. She sat up straighter, noticing the time. It was later than she expected, and the tour bus was already at the Swiss Miss. Poor Esther! They'd better hurry back.

She rose. "Naomi, we should go."

Naomi nodded, but Cheryl could see reluctance in her gaze. The mother hen in the older woman wanted to tend to these women and their children, but now was not the time. With a sigh, Naomi rose.

"We have the address, and I will put some seeds in the mail tomorrow," she told the young woman next to her.

A baby slept in a car seat near the woman's feet, and the woman's face brightened at Naomi's words.

"Seeds?" Cheryl asked, walking to Naomi's side.

"Yes. Heirloom seeds for bush beans and winter squash. When you grow plants from heirloom seeds you can save the seeds from the vegetables and replant them."

Cheryl felt her brow wrinkle. "Wait, can't you do that for all seeds?"

"No." The young woman stood. "You can't do that with vegetables bought from the store. They are usually sterile. But my grandmother had passed down her heirloom seeds..." The woman's voice trailed off. "I, uh, left behind my seeds."

"I'm so sorry." Cheryl didn't know what else to say.

The woman smiled up at Cheryl. Tears rimmed her eyes. "I was thinking about those seeds last night..." The woman sat again and lowered her head, staring at her hands folded on her lap. "They seem like such a silly thing to worry about."

Naomi placed a gentle hand on her shoulder. "God sent us here for a reason. I have no doubt that He heard your prayers. Sometimes He wants us to know that the little things that matter to us matter to Him too..." Then Naomi looked to Cheryl. "We did not realize how God was going to use us today, did we?"

Cheryl swallowed down the lump of emotion. Only God could use their searching for a thief to help these women be reminded of His ever-present help and love.

"No, not at all." Her eyes fixed on Naomi's. "Maybe this wasn't a rabbit trail after all."

Still, coming here wouldn't help them figure out who their thief or intruder was...or if they were one and the same. It did tell Cheryl who it wasn't.

She left Naomi's side and walked over to John-John. "We're leaving now, but if you stop by the Swiss Miss again next week, I can find a few more things—gifts for the women."

Seeing them, knowing them, she wanted to give. And maybe that's why Aunt Mitzi had been so generous. As a part of the community for so long, Mitzi was familiar with the numerous needs. And once you knew a person's needs, how could you not help?

"Do you have any peaches or other canned fruit?" John-John asked. "Violet promised to make some pies, but I only have one can of preserves so far."

Cheryl's eyes widened, and she remembered Naomi had indeed seen the man with a jar of her preserves. "Naomi might, but can I ask where you got the first jar?"

"It was the strangest thing," the man said. "I'd set my box just inside the library door. I was running inside for a book, and I didn't want to lug that heavy box up and down the bookshelves. For a moment I was worried someone would take something. Instead, someone left something. After I found the book and checked it out, I went for my box. There, sitting on top of some quilted placemats that Agnes from the quilt shop gave me, I found the jar."

"Did you talk to anyone? See anyone?"

"The only person I talked to was Pam—the librarian. She asked me how things were going. She knew my sister..." His voice trailed off. "I asked Pam about the preserves, but she hadn't seen anyone around the box. The only other people who'd gotten closer were some teens who were there for some type of club meeting. I really wasn't paying attention."

Cheryl nodded and then remembered they must leave. "Please come by next week. I'll talk to Naomi, and we'll see what we can do. I'd be happy to buy more canned peaches from her for you. Peach pie is one of my favorites."

"Buy them?" Naomi's voice filled the room.

Cheryl turned, unaware her friend had listened to their conversation.

"You will do no such thing," Naomi continued. "God has given us plenty to share."

Cheryl could tell from Naomi's furrowed brow that she would not accept any payment, other than the knowledge of making a hard holiday easier for these women.

They hugged their new friends good-bye, and suddenly the worries she'd carried in seemed lighter as she carried them out.

"Do you think Esther's going to disown us when we return?" Cheryl quipped as they returned the way they'd come.

"Oh dear, I hope not." Naomi's voice was more serious than Cheryl expected. She glanced over and noticed a faraway look in Naomi's gaze. And for the first time, Cheryl wondered about the struggles Naomi had faced over her lifetime. She related to those young women in a way Cheryl hadn't expected. But then again, who didn't live this life without experiencing pain?

Whatever it was, being there had stirred up old memories in her friend. And also stirred up a few emotions in Cheryl as well—feelings of being hurt and abandoned—pain she usually worked so hard to hide.

CHAPTER FIFTEEN

Two buses were parked down the road from the Swiss Miss, and the store was filled to the brim with customers when Cheryl and Naomi returned. Relief flooded Esther's face, and both women set to work, helping where it was most needed. It wasn't until the last customer left and Cheryl sat down on the stool behind the counter that she realized they'd yet to inform Esther about what they'd discovered in Millersburg.

Their experiences spilled out of Cheryl and Naomi—about the women, the children, and their many needs. The two friends had only visited for thirty minutes, but seeing those women and spending time with them had made a lasting impact.

"It also made me reconsider my assumptions," Naomi said. "When I saw that man with my peaches—and the condition of his clothing—I thought for certain he was camping at our place."

"It's good to know we can mark John-John off our list." Cheryl rubbed Naomi's paper in her pocket. "But that doesn't help us figure out who it is."

"If we had more time, we could talk with the other shop owners, but with Thanksgiving next week I doubt that will happen." Naomi sighed. "And speaking of Thanksgiving, I am afraid I cannot come in tomorrow, Cheryl. I need to do some baking yet at home. I am hoping to have a large crowd."

Cheryl nodded and then turned away. She hadn't thought much about Thanksgiving—other than it being the start of the holiday sales season at the store. She hadn't considered where she'd spend the actual day. In years past, she often flew to Seattle to visit her parents. For the last few years she'd been with Lance's family. Maybe this year she'd just make a small meal and enjoy a good book. She hadn't had much time to read lately.

The rest of the day passed quickly, and no other mention was made about Thanksgiving. A few customers came in and bought the last of her Thanksgiving decorations, yet no one had asked her about what she was doing that day.

When Beau wasn't napping under one of the tables, he jumped into the display window and watched the people on the street. Cheryl noticed that all of them seemed to have smiles on their faces and an extra hop in their steps. She had no doubt their minds were filled with plans for the holidays to come—good food, time with family, and a break from work. With Black Friday coming after the holiday, the only thing Cheryl could think about was what items to put on sale and how much to mark them off. She wished Aunt Mitzi was available to answer questions about that too.

As the workday ended, Esther eyed her mother, wearing the same smile she had all day. Cheryl wished life had been so uncomplicated when she was in her teen years. She'd been striving for too many things and worrying about even more at that age. Esther would make a wonderful wife someday.

Seeing that it was closing time, Esther removed her work apron. She smoothed her simple blue Amish dress and exhaled a long breath. "Tomorrow will be a busy day in the shop, but Cheryl and I can handle it."

Cheryl cocked an eyebrow. "Yes, it will be busy, and the work will start earlier than normal."

"What do you mean?"

"LeRoy is coming to fix the front awning. While he's here, I'd like to talk to him about taking a look at the bathroom sink."

"LeRoy is coming by?" Esther's voice perked as she said those words.

Cheryl noticed pink rising up Esther's cheeks and tried to hide her smile.

With a lightness to her step, she went to the office and retrieved her coat and her mother's. "He could use a friend, being from out of the area and all."

"Oh, he is from out of town?" Naomi asked, accepting her coat from her daughter.

"Ja, we have chatted a little when he has come in to look for work."

Naomi eyed her daughter, curiosity in her gaze. Cheryl had seen that look many times, but this time it seemed the older woman was seeking a different type of clue—insight to her daughter's heart. "Have you asked why he moved to Sugarcreek?"

"He said something about trying to help his brother, but...well, I do not think of what to ask until he is gone."

Naomi put on her cape, and she glanced out the window as if checking for Levi's buggy. "Depending on where he is from, we might know his family. Make sure you ask tomorrow, will you?"

"I will try to remember, but he makes me so..."

"Unfocused." Cheryl interjected. She chuckled, remembering how she'd felt every time Lance was near. She'd get so excited over the idea of seeing him, and then when they went on a date, it felt as if her windpipe shrunk to the size of a spaghetti noodle and she couldn't breathe. When had things changed? They'd fallen in love—or so she thought. They'd planned on getting married. Then they'd fallen into a routine without excitement, without joint goals.

Talking to Lance on the phone or meeting him for dinner had become as ordinary and uneventful as checking the mail. It was no wonder he'd backed out of their engagement. That shouldn't be how happily-ever-after started, right? The only problem was Cheryl now had those same throat-tightening, heartbeat-pounding feelings again, but with someone unobtainable.

Cheryl moved to the window, looking out for the black buggy and handsome driver—for Naomi's sake, of course.

"Oh, and don't forget to read that paper Seth found in the buggy. We will also have to think of another time when you and I can go around and ask business owners about clues."

Like we have time for that. It sounded like a good idea, but Cheryl was barely keeping up with the store as it was.

A buggy pulled up and parked just outside the shop. Levi sat on the driver's seat. With quick movements, he climbed down.

Cheryl hoped he'd walk into the shop to get his mother, but instead he got out the lap blankets from the backseat and waited.

Cheryl sighed and turned back to Naomi. "The paper from your buggy, yes. I promise I'll read it tonight." She patted her apron, and a sudden weariness overwhelmed her. "I'll also make sure that I come to work early tomorrow and let Agnes know that our 'Mr. Johnson' is not the thief."

"And he is not sleeping in my winter buggy," Naomi added. She pushed open the front door, and a few dry leaves blew in. "I do not know, Cheryl. These mysteries may stump us after all."

Naomi rushed out to the buggy before Cheryl could answer, and Esther followed, offering a small wave.

She moved to the front door and locked it.

No, she wouldn't let these mysteries stump her. She had to find answers, otherwise there would be no peace this season.

Cheryl turned and scanned the shop, looking for Beau. She didn't see him right away, so she started checking under tables. He seemed to like resting among the boxes and dust hidden by the long tablecloths. She finally found him near the back. She bent down and scooped him up, eager to get home. She was happy the trip to Millersburg had gone well, but she wasn't any closer to answers.

"The questions keep building, Beau."

He purred a response and yawned.

Outside, a gentle rain started to fall, and she shivered thinking about walking through it. "Maybe we'll sit tight for a few minutes. Wait and see if the rain lets up."

Settling down on the stool behind the counter, Cheryl pulled the piece of paper from her apron pocket. The page was filled on both sides in the same scribbly script.

The woman paused and then leaned over the counter. "Please, miss, would you let him come inside? The temperature is dropping. He has nowhere left to go."

"I'm not sure," Meryl said, smoothing down her long skirt and apron. "Where did you find him?"

Meryl looked out the window. She'd only been in the Brandywine Valley for six months, and she was not used to this cold weather. The dirt roads outside were getting muddy after the rain. The plain wooden storefronts looked to be various shades of gray because of the rain and fog.

A few wagons drove down the street, their old horses walking with burdened steps. She wished she had a wagon to ride home in. It would be a long, cold walk, even if she left now. If she waited, there was no certainty she would make it home before dark. And worse yet—she didn't have enough kerosene for the lantern in her shop to last the night or enough coal for the fire. Whatever should she do?

Meryl shivered as she thought about letting the man inside. He slumped against the outside wall, weary from his journey. But where had he come from?

She could help him get warm, but what would happen when the coal ran out? She wouldn't be able to help him if she couldn't help herself.

Meryl had another worry.

Was the man safe to be around?

She knew someone who could help, but the Miller home was a few miles away—too far to walk. She'd never get there before dark. And that still wouldn't help the man who was slumped outside her door passed out.

She pressed her hand to her chest and wished for her brother Hank to return. He'd gone to buy more coal and hadn't returned. If he did make it back, would it be possible for Hank to ride out to the Miller farm and request help? There was no place that provided more hospitality, peace, and comfort as the Millers. Walking onto their property was as welcoming as the sun after a storm.

Meryl looked to the young woman who stood before her. She waited, expecting an answer. Without Hank, Meryl had no chance of reaching the Millers. And she could not leave the man in the cold.

"Can you help me drag him inside?" she asked.

"Ja, miss." The young woman glanced over her shoulder. "I will help as I can."

Meryl stepped out into the cold. It bit at her cheeks and whipped her skirt around her ankles. She knelt down by the man. "Sir, are you feeling sickly?"

"Have I made it?" His voice was raspy.

"That depends." She moved around to get a good grip under his arm. The young woman did the same. "Where were you going?"

"I was coming to find…"

Cheryl turned over the page. The words ended just like that. A few notes were written on the top of the back page. *Character motivation clear? Dialogue true to time period?*

"What in the world?" Cheryl mumbled to herself. Seeing this changed all her ideas of the type of person who'd been sleeping in the buggy. The person was smart, creative. Could Gage have written this? Maybe. It was more likely he was involved in the thefts alone. But who would write about this "Meryl"? Who would ever come up with this story? And where was the rest of it?

None of her suspects seemed like people who could write like this.

Cheryl tucked the paper back into her apron pocket and then put on her coat. She felt no closer to an answer than she did a week ago.

"Aunt Mitzi, what did you get me into?" Cheryl muttered as she picked up Beau and locked up the store. It was nearly dark outside, and as she got into her car she wished she had somewhere else to go—someplace full of light, full of life, full of people. As she drove home, the idea of spending Thanksgiving alone added another burden to her already full load. It still bothered her. Why hadn't Naomi even asked what she was doing that day?

I wonder if the Millers' intruder expects an invitation too.

She thought about the most recent discovery—this story that Seth found—and she couldn't help but chuckle. Was imitation the greatest form of flattery? Even fictional imitation?

"Was Mitzi ever written into a book?" Cheryl said to Beau, who lay curled up on the passenger seat. "I suppose I should be honored."

She patted her pocket. The writing wasn't bad either. At least it was something worth writing Mitzi about. Cheryl was sure her aunt would love a letter from...Meryl. It might be a nice distraction. Not as good as a hot bath, but close.

CHAPTER SIXTEEN

Cheryl paused her steps as she approached the Swiss Miss the next day before the late fall's dawn tinged the sky. She expected the awning to be down. She expected there to be quite the mess on the sidewalk in front of the store. She was surprised that most of it was still up. The old fabric had been stretched over fresh new boards. How had LeRoy finished the job so quickly?

LeRoy climbed off a ladder leaned against the wall. His back was to her as he poured himself a cup of coffee. He shuffled from side to side as he drank it, obviously cold. He walked closer to the door of the Swiss Miss and peered inside. Was he looking for her?

Cheryl stepped forward. "Here, let me open that door."

He jumped slightly and then turned. Instead of his Amish hat, a stocking cap was pulled down to his eyebrows. He wore a thick work coat today too, and if it weren't for his handmade pants, one would never know he was Amish.

He finished his sip of coffee and then returned the lid to the thermos. "I jus—just have a little more." His words came out in a puff in the cold air. "Then I'll come in."

"No, it can wait." Cheryl unlocked the door. She stepped inside and flipped on the lights, swinging the door open wide for him. Warmth from inside rushed out to meet her, welcoming her in.

"If I can just finish first..."

Cheryl waved him in. "Nonsense. Your cheeks are red, and your crimson nose would put Rudolph to shame. Sit inside for a moment and thaw."

He nodded and put a few of his tools inside a large wooden crate. It had a handle and appeared to be made of old pallets. When he picked it up, she noticed something hanging from the bottom of the crate where there was a two-inch gap. It looked like a red handkerchief or something.

"You're losing something out of the bottom." She pointed. When he stepped inside, she shut the door behind him.

"Yeah." He reached under and pushed the piece of fabric back up inside. "I need to fix this work box." He set it on the ground. "I left my old toolbox back in Illinois. At least this sort of works."

Cheryl was about to ask exactly where he'd come from when the front door opened and Esther rushed in. She paused when she saw LeRoy and then closed the door behind her. Esther opened her mouth as if to say something, but then seemed to change her mind.

"Why, look what the wind blew in." Cheryl said louder than needed, hoping to break the ice between them. "I'm so glad you could come in early today."

"Levi was coming to town, so I thought I would catch a ride." Yet even as Esther said the words, her gaze was fixed on the Amish bachelor.

LeRoy pulled off his gloves and rubbed his hands together. Cheryl wished she had something warm to offer him, but she did have something else she believed he needed.

"It's clear you'll be done with the awning soon. Are you looking for more work?"

A soft smile touched LeRoy's lips. He looked to Esther and then back to Cheryl. "Ja, I need more work... Anything would be helpful."

"There is something wrong with the bathroom sink. I think the whole piping underneath needs to be replaced. I'm not sure if you..."

"I can do that," LeRoy interrupted. "I worked on a construction crew for a few years."

Esther removed her coat and carried it to the back, and LeRoy's gaze followed her. Even though this was her store, Cheryl suddenly felt like the third wheel.

"I'll take a look at the sink as soon as I'm done with the awning. But I might need a little help." He sighed. "I don't have transportation or a buggy here in Sugarcreek. If we need a trip to the hardware store, I will need a ride."

Cheryl pointed outside. "And how did you get that lumber for the awning?"

"It's leftover from some I used at Dutch Creek Foods. They had me build new shelving in their back storeroom. I asked if I could use some of it for your awning, and they didn't mind. In fact, Becky said she had an old file cabinet if you need one."

"That's so kind." Cheryl did need to organize the office, but not now. Not during this busy season. She looked to Esther and nodded, signaling her approval of this Amish bachelor. "I don't need a file cabinet right now, but thank Becky for thinking about me. As for supplies, I'd be happy to drive to the store."

"I'd appreciate that," LeRoy said enthusiastically as if she'd just given him a thousand dollars. "But first I need to finish the awning and check out the sink. It shouldn't take more than an hour."

An hour of Esther staring mindlessly out the window, watching the bachelor.

The morning went by quickly. Cheryl was pleased with the finished awning. After taking a look at the sink, LeRoy discovered that whoever had installed the plumbing on the bathroom had done it wrong, causing one of the pipes to collapse.

"It might have been my uncle Ralph, Aunt Mitzi's husband." Cheryl chuckled. "He was a quiet man—a bookkeeper. He wasn't too handy with tools, but my aunt insisted on asking him to help out anyway. I remember hearing my mom talking to Mitzi on the phone saying it would be easier hiring help to start off, but I'm not sure Mitzi took that advice."

"It's a good thing that sink isn't used much," he said. "If it had been a kitchen sink, it could have broken completely and flooded, causing a big mess."

"Will it be hard to fix it?" Cheryl asked.

"Ne. It'll just take some new pipes and a few other supplies. In fact, I won't need a ride after all. It's just a short walk to the hardware store, and I don't need much."

"Are you sure?" Cheryl looked toward the front of the store where numerous customers lingered. "I need to give Esther a lunch break. If you can run to the hardware store, I'll watch the front while she goes to lunch."

Disappointment clouded LeRoy's face. "I can do that." He slid his arms into his jacket, and his shoulders slumped.

Had she said something wrong? Then she realized the problem. LeRoy had probably hoped to go to lunch with Esther.

"Would you like to go to lunch with Esther?"

He shook his head. "Ne, it's no problem. It'll just take me thirty minutes or so to get all the supplies, and I'm sure Esther doesn't need me tagging around." He shrugged and then looked back at his work box. "You don't mind if I leave my box here, do you?"

"You can leave it, yes. And Esther could pick you up some lunch."

"Sure." He offered the smallest hint of a smile. "I'd like that."

Cheryl took over the front of the store, and she watched as LeRoy walked Esther across the street to the Honey Bee Café. He waited while she entered, and then he headed down the street to the hardware store. Cheryl let out a heavy sigh, disappointed in herself for speaking before thinking. She hoped LeRoy didn't think she was discouraging him from pursuing Esther because from what Cheryl saw he was a nice young man. A hard worker too.

When the last customer left, she took a deep breath and viewed the store. She'd been so busy lately she hadn't taken time to check her stock. Then again, the store had been so full of people she was pretty certain a crook would have no chance to sneak out anything. It would be nearly impossible to do with so many people, so many eyes.

Still, Cheryl walked around and eyed the shelves. Everything seemed in place until she came to the table with Katie's Fudge. Or rather, the table where Katie's Fudge had been. It was empty. *Surely we haven't sold every box.*

Cheryl's heartbeat quickened. She strode to the counter and looked over the sales notes for the last week, hoping for an explanation. Since things had been busy over the holidays, she, Esther, and Naomi had developed a system to remind Cheryl of what to order. Whenever they sold the last of something, they'd write it on the list. Yet no one had mentioned she needed more fudge. Had they not noticed?

Cheryl paced the area in front of the display table.

She wanted to believe that somehow she had simply missed ten boxes of fudge moving through the store over the last week.

She wanted to, but she couldn't.

Her thoughts traveled to the next conclusion—one she couldn't ignore.

If the fudge hadn't been sold, then it must be stolen.

Knots tightened in her gut. Those boxes of fudge weren't cheap, but worse was the knowledge the thief was still active, as bold as ever.

Bold, yet invisible.

Had anyone come in with a large shopping bag or a box—something they could have slipped the boxes of fudge into? No one came to mind. Cheryl picked up the phone to call Naomi, to ask if her friend had somehow forgotten to make a note, but just as she did, the door opened and LeRoy entered. His arms were full of pipes and a bag of supplies from the hardware store.

Cheryl returned the cordless phone to its cradle. "Would you like help with that?"

"I'll just drop it all in the back, but thanks." He sauntered by, and although the Amish bachelor attempted to force a smile, it wasn't convincing.

She felt a twinge of regret, knowing her mistake. She wished she had let LeRoy know she saw him as a new friend, not just paid labor.

She couldn't change the past, but she could make things better now. She'd make a point to find out more about LeRoy—and not just see him as someone who'd help her get the store in better shape.

The perfect opportunity came ten minutes later when Esther returned with lunch for LeRoy. Instead of allowing Esther to take it back to him, Cheryl set up three chairs behind the counter and put out the Be Back in Fifteen Minutes sign in the front window.

"LeRoy, lunch is ready. I thought we'd take time to visit while you eat."

LeRoy seemed both pleasantly surprised and unsure. He scratched his ear and looked to the front door as if not believing what he saw. "Danki. That was kind of you. But isn't there a place I can sit in the back? Maybe in a storage room? You don't need to close your store. And I don't want to be in anyone's way."

"It is cold in the storage room," Esther interjected. "You will not be in the way, honest."

"Esther's right," Cheryl added. "If a customer needs something, fifteen minutes isn't too long to make them wait. It's important to make time for friends."

LeRoy looked at her and then quickly away. He'd been so friendly before, but now that he had their attention, he seemed shy and hesitant. He wiggled in his seat and folded his hands in his lap.

"Ja, danki." He looked to Cheryl. "You are very thoughtful."

With a smile, Esther handed LeRoy a paper bowl filled with creamy potato soup. It was thick, with cheddar cheese sprinkled on top.

"Thank you."

He stirred the soup with the spoon and then looked back over his shoulder again, eyeing his toolbox. Was there something in it he needed? She couldn't tell.

Cheryl sat down in the chair next to Esther. "I know what it's like to be a new person in a new town. I'm pretty new to Sugarcreek too." She also thought of the women and children she'd met at the shelter yesterday. "And things are even harder if you ended up in Sugarcreek because of...well, challenges. Or because of other people's choices." She hoped by saying that LeRoy would open up.

LeRoy didn't respond, and she didn't press. Instead, LeRoy took a big bite of the soup. He smiled, and his eyes fluttered closed. "I sure miss my maam's cooking."

"And I am sure she misses you," Esther said.

"Is there a reason you moved to Sugarcreek?" Cheryl asked, realizing that beating around the bush wasn't going to work with him and knowing Esther would be too shy to ask.

"The truth?" He lifted his eyebrows. Then he lowered his head and continued eating. "It was my brother. He's in his rumspringa and getting himself into a lot of trouble. He moved to Sugarcreek to be near a girlfriend, and I've never seen my maam so distraught. I told her I'd move closer. I'd watch over him."

"Does he know you're here?" Cheryl asked.

"Ja, but he tries to ignore me. Pretends I'm not."

"Do you think he's going to change his ways—that he'll return?" Cheryl thought of Ben and Rueben Vogel. How many years had Ben's leaving put a wedge between the two brothers? She also thought of Seth's and Naomi's oldest daughter, Sarah. How many prayers had been prayed for the young woman over the years?

LeRoy paused with the spoon halfway to his mouth. "If you want the truth, I'm not nearly as concerned by my brother's actions as I am about my mother's heart."

Esther leaned forward. She folded her hands on her lap meekly, but under her long skirt her foot bounced. "It must be breaking right now, with not one but two sons so far away."

"Ne. I mean her actual heart. She has an irregular beat. Too much stress and it's worse. She was in bed for most of the month of October, but since I've been here…well, it helps her to know he's being watched. It's helped her health."

Esther glanced over at Cheryl, and Cheryl surmised what the young girl was thinking. *We have to find a way to help him—help his family.* Esther was like her mother in so many ways.

Cheryl felt the same. She'd donated items to businesses and organizations in order to help various causes in the area, but hearing his story, she wanted to do more. This young man was giving up his life—his future—to help his maam.

"Listen, after you're done with the sink, I have another job for you. It's a bit bigger... if you're interested."

The man's eyes brightened. "You would do that for me?"

Cheryl was surprised that he didn't ask what it was. "Yes, I'd love to make sure you have work. I'm sure it makes all the difference."

"It does. I've been sending money..." He didn't finish, but she was certain that LeRoy was about to say that he was sending money home to his maam. Was LeRoy's father out of the picture? Had he passed away? Cheryl thought about asking but then changed her mind.

"Ja, it would help," he stated simply.

Cheryl stroked her chin. "As for the next project, I was thinking that maybe I'll take that file cabinet after all. I know it's probably the wrong time for it, but if you could exchange that cabinet and maybe put up some bookshelves for me, well, I'd like to make the office my own."

"Ja, of course." His face brightened. "I could even build an in-the-wall safe if you'd like."

"A safe?" Cheryl's eyebrows furrowed, and the peace she had a moment earlier sank like a weighted balloon.

"If you don't need a safe, it's not a problem. Just with all the thefts...and now that you know Mr. Johnson isn't the crook..."

Cheryl tilted her head and eyed him. "How did you know about, uh, Mr. Johnson?" She thought better of using his real name until she figured out what LeRoy knew.

The man looked up and to the left and then back to her. "It was just a guess, really. I mean I didn't hear you talking about him when you returned. There were no police called, and when you came back, you gathered a few more items off the shelves and set them in back. I assumed they were for the shelter."

Cheryl eyed him. "Wait...you weren't here when I got back."A chill traveled down her spine, washing away the friendliness that she felt a moment before.

LeRoy's booted foot bounced, and she could see his mind spinning. Then he looked down at his soup. "I wasn't inside. But I was outside, uh, measuring for the awning."

Cheryl nodded and released a breath. She hadn't seen him, but with the glare of the interior lights, it was hard to see outside once dusk set in. Besides, why would she question his word? She had no reason to think LeRoy wasn't truthful.

He was observant. What else had he observed when he worked in the various shops? She thought about asking him—to see if he'd seen anything unusual, but she reminded herself not to think of LeRoy as someone who could help her, but as someone who first needed a friend.

Cheryl cleared her throat. "I'm excited you're willing to tackle these projects. I suppose we'll see a lot of you while you work on them. They're big projects." She looked to Esther. "And if I'm not here, Esther can help with whatever you need."

"Ja, wunderbar. I appreciate that." LeRoy took another bite of his soup, and Cheryl noticed he was trying to hide a smile. To her left, Esther was too. Cheryl had no doubt that there was interest between the two of them…but was it enough interest to lead to more? Deep down, she hoped so.

There were a lot of concerns about the events happening in Sugarcreek lately, and a lot of questions filled her mind, but at least Cheryl could count on one thing. Sweet romance could happen anytime, anywhere. And good could come out of anything, even a crumbling awning and a broken sink.

Cheryl jerked awake. The room was dark. The golden light from the moon gave the room a soft golden glow, and she struggled to figure out where she was and what had awakened her.

She looked around, taking in the walls of framed photos, the ceiling, and the pillows stacked next to her, trying to figure out where she was. Trying to reassure herself that she was still in Sugarcreek and that she was safe—at least for the moment.

Her dream had carried her back to her apartment with its Pottery Barn furniture, oriental rugs, and framed travel posters. She rubbed her eyes, wondering where that had come from and turned to the window, gazing out at the white painted birdhouse on a tall pole outside. Beau sat in the window looking at it, as if dreaming of a midnight snack. Is that what he usually did while she slept?

Cheryl stood and slid on her bathrobe. She moved to the window and stroked Beau's fur. "You're up awful early. Or maybe you didn't fall asleep."

She was headed to the kitchen for a glass of water when she noticed movement on the street. Someone was out there, walking hurriedly down the sidewalk. She couldn't tell if it was a man or a woman, but they were hunched over and carried a large pack. Or was it a garbage bag? She couldn't be certain.

As she watched, something about the hunched stride was familiar.

Did she know the person?

She pressed her nose to the glass as she followed the person's progress. If she knew them, it was buried in her subconscious.

What was someone doing out after midnight? Maybe it was the person who slept in the Millers' buggy shed. Yes, maybe he or she found Goldilocks—Levi—sleeping in the shed and had to find a new place to sleep? No, that couldn't be right. The person outside was walking away from town. It was possible that they were heading to the Miller farm, and if that happened, she'd hear about it when Esther arrived at the store.

Or maybe it was a person out walking who had no connection to either the thefts or the Millers' farm. Not everything was connected to those mysteries. Who would be out this late at night? And why? Did they work the late shift? Couldn't sleep?

Cheryl yawned and stretched. She didn't want a drink anymore, but returning to bed sounded great. As she slid between the rumpled sheets, she tried to remember what had awakened her. It was a dream. A bad one. In it, she'd been back in her apartment, but on every surface were boxes of fudge. Yet when Cheryl walked around and opened them, all the boxes were empty.

Is there something You're trying to tell me, Lord?

She bit her lip, wishing she had paid better attention in her college psychology class when her professor talked about the meaning of dreams. What it did remind her is that she'd yet to talk to Esther about the chocolate. Hopefully, by some miracle, it had all been sold.

Cheryl rolled to her side and tried to push all those thoughts out of her mind. Tomorrow—she'd think about it all again tomorrow. Tonight she needed sleep. Tonight she needed peace. And the last thing she needed was to replay the image of that person walking down the street. And the knowledge that she recognized that stride and that hunched walking stance…if she could just remember where she'd seen that recently. If only she could just remember who.

Cheryl sat cross-legged on the couch, a quilt spread on her lap as puddles of morning light fell on the blanket. She was up, dressed, and ready for work early. She'd made sure to do that so she'd have time to write Aunt Mitzi. Her letter to her aunt wouldn't make it before Thanksgiving, but she at least wanted her aunt to know that she was thinking of her…and that she should possibly be called Meryl from now on. A smile filled her face at that thought. No matter how disturbing she found it that someone was writing about Sugarcreek—about her, she couldn't help noting the humor too.

Cheryl joined her hands and stretched them toward the ceiling then with the urgency of a high schooler with a term paper due in an hour she poured out all the news of the past week to her aunt, writing on the stationery with long strokes.

While retelling the story found in the winter buggy started the letter off light, her words sobered as she continued. Tears filled Cheryl's eyes as she relayed their visit to the shelter. She also told Aunt Mitzi about LeRoy and his repairs. The young man might have captured Esther's attention, but his heavy burdens might hold him back from pursuing her. Hopefully not for long. Cheryl hoped LeRoy would find healing in this quiet town, just as she was finding healing from her breakup with Lance.

Then there was Gage. Cheryl hadn't seen him in a while, but she couldn't get the young man off her mind. In all three cases, the pain these young people experienced wasn't their fault.

"Oh, Beau. Why do things have to be so hard, especially when you're doing all the right things?"

Cheryl finished the letter and then eased off the couch. She moved to the front window, appreciating the morning sunlight that draped the wide front porch. How many times had Mitzi stood at the window, looking into the new day? Had she worried about her friends around Sugarcreek? Had she fretted over her relationships or her choices? Was she second-guessing her move to Papua New Guinea even now?

Cheryl tried to picture herself back in Columbus. The dream last night had taken her back there. In Columbus, she'd lived by her calendar and the alarms on her phone. She drove more in one week there than she did in a month here in Sugarcreek. Just getting to appointments and meetings had consumed hours in her day. While she appreciated the slower pace of Sugarcreek, she had to admit it was lonely at times.

Beau jumped onto the windowsill, and Cheryl tucked the letter into an envelope. Once it was addressed and stamped, she set it on the side table next to her remote control and then folded the quilt and returned it to the sofa's back.

"Ready to head out?" she asked her cat. "Unless you're interested in a quiet time at home today. I have to admit that if I were you, I might take that option. At least you'll get a quiet nap."

Beau softly meowed and then lay down on the windowsill.

Cheryl tucked a strand of red hair behind her ear and then chuckled. "Well, I suppose that's my answer."

Out the window, a car traveled down the street. Cheryl watched as it slowed and then stopped. Then a woman got out. She walked over and picked something up. Cheryl couldn't tell what it was.

Next, the woman got back in the car and pulled over to the sidewalk in front of Cheryl's house before parking, facing the wrong direction. She looked up and down the street and then turned and met Cheryl's gaze. Seeing Cheryl in the window, the woman waved. She held something in her hand and then hurriedly walked to the door.

Cheryl opened the door before the woman could knock.

"Oh, I'm so glad that you're home. Does this belong to you? Or do you know who it belongs to?" The woman held up an Amish-style handcrafted miniature doll. It still had the price tag on it. It wasn't the same style that Cheryl had in her store, but she'd seen them in Sugarcreek Sisters Quilt Shoppe.

"That's not mine, but I know where it came from." She pointed to the price tag. "I run the Swiss Miss, and I know Agnes who manages the quilt shop next door."

"Oh, I do love the Swiss Miss. Mitzi always finds the sweetest things. Do you want this? I'm not sure how it got out there, but if you can find the owner..."

Cheryl held out her hand, and the woman offered her the doll.

Cheryl turned it over in her hand. "It doesn't look too dirty, maybe it was dropped yesterday. I can ask Agnes if she remembers who bought it. Maybe someone dropped it on their walk home..." An image filled Cheryl's mind, and she remembered an image from last night. Someone had walked down the street. Had whoever that was dropped the doll? Had he or she stolen it?

Cheryl's mouth circled into an O. Had everything in that Santa Claus bag been stolen?

"Is everything all right?" the woman asked. And then before Cheryl had a chance to answer, a tinkly alarm sounded from the car's open door. "I have a meeting I'm late for. Thanks for taking care of the doll."

Cheryl pressed it to her chest. "I'm happy to take it to Agnes..."

"Thanks!" the woman called, cutting off her words. "I'm so glad. A sweet toy shouldn't be in the road."

After the woman drove away, Cheryl turned the doll over in her hands. Once the car was out of sight, Cheryl walked out into the street.

The roadway was quiet, and there were no other cars or people. She looked around to see if anything else had been dropped, but saw nothing. Just some garbage. She leaned over to look at the trash closer.

Cheryl's mouth dropped open, and she squatted down and picked up one of the crumbled papers. It was a wrapper, and she recognized it immediately. It was the type used on the boxes of Katie's Fudge. Whoever had been carrying that bag last night had eaten her fudge while he or she walked. And doing it right in front of her house! She tried to think about where they were going. Beyond her house were more houses, mostly small rental cottages that tourists rented for a week or a month.

She turned and strode inside. Shutting the door behind her more firmly than necessary, she closed her eyes and tried to remember any other details about the person, but it had been too dark.

All she remembered was a dark form carrying a bag and the hunched-over stance and long-legged gait. There was some familiarity to how the person had walked, but she still couldn't put her finger on it. Whoever was behind the thefts stayed one step ahead of her, and with the busy store she questioned if she'd ever keep up let alone find the thief.

Cheryl gritted her teeth. Whoever it was obviously had no plans for stopping their thefts. Why should they? So far they were getting away with them. In fact they seemed to be stealing more and getting bolder. And why?

Why would someone focus on Amish merchandise?

CHAPTER SEVENTEEN

To one customer: "Have a happy Thanksgiving."
To the next: "Are you going anywhere for Thanksgiving?"

All day the words flowed with each customer until she was tired of saying them.

"What are you looking forward to this Thanksgiving?" Cheryl's voice rang in her ears, and she pasted on a smile. The customers loved when she asked, and they all had wonderful plans.

Thankfully, no one asked her plans in return, especially after Esther arrived. How would she respond? "Oh, I'll have a TV dinner while I watch the Macy's parade and then enjoy a good book." It seemed so...boring.

It was boring. And pitiful. And made her so glad no one had asked.

Instead, Cheryl dreamed of pumpkin pie every time she sniffed another whiff of pumpkin candle, and she pasted on what she hoped was a convincing smile.

Even as she worked, Cheryl couldn't help noticing Esther move around the shop, helping the customers with little energy today. The young Amish woman did her best to give equal attention to the clusters of tourists, yet her delicate features seemed downcast. Had something else happened at the farm last night? Were things moving from bothersome to dangerous?

Cheryl rang up a woman's order and then approached Esther. She needed to ask about the fudge before someone else required her help.

"I have a question," Cheryl asked.

Esther jumped slightly, causing Cheryl to change her question. "Are you all right?"

The young woman shrugged and fiddled with her kapp strings. "It is just that Maam finally told me the whole story—about the notes and about things disappearing from the cellar. She was not going to tell me, but I insisted. I wanted to call a friend, but they would not let me leave. That is when I made them tell me the whole truth."

Cheryl's heart sank. She'd assumed Esther knew the whole story before, but she understood why Naomi had held back. Naomi was a nurturer, and she didn't want to startle her daughter. Cheryl thought about the person walking down the street last night. If that had frightened her—just a form walking in front of her house—how would she handle it if she were in Esther's shoes, knowing a stranger was so close? She'd feel fidgety and unsure, just like the young woman in front of her.

"Esther, your daed and maam aren't listening to me. I wish they'd call the police about the intruder. Do you think you can talk to them?" Cheryl considered telling Esther about the doll and wrappers, but changed her mind. Esther had enough to worry about.

"I have tried, and my parents say they will take care of it. They are still concerned about the person. They do not want to get him or her in trouble. Last night Levi even said he would stay up to confront whoever it was, but I found him asleep on the sofa. He must have gotten cold and returned to the house sometime in the night. I tried to wake him, but it was impossible. Meanwhile I had a hard time sleeping." Esther's voice had a delicate tremble, and her eyes wore an expression to match it. "My room is closest to the buggy shed. I have a hard time sleeping knowing someone could be out there."

The tour bus parked outside, and as much as Cheryl wanted to comfort Esther's fears, she had another pressing question. Even though she wouldn't mention the wrappers, she had to ask about the fudge.

"Esther, we're out of Katie's Fudge. There were five or six boxes yesterday. Did someone come in and buy them?"

"The fudge?" Esther hurried to the display table where the fudge had sat. Her mouth gaped open. "You are right. They are not here." She placed a hand on her chest. "But I did not sell it, and Maam has not been in lately. If it was not you or me who sold those boxes, then where did they go? Were they stolen just like those Amish carvings?"

Esther blinked quickly, and Cheryl was certain the young woman was ready to burst into tears. With her growing interest in LeRoy, the worries about the person in her buggy shed, and now the most recent theft—the young woman's emotions were both up and down, like her nerves were right on the surface.

Maybe things would be easier once Naomi got here. She always did seem to know how to calm her daughter.

Cheryl released a breath. She patted Esther's hand. "Let's not worry about that now." Her words were barely a whisper. "We'll figure it out. Let's just get through the day." Cheryl looked around. "Will your maam be in?"

Esther nodded. "I think she will later."

"And LeRoy? Have you heard from him? Seen him?"

Esther shook her head. "Ne. I have not seen him since we left last night." She bit her lip, and Cheryl could tell she was worried about him too. "I thought he would let us know if he was not coming."

"Excuse me?" A woman approached. "I have a question about some candles."

Esther turned to the woman, but then Cheryl stepped forward. "I can help you. We have a lovely selection."

Cheryl helped a woman pick out some seasonal scented candles and thought about walking next door to chat with Agnes—and showing her the doll. But the store was busy, and she didn't feel comfortable leaving Esther alone.

Instead, she plastered on a smile and went about her work as if everything were right in the world.

And it would be right again sometime, wouldn't it? Cheryl released a breath, praying it would be so.

The day was busy with customers, but one customer stood out among the rest. The young blonde woman wore the same army jacket she'd worn last time and carried the same pink backpack too. Only this time she walked around with a small notebook in her hands.

She was listening to customers again, eavesdropping on bits of conversation. She also strolled around, taking notes on items and watching the customers and staff. Every time Cheryl attempted to approach her, the young woman would strike up a conversation with another customer about a product or an item, as if it were the most fascinating thing she'd ever seen.

What in the world can she be up to?

Soon customers cast the young woman curious glances too.

When more than an hour passed, Cheryl was no longer able to pretend she didn't notice the woman's strange behavior.

As the young woman picked up a decorative kerosene lamp and turned it over in her hands, Cheryl approached. "Excuse me. Is there something I can help you with?" She pointed at the woman's notebook. "You've taken a lot of notes and been in here a long time."

The young woman swallowed hard and then lowered her chin. "I'm creating…" She looked up into Cheryl's gaze. "I was actually wanting to, uh, create a place like this." She tucked a strand of blonde hair behind her ear. "It sounds sort of silly, I know, but I've thought about it a long time."

Her eyes were large and earnest, and if she was lying she should move to Hollywood. Acting like that would win a lot of awards.

Should Cheryl believe her story? The last time the young woman had been in, she'd claimed she was a journalist for the *Little*

Rock Times, and that proved to be false. Should she believe anything this woman said?

The young woman shuffled slightly. Cheryl almost thought she'd bolt, but instead she extended her hand. "I'm Cassie by the way. I do have a journalism degree." She readjusted her backpack on her shoulder, and then she looked around. "I *am* here to research, but for something else entirely. My goal is to recreate a place like this. I hope you don't mind."

"Will it be my competition?" Cheryl cocked her head. "Because that would be a problem."

"Oh no!" Cassie shook her head. Her blonde hair fluttered as she did. "Not at all. It's a completely different location." A glimmer of excitement filled the young woman's gaze, and Cheryl couldn't help warming to her.

Yet in addition to the glimmer in her eyes, there was a sly smile on Cassie's face. Cheryl was certain the young woman was hiding something. What could Cheryl say to that? Did she say yes so that Cassie would hang around—so she could catch her stealing? Or no, to make sure she stayed out of her store. But then she might just go rob someone else.

Cheryl also had Esther to worry about, and she had no idea where LeRoy was. Thankfully he'd fixed the sink, but the old pieces still lay on the floor. The bathroom was a mess, which meant she'd had to send more than one person next door to the quilt shop to use their bathroom.

Cheryl was still trying to decide what to say when an elderly woman approached.

"Excuse me," the woman said. "I'm looking for more of these Hollyberry candles. Do you happen to have more in the back?"

"I can check. It'll just take me a minute." Cheryl looked to the young woman to excuse herself, but Cassie's attention had already turned to some hand-dipped candles. She studied them with awed interest, as an art enthusiast would study the *Mona Lisa*.

Cheryl hurried to the back and found the jarred candles the woman needed. By the time she made it back up front, Naomi rushed in, tucking gray hair back in her kapp. "I am so sorry I am late. I had to buy some things for our Thanksgiving dinner. I wanted to get the items I needed before the stores sold out next week."

"You're a smart woman." Cheryl smiled, pretending Naomi's words didn't sting. Naomi was her closest friend in Sugarcreek, and the Millers felt like part of the family. But since they hadn't invited her to dinner, maybe her feelings were one-sided.

Cheryl took in a deep breath and then blew it out slowly. She had to make a plan. Since John-John hadn't come by for the additional items, maybe she should just take them down to the women's shelter herself. And maybe instead of pouting about Thanksgiving, a better idea would be to call Violet and see if she could serve the women that day. She guessed Violet could always use another pair of hands in the kitchen.

"Did you see LeRoy around town?" Cheryl asked Naomi.

"Ne. Did he not come today?"

"No. He didn't."

"Esther mentioned you have another project for him. You did not pay him in advance, did you?" A look of concern flicked on Naomi's face.

"I only paid him for the work he's finished." She bit her lower lip. "I hope he's all right. I don't have a way to contact him. If he lives on his own, how would anyone know if something happened?"

Two people walked in the shop, one right after the other, interrupting her thoughts. First, it was the foster boy, Gage. The young man made a beeline path to the game of checkers. Gage's long stride caught her attention and so did his hands tucked into the pockets of his bulky sweatshirt. It seemed there was plenty of room in there to hide things.

Cheryl's gaze followed him for a second, but then all her attention turned to the second person. Levi Miller walked with a more relaxed gait. He paused just inside the door and looked around. His eyebrows lifted as he noted the number of customers. Then his eyes skimmed the room, resting on hers. Her breath caught.

"Maam, can you help me at the register?" Esther called.

"Ja, of course." Naomi hurried over to help bag up the packages.

Levi removed his black felt hat, and then he stepped forward. He turned it over in his hand. "Cheryl." He stated her name simply, but just the sound of it caused small flutters of butterflies in her stomach.

"It's good to see you, Levi. Did you need your maam?" She pointed to the counter and the register, where Naomi was wrapping jars of jam in paper and placing them in a bag. "I'm sure she'll be done in a minute."

"Ne. Actually I came in to talk to you. I need to apologize for the way I acted the other night."

"The other night?"

"Ja, okay more than just a few nights ago. I did not treat you very kindly, and it has been bothering me. I should have come sooner, but I know you are busy."

A customer glanced in Levi's direction, and her eyes widened. She alerted her friend who also looked. Around Sugarcreek the Amish were the superstars, and someone as handsome as Levi drew the same type of attention as Brad Pitt did when he was spotted on Rodeo Drive.

"I was really out of place," Levi continued, unaware of the customer's intense gaze.

The woman continued to stare, and she approached Levi's left. Cheryl tried to watch her out of the corner of her eye. The woman tried to be sly as she took a picture of Levi, and Cheryl hid her smirk.

Her Amish friends got that a lot. People tried to be sneaky as they took photos of the Amish, but they fooled no one. Even Levi must have noticed the woman and her camera because he glanced over and smiled. She quickly snapped a shot, and then he returned to his pensive look, focusing on Cheryl again.

A soft smile rose to Cheryl's lips, and she tried to ignore the woman. "Apologize?"

Levi leaned closer, and his intense gaze fixed on her. "I am sorry for how I treated you last week. I told you that you were bringing your big-city problems..."

Cheryl held up her hand. "I know what you said," she whispered.

"Anyway, I should not have said that. I know you were just concerned. And maybe we should have listened sooner." Levi swallowed, and his Adam's apple bobbed. "I tried to stay up last night to catch the intruder." He looked away shyly. "But I ended up coming into the house sometime in the night. It was freezing. Whoever is staying out there is tougher than me."

Cheryl noticed more movement and more attention on Levi. It was the young woman Cassie. She watched Levi intently, peeking over the stand of candles. Every now and then she lowered her hand, and Cheryl wondered if she was jotting down more notes— as if staring at a handsome Amish bachelor would be any help to her opening her own gift shop.

"It has been cold lately. I'm thankful for a nice warm house." She tilted her head as she looked at him. "Are you going to try again—sleeping out there in order to find your guest?"

He shrugged. "I do not know what to do. Maybe we could talk about it."

"Talk?" Cheryl tucked her hands into her apron pocket, and her fingers brushed the papers they'd found in the winter buggy. She wondered if Levi knew about the stories—about Meryl—and she guessed he did.

"Maam said things have been busy here, but I was hoping that you had time to talk still."

"Perhaps go for a buggy ride?" Cheryl glanced over to Naomi, who was pretending not to watch.

"Ja, just around town for a while, and then we will pick up Maam and Esther and take you out to our house for dinner. After dinner I would be happy to give you a ride home too."

"Dinner, that does sound wonderful. So does the ride." Cheryl pulled her hand from her pocket and rested it on her stomach, emphasizing her words. "When? Later today?"

"How about now?"

Cheryl glanced around the busy store. She still had to get her overdue books back to the library. She had to put in a few orders for Christmas. And she still hadn't gone next door to talk to Agnes about the doll. She'd been planning to do that as soon as Naomi arrived.

"Now? Well…" Cheryl looked at Cassie and Gage. The two people she still suspected of stealing were both in the store. She should stay and watch them then maybe she'd have the answers she needed.

"Another time would be better." Cheryl crossed her arms over her chest. "There is so much going on today."

The light in Levi's eyes faded, and he tucked his hands in his jacket pockets and looked down at his boots. "Ja, you are right. Maybe a better time." He pulled his hand out of his large jacket pocket and held something wrapped in wax paper in his hand.

A sweet, yeasty aroma filled the air, and Cheryl breathed in the scent of cinnamon rolls.

Levi extended his hand. "I suppose I should leave this with you then. It is a treat from the Honey Bee." He chuckled. "If I keep it, I will eat both."

"That is so nice." Cheryl reached for it and then paused. She considered what Mitzi would say... *live the adventure, let yourself enjoy life once in a while.* After all, the store would still be there the next day. And the next.

But still, there was too much happening. She had to keep her eye on the suspects. If something turned up missing later, she'd regret leaving.

Cheryl blew out a soft breath. "You know, actually I think I would like to go on a buggy ride, but can you wait an hour?" She pulled her hand back, and then she pointed to the clock on the wall. "I can get off a little early, but I just can't leave your maam and sister like this."

Disappointment flashed in Levi's gaze, but he smiled anyway. "I would not expect anything less from you, Cheryl. You are always thoughtful like that."

Levi sauntered out, and for the next hour Cheryl did her best to help her customers and to watch both Gage and Cassie. The tour bus left, filled with happy customers and overflowing bags, yet both her suspects were there when Levi returned.

Seeing him, Cheryl approached Esther.

"Can you watch *them*?"

Esther's gaze darted from Cassie to Gage and then back to Cheryl again. "Ja, of course."

Levi walked up to her, and he paused before the two women. "Ready?"

"Do you mind if I get my coat?"

He smiled. "Of course not. It is cold out there."

Cheryl walked to her office, stepped inside, and sighed. "What in the world is this about?" She placed a hand over her heart and told herself that Levi was just being friendly, that's all.

"He felt bad for his words... and you have been worried about too many things." It was Naomi's voice from the doorway. Cheryl turned.

"I am glad you are going, Cheryl. You need a break."

Yet seeing her friend's smile, Cheryl's heart sank. Had Naomi put Levi up to this?

"You're always taking care of everyone, aren't you, Naomi?"

Naomi shrugged. "And if I do not, who will?"

"And what about you?" Cheryl stepped forward and took her friend's hand, telling herself she needed to be thankful that Levi agreed with Naomi's plan. "Who's going to take care of you?"

Naomi's face displayed peace even though the noise and the crowds were just a few feet beyond the office door. "The goot Lord takes care of me."

"And He takes care of me too." Cheryl gave Naomi a quick squeeze. "After all, He gave me you as a friend."

Then, with tentative steps, Cheryl walked back to the front of the store. Levi waited by the door, and Cheryl wondered if this wasn't the biggest mystery of all. Levi was open to being a friend, just when Cheryl was sure that she needed one most. At least she should be thankful for that.

Chapter Eighteen

Cheryl held Levi's hand as she climbed into the buggy.
"Is this the winter buggy?" she asked.

"Ja." Levi climbed up beside her. "The glass protects us from the elements. It is small, but it works." He chuckled. "We stay warm because we are pressed together." He reached in the back and grabbed a blanket. "I am sorry I do not have a heater like your car. Do you mind if I tuck this around you?"

Cheryl tucked her scarf tighter under her chin. "Not at all. Thank you."

He placed the blanket on her lap. It was thick and warm. Then he gently tucked it around the sides of her legs. Levi's neck was close to her face, and he smelled of hay and wood shavings—a delightful smell.

Cheryl couldn't remember the last time someone had tucked her in. His tenderness warmed her, even though the buggy was cold inside. She liked this protective side of Levi that tended to her.

Levi sat beside her and placed a second blanket on his lap. She resisted the urge to snuggle close to him. This was simply a friendly ride, that's all—nothing to write Aunt Mitzi about.

Levi looked so handsome in his dark jacket, smoothly shaved face, and thick wool hat. After seeing she was settled in, he flicked the reins. In one smooth motion the horse lurched forward.

She glanced around at the buggy. It was noticeably different than the one she'd ridden in last time on the Millers' farm. That buggy had been open, and the crisp fall air brushed her cheeks as she rode.

This buggy was walled in with glass. Even though the windshield on Levi's side of the buggy was open for the reins to fit through, there was a window in front of her. The glass went all around the back and around the other side, blocking out the cold wind.

With another tug of the reins, the horse veered on to Main Street. The horse's hooves clomped on the black asphalt. Cheryl sucked in a breath and then glanced over her shoulder, looking for cars.

"Do not worry." Levi chuckled. "I have a mirror, and no one was coming."

She folded her gloved hands on her lap. "I'm a horrible back-seat driver. Just ask..." She'd almost said, "Just ask Lance" but she didn't want to explain. She glanced over and smiled. "I'm as bad a passenger in a buggy as in a car."

He flicked the reins once more and the horse started to trot in a steady rhythm, picking up speed. "I never said you were a bad passenger." The gentle rocking of the seat was calming.

They neared the end of the block, and Cheryl noticed Agnes standing on the corner talking to someone...that woman with jet-black hair and purple glasses. The same woman who'd been a customer at the Swiss Miss earlier that day. Cheryl's heart skipped a beat, and she wondered if Agnes was confronting the woman. Did Agnes think she was the thief?

Then a smile filled Agnes's face, and Cheryl guessed she was off base. As they passed, Agnes glanced at the buggy. She looked toward Levi first then Cheryl. Her eyes widened and she waved excitedly, as if trying to get Cheryl's attention. Levi was looking the opposite way, and for the briefest moment, Cheryl planned on telling him to stop. Maybe the woman had news about the thefts.

Cheryl needed to talk to her too. She'd left the little Amish doll from Agnes's store in her office and still had the wrappers from the boxes of fudge to show Agnes.

She also hadn't heard any reports from Agnes in the last week. But as much as she needed to talk to the quilt store manager, she wanted to be here with Levi. He said he wanted to talk to her about whoever slept in their buggy. She'd almost turned him down—then made him wait. She didn't want to ruin it now.

So instead of looking over to Agnes, Cheryl kept her gaze ahead. And instead of asking Levi to stop, she snuggled down farther into the seat.

"So this is the buggy where the guest has been sleeping?" she asked, hoping Agnes wasn't trying to run after the buggy and almost giggling at the thought of her chasing them down the block.

"Ja." He nodded. "We park it in the buggy shed. The windshields keep the cold air out, making it warmer, but not warm enough for me. I tried to sleep in it last night and gave up."

"Is there a way to lock the door to the buggy shed?"

"There is a way . . . it just has not happened yet."

She thought about suggesting he hire LeRoy to install a lock, but changed her mind. Levi no doubt had the ability, so why hadn't he done it?

"I have to admit I am torn over whether I want to install a lock."

"What do you mean?"

He glanced over at her, studied her face for a minute, and then focused on the road ahead once more. Then his attention turned to a man walking down the street. Levi's hands were on the reins, but the horse seemed to be leading the way. She supposed that was one way driving a car differed from driving a buggy. In a buggy you just had to set off and head the right direction. There was little steering until you needed to turn another direction.

"That is what I wanted to talk to you about. Out of everyone, I knew you would give me an honest answer. I am torn because the Good Book says we should care for our neighbors. If someone strikes us on the cheek, we turn the other to them also. If we have two cloaks, or coats, we should offer one . . . I know you have read it."

"Yes, but that means *neighbors*, not strangers freeloading on your property." She said the words, and she could almost anticipate his answer.

"In that same passage it says, 'Bless them that curse you, and pray for them which despitefully use you.'"

Cheryl sighed. "Yes, there's always that. Those things make sense when you read them, but they're different . . ."

"They are harder when you try to live them out. And when you are worried about your family, I know."

Cheryl crossed her arms over her chest, trying to imagine what she would do. How would she feel if there was obviously someone in need but she worried for her family? It was hard to say, but something inside told her she'd put her family first. But is that what God wanted?

"There is not only that," Levi continued. "What about the Good Samaritan? He helped the man who was injured on the roadway. He risked his own life by stopping, but he still did it... because the man was there. The Samaritan did not know the man. They were also considered 'enemies' by their culture, just like an intruder and a home owner I suppose."

Cheryl shuffled slightly in her seat. She could understand what he was saying, but there was the safety of his family to consider.

"I could see how you'd want to help someone who came to the door. Or someone you find on the road, but this person is in hiding... and doing who knows what else. You really have no idea, do you, what their motives are?"

He glanced over at her and winked. "Writing, or at least that is what it appears."

"Yes, that is the strangest part." She focused on his blue eyes, realizing again what the closeness did to her pounding heart. "Did you read it?"

"The story about *Meryl?*" He emphasized the last word. "You should be honored to be the subject of such a great story."

She chuckled. "Yeah, do you know what I think? I think you're in the story too."

"I am?"

"I'm certain of it. You're that guy who was passed out, leaning against the front of my shop."

"Meryl's shop..."

"Yes, *Meryl's* shop." She nudged him in the ribs, and he jumped.

"Ouch." He smirked. "So I am the bum?"

"How do you know he's a bum? I think he's there for a reason, right? That's what brings intrigue to the story. Maybe it's the hero and—" Cheryl stopped short. Maybe it was a romance book, but that would give Levi the wrong idea.

"And the hero saves the day and finds the thief?"

"Exactly." She nodded. *And rides off with the girl,* she wanted to say.

They continued on, and Levi turned the buggy to go down the road behind Main Street. Then reaching into his pocket, he pulled out the cinnamon roll. He chuckled. "You are lucky I did not eat that."

"Thank you. Do you mind if I save it?"

"Not at all. Did you have a big lunch?"

"Something like that." She wasn't about to tell him that his nearness made her lose her appetite...but in a good way.

They passed the Berryhills' house, and Marion had just parked her car and was climbing out. Cheryl waved, and Marion waved back. She looked surprised to see Cheryl's form of transportation today.

Marion's coat didn't button over her stomach, and Cheryl wondered how many days until the new baby would be joining their family. How would Gage handle that? Was he going to feel left out? Or was he excited that his new family was growing?

Cheryl sighed. "So I suppose if I've already pegged you as the hero of the story, you might want to do something risky and help the person in need."

"Are you talking about me or the story?"

"Honestly, I'm talking about both."

He was silent for a moment as if considering her words. "Funny, I thought you would be the one telling me to call the police."

"I would have said that . . . if you hadn't quoted scripture."

"Ja, that is the problem that I keep returning to. Either that or the solution."

It was warmer now in the buggy. Maybe from the blanket. Maybe from the closeness to Levi or the warm air of their breaths.

"So what will you do now?" Cheryl asked. The buggy turned the corner again and then crossed the road, heading toward her house.

"Well, Maam left a note, telling whoever it was to come to the house if they need food and whatnot, but I may write my own note."

Cheryl sat straighter in the seat. "Really?"

"Ja, but now I am trying to figure out what to say. I should offer my bed . . ."

She gasped and placed a hand on his arm. "Offer your bed? As in letting the person stay in your house?"

"But I am not stupid. Sometimes big-city troubles do find the countryside. I suppose I have until dinner to think about it. Our visitor usually does not slip in until late."

"Maybe today will bring more answers." She thought of Cassie and Gage. She wondered if Esther would see anything that provided additional clues. "And I know you, Levi. You'd never put your family in harm's way. God will help you figure it out. I know He will. But I appreciate you talking to me about it, even if I don't have answers."

"The fact you did not rant and call me foolish for considering offering my bed is an answer."

She smiled. "Well, if you're going to bring God's opinion into it and all . . ." She joked. "Then I suppose He knows a thing or two about how to deal with people."

Her comment got the smile she hoped from Levi, but it was more than that too. Having him open up to her in this way made her see he'd been thinking about what she had to say. And that he trusted her.

As her house came into view she knew this was a big step—not only for Levi, but for her. Levi saw her as someone he could turn to. And with friendships like that starting to take place, Sugarcreek was feeling more and more like home.

CHAPTER NINETEEN

After a day of mounting questions and worries about thefts and intruders, the buggy ride had helped to calm Cheryl. She hadn't known how much the queries had weighed on her until the gentle sway of the buggy had lulled them away. Cheryl shrugged her shoulders. Even her neck felt looser after the ride. Who knew listening to the horse's hooves clomp and sharing simple conversation could do so much.

With a lightness to her step that hadn't been there for weeks, Cheryl returned to the Swiss Miss to help Naomi and Esther close the shop. Then she drove home with Beau.

She gave him fresh water and filled his dish with food. "Tomorrow night we'll sit, and you can curl on my lap, and we'll watch mindless television. I promise."

She had only a few minutes to freshen up before Levi drove the buggy to her house to pick her up for the ride back to the Miller farm. Cheryl had considered telling Levi she could drive herself. It would be faster and warmer, and he wouldn't have to worry about taking her home. But she liked the idea of him driving her home tonight. *By the light of the silvery moon.*

Several minutes later, she joined the Millers in their buggy. She insisted Naomi sit in the front seat next to Levi, and she climbed in the back and sat next to Esther. They chatted about Gage, Marion's new baby who was due any day, and the young woman who now claimed she was opening a gift shop.

"There's something else I haven't told you about. The other night I woke up after a bad dream, and Beau was watching something intently out the window. Well, at least I thought it was something. It turned out it was someone. And they were carrying a sack full of things. Then this morning someone found a little Amish doll in the road... and wrappers."

Esther cocked an eyebrow. "Wrappers?"

"Yes, wrappers just like the ones from the boxes of fudge."

"Do you think it was the person who has been stealing things from the stores on Main Street?"

Cheryl nodded. "I think so. Who else would be lurking around like that?"

Naomi turned in her seat. "A guy? A girl? Did you see?"

Cheryl shook her head and puckered her lips. "Unfortunately not. The person was wearing dark clothes. He or she had their head down. Whoever it was walked quickly away from town—as if they had someplace to go."

"What is down that street?" Levi piped up from the front.

"Just more houses, apartments..."

Naomi's eyes widened. "There are some abandoned houses down that way. It is possible that the person could be hiding the stolen items in one of them." She tapped Levi's shoulder. "Do you remember when some of your friends used to have those wild parties there during their rumspringa?"

Levi turned her direction. "They were not close friends, but I knew them. And ja, I remember. It seems that it has been on the agenda of the town council for a very long time to get those places torn down."

"That would be a shame." Naomi clucked her tongue. "Do you know when we were visiting with those women at Every Woman's House that Violet told me their greatest need was for transitional homes—places for the women to go once they felt safe again. It is hard enough to leave everything behind because of domestic violence, but the next step is starting over on your own. Maybe we can talk to the town council about that. And maybe instead of a barn raising, we can bring everyone together to remodel those homes."

Levi nodded. "It is a goot idea, Maam, but I think you are getting ahead of yourself. It is a goot idea to stop by those houses and look. Maybe I will do that tomorrow."

"Tomorrow I'm going to talk to Agnes," Cheryl said. "I haven't heard one thing about what's happened with other businesses or if Officer Ortega has made any headway. And today got away from me."

Naomi glanced over her shoulder. "I suppose every other shop owner has discovered what we have. The busy holiday shopping season has descended on Sugarcreek early."

"Yes, Aunt Mitzi will be pleased with the sales. I think she'll also be pleased with the repairs to the awning and the bathroom."

"It is strange how I—we—never heard from LeRoy today." Esther's voice was soft, and Cheryl wondered if the comment was for her ears only.

"I wondered too. I hope he's not sick. He was working out in the cold for a long time yesterday morning."

"I am more worried about his maam." Esther rubbed her gloved hands together. "Or his brother. It must be hard trying to take care of them both while trying to find work in a new town."

Levi's hands lightly held the reins, and he focused straight ahead. "Why not get a regular job? There are always places hiring—the factories or local farms. It would be easier to find full-time work than going around town trying to find odd jobs."

"Maybe he needs to be flexible, like needing to leave to care for family at a moment's notice," Esther countered.

It was barely perceivable, but Levi shook his head. "Seems he could have stopped by to talk to Cheryl. Or leave a note on her front door. It is not right that he left her place in a mess like that."

Esther placed a hand on Cheryl's blanketed knee. "I told Levi about what had happened, and he did not want to leave you with that mess in the bathroom. We cleaned it up for you. It only took us ten minutes to haul out all the old stuff and clean it up."

"Thank you for doing that..." Cheryl looked to the back of Levi's neck. "That was kind of you." She didn't know what else to say about LeRoy. She didn't want to point fingers like Levi without knowing the problem. She also didn't want to defend him like Esther since she agreed with Levi. LeRoy should have left a note.

They rode quietly the last five minutes. Cheryl felt her eyes fluttering closed more than once as the quietness of the buggy and the clip-clop of the trotting horses soothed her. While she loved her car, its heater, and her radio, she could see how a buggy ride home every evening would help to separate one's mind from the worries and demands of the day.

Autumn still hung on, but barely. From the clouds building in the darkening sky, it seemed winter wished to push across the landscape.

When they neared the Miller farm, Cheryl almost drifted off, but startled when Esther straightened and leaned forward.

"Is something wrong?"

Esther pointed out the front of the buggy. "Look."

Seth waited for them in the driveway. He was wearing his work jacket, and Cheryl guessed it was chore time, but that didn't explain why he stood there waiting.

He held what looked to be a plastic bag filled with garbage in his hand, and his furrowed brow proved he wasn't happy about it.

Levi pulled up near the buggy shed, and the front doors were open.

She was the last one to climb from the buggy. She was thankful for the hand down from Levi, but his scowl alerted her that Seth's actions weren't a common occurrence. Something was clearly wrong.

"Well, it seems the buggy shed was too confining. It seems whoever moved in is taking over more and more of my barn." Seth held out the plastic bag as evidence. "What is going to happen next? Are they planning to move into the house?"

Cheryl glanced over at Levi with those words. Levi's jaw twitched slightly, but he kept his eyes focused on his daed's.

"Whoever is staying here hid a plastic bag full of things under one of the haystacks," Seth continued. "We never would have found it except our 'guest' made a mistake. They left peanut butter crackers in there. Rover dug it out, and when I went to do chores, the contents were strewn over the barn."

Cheryl's chin shivered, and it wasn't just from the cold. "Are they moving in slowly?"

Seth shrugged, and Cheryl knew she was asking questions no one except the person could answer. But the more stuff they found around the barn, the more it was an indication the person planned to stay awhile.

Naomi approached her husband. Curiosity creased her brow. "What was in the bag?"

"Come. I will show you." He pointed to the barn. "Let us get out of the cold."

Cheryl's breath made frosty puffs in front of her mouth as she followed.

They entered the barn, the large door creaking. Naomi closed it behind them, and then she spoke in a soft greeting to the animals. She walked by the milk cow and stroked its wide forehead. She passed the horses next. A black pony stretched out his neck, and Naomi scratched it between the eyes.

The building was also larger inside than it appeared. It was warmer in the barn than it was outside—maybe from the heat of the animals? And that was another mystery, why hadn't the intruder slept in here? It was warmer than the buggy shed.

Seth led them to a neat pile of feed bags. On top he'd laid out a variety of items. A plastic coffee cup with a lid from the Handi-Stop gas station down the road and what remained of packages of peanut butter crackers. A thick cardboard envelope that had been chewed on the edges and a notebook. The envelope was sealed.

Seth pointed to the notebook. "It was open and I saw our names."

Cheryl stepped forward. "Your names?"

Seth handed her the notebook. "Ja."

Cheryl opened the cover. "Chapter one," she read at the top of the first page. Then she proceeded to read.

Naomi Miller did not know what her son, Levi, was up to. He walked out of the big red barn with a shovel. He whistled as he walked.

"Going out to the old oak tree, Ma!" Levi called over his shoulder.

Cheryl paused her reading. "Ma?"

Naomi shrugged. "Levi has never called me Ma since I have known him."

Cheryl smiled. "Well, there is a television show called *Little House on the Prairie*. I used to watch it as a kid. They wore bonnets, and the children called their maam, Ma. Maybe that's where they got it?"

Naomi crossed her arms over her chest. "Ja, but I do not like it. I became worried when whoever-this-is called you Meryl. To use our real names... that seems so personal."

Cheryl nodded. She was intrigued by the story—mostly how the writer was mixing in real people. "There is something strange about a person not only sneaking around your farm, but writing all of you into a story."

She continued reading.

Levi Miller walked with a hop in his step. He was tall with blue eyes, a few freckles, and brown hair cut straight across his forehead. He would have been handsome if he had a better haircut and wore a nice pair of jeans instead of homemade britches. But Levi didn't worry about that. He'd had a dream. In his dream his great-great-grandfather had visited him. The man told him a treasure was hidden by the big, old tree. In it was a time capsule, and within the capsule were stories of those who'd visited the farm over the years.

Cheryl turned the pages. Page after page there was more of the story. As it went along the modern day story ended, and the historical stories changed each time the time capsule was opened.

Levi looked to his daed. "Did you read the whole thing?"

"Ne. Only about ten pages," Seth said as if embarrassed by the fact he'd read so much. "I had to keep going. I wanted to know what Levi discovered."

Cheryl flipped through a few more pages. "Well, we know one thing. Your guest is a woman."

"How can you be sure?"

Cheryl pointed to the description of Levi. "First of all, the story sounds as if a woman wrote it. No man would describe Levi this way." Cheryl agreed about everything except the haircut. Levi's haircut was part of what made him Levi.

Naomi nodded. "I think you are right. Also, look at the other items in the bag—a pink plastic coffee cup, sugar-free chewing gum, and some lip gloss. Those things do not seem to belong to a man."

Cheryl shivered, and Naomi motioned to the house. "Why don't we get inside? We can look through this and talk as I get dinner on the table."

She followed the Millers into their home. It was warm inside, and the only sound was the wood crackling in the fireplace.

Cheryl slid off her coat and hung it up on the rack by the door. She followed them into the kitchen. "I'd be happy to help with dinner."

"There is nothing to help with. I made a pot of vegetable soup last night, since I knew I would work today. It is in the icebox. I just have to reheat it."

Cheryl sat at the table. "Sounds wonderful."

"It will taste wonderful too." Levi sat beside her. "Well, this answers my question."

"About leaving a note."

"Ja, I would not feel comfortable offering my bed to a woman. Even if I slept in Eli's room, it would not look right."

Esther's mouth gaped open. "And you think it would have looked right to offer a strange man your bed, with me right next door?"

Levi glanced over to Esther. "If you say it like that, I suppose it is not a goot idea." He placed both palms on the table. "I wish there was an easy answer."

Esther started setting the table. Cheryl rose to help, but Esther motioned her to sit.

"It is just the five of us tonight. Elizabeth has been in Charm helping a cousin who just had a baby, and Eli and Caleb are away too. Everyone will be home for Thanksgiving."

Cheryl forced a smile. "I wondered why it's so quiet." She didn't mention Thanksgiving and neither did they. Levi continued reading the notebook while Cheryl picked up the envelope and turned it over. If it hadn't been sealed, she would have opened it. Maybe something inside would give them a clue about its owner.

Naomi placed freshly baked bread on the table and went back to stir the soup. Laughter rumbled from Levi. "Here you are, Meryl, in 1931 Sugarcreek. I know why that old page was torn out too. Instead of the man being slumped against the wall outside the shop, he rides in slumped on a horse, passed out from loss of blood."

Cheryl placed a hand over her mouth, trying to stifle a laugh. "That *is* more dramatic."

A few minutes later Naomi set a pot of soup in front of them. They all washed up, and then Cheryl waited while they lowered their heads in silent prayer.

Thank You, Lord, for these good friends. And I pray for this person, whoever she might be. I pray that the Millers will be able to give her the help she needs in a safe way.

Cheryl didn't know why the young woman chose the Miller house out of all the others, but she knew God allowed it for a reason. If anything, she enjoyed how this mystery was bringing them together.

CHAPTER TWENTY

Cheryl still walked on cloud nine as she traveled to the Swiss Miss the following morning, thoughts of Levi Miller filling her head. She hadn't stayed too late after dinner at the Millers' house. Early-to-bed Levi was already yawning as he helped her back into the buggy. It had been a quiet ride home, and she'd pointed out stars and constellations along the way. Levi had listened and even shared a few stories from growing up. It had been a perfect date in her opinion. Her heart told her the same. The only problem was it hadn't been a date.

Esther had offered to come in early to open the store, and Cheryl had run by the Silo Church to drop off a few things for the box the women's group was putting together for Aunt Mitzi. She included the lone box of Katie's Fudge she'd taken home for herself and a few more of her aunt's favorite treats.

As she carried Beau into the shop, she hoped the morning would usher in a normal day, slow until the first tour bus arrived so she could check the shop's inventory for any other thefts. Then after the bus, she'd visit Agnes. When she walked through the Swiss Miss's door, Cheryl heard pounding and the Christmas music louder than normal.

She glanced at Esther with raised eyebrows. "So LeRoy's back?"

Esther nodded. "Ja. It is like I thought. His brother was in an accident. The car was dented up, and his brother has a concussion. LeRoy had to sit with him for twenty-four hours. He apologized for not letting us know."

"And what's that banging?"

Esther shrugged. "He said something about putting in new shelving that matched the new file cabinet. I thought he had talked to you about it."

"No, but…" Cheryl paused. Something wasn't right. Even as Esther talked to Cheryl, her eyes were fixed on the checkers table in the front corner of the store. Cheryl turned and followed her gaze.

Gage watched Ben and Rueben playing a game of checkers. He wore the same green sweatshirt, and he leaned against the table that once held the carvings of Amish children. A dull pain hit the pit of Cheryl's stomach when she noticed the large pocket in the front of the sweatshirt. It was bulky, sticking out away from his body. *What could be in there?*

She thought about approaching him and asking him to show her what was in his pockets. Was that legal? It was something Aunt Mitzi hadn't told her about. Could she get in trouble if she falsely accused someone of shoplifting?

Cheryl considered going to her office, asking LeRoy to step out for a few minutes, and calling Chief Twitchell to ask about Gage. Then she'd have to figure out what to do about LeRoy. She hadn't talked to him about new shelving. She moved the direction of the office and then paused.

Esther's eyes widened, and a worried look crossed her face. Cheryl glanced over her shoulder and saw the game had finished. With arms stretched into the air, Rueben declared himself a winner. Gage looked up, glanced around the store. He noticed Esther's gaze and moved to the door without a word or another glance. Even his footsteps were quiet as he left.

The bell on the door confirmed his departure, and Cheryl decided to follow. She took a few steps toward where Esther stood.

"I'm following him," she told Esther in a loud whisper. "Keep an eye on LeRoy."

Cheryl wasn't sure why she said that last part, but something about LeRoy's excuse didn't sit well with her.

Esther nodded and then approached a customer.

Cheryl buttoned her coat back up and then hurried back into the cold day. She looked to the left and then the right. *There.* She spotted Gage walking toward the bookstore. Yet instead of continuing on to the store, he turned down a side street.

Cheryl quickened her pace. The cold air stung her lungs as she hurried on. She passed a few ladies she knew from church, including Aunt Mitzi's friend Laurie-Ann. Laurie-Ann paused and lifted her hand in greeting.

"Can I call you later?" Cheryl asked, knowing the woman wanted to talk. "I'm on an errand right now."

She didn't wait for the woman's response and hurried on. She got to the end of the street and rounded the corner where Gage had turned. The next block was a mix of businesses and vacation rentals, and Cheryl wondered if her suspicions were right. If Gage was the thief, he had another place he stored the items. Like maybe in one of those abandoned houses? Had Levi had a chance to look? She believed Marion when the woman said she hadn't seen any things around the house. Maybe Gage had found an empty rental house or someone's shed to hide things in.

She saw him turn down the street again, and he approached a small apartment complex. Without hesitation he walked up the sidewalk to the first door. He looked down at his feet as he waited.

Cheryl paused by the mailbox out front and waited. She would never make a good spy, but at least Gage hadn't turned around and spotted her.

He knocked again, and worries flooded her mind. What if this went beyond just stealing gift items? What if Gage was involved in something bigger? What if she was about to witness a drug deal or some other illegal act? *Maybe I shouldn't have followed him.* Then again, this was Sugarcreek and not Columbus.

The twinge in Cheryl's gut worsened. She'd wanted to do her part in catching the thief so the citizens of Sugarcreek could have peace, but it wasn't working. Maybe she should have followed Agnes's advice and turned the information over to the police and let them handle it. Maybe she should have called Chief Twitchell days ago.

The door opened, and Cheryl's breath caught. She sucked in another breath of surprise as an elderly woman stepped out. Cheryl didn't know the woman's name, but she recognized her from church. She hadn't seen the woman in a few weeks, and now Cheryl knew why. The woman wore a faded housedress, and she had a boot cast on her foot. She held a small white Maltese in her hand, and with a sweep of her arm she welcomed Gage.

They talked in the doorway, and Cheryl wished she could sneak closer to hear. Then Gage shook his head, and from his sweatshirt pocket he pulled out what looked to be small cans of dog food and handed them to the woman. The woman accepted them with a wide smile. She tried to offer Gage some money, but he shook his head and slumped away.

Cheryl looked around, trying to figure out where to go, where to hide—but there was nowhere. She noticed a piece of junk mail on the ground, so she knelt down to pick it up as he passed. She didn't look at him. Had he noticed her? How could he not with her red hair and her work apron peeking out from her coat?

When he was a few feet past her, Cheryl rose and walked the opposite direction. She supposed one act of kindness didn't mean Gage wasn't the thief, but what she'd just witnessed didn't mesh with what she would have anticipated. She'd expected him to pull something small from her shop out of the pouch…not dog food. She'd expected him to meet someone shady instead of an elderly woman who needed help. Maybe Levi was right. Maybe she did allow her big-city experiences to color the people she met in Sugarcreek. Maybe Gage was just a lonely teen trying to fit in and not knowing what to do with himself other than watch those around him like the brothers playing checkers. If she still felt displaced several months after moving to Sugarcreek because she wanted to, how did he feel being moved here for a foster home? She'd chosen to leave her life in Columbus. She'd chosen to pack up her things and start afresh in Sugarcreek. But Gage hadn't. Other people's choices had led to his being moved to a new place, a new home.

She glanced over her shoulder and noticed Gage's hunched walk as she rounded the corner. Had he made any friends? Or had he felt everyone's distrustful stares?

Cheryl swallowed down guilt that she had been part of the unwelcoming stares. She'd been so focused on solving a mystery she'd missed seeing the people who God was placing around her—a boy in foster care, a man who'd lost his sister, a young woman away from home finding solace in her store, an Amish bachelor trying to make ends meet while watching his brother.

Each of them was searching for "home" just as she was. Yet she was one step ahead of them. She had many acquaintances and some friends, especially the Millers. She had arrived with a place in the community thanks to the store and church connections.

Had she missed the whole point of these last weeks? Had God brought these people into her life so she could figure out who was stealing? Or was she supposed to extend a hand of kindness?

Cheryl walked with slower steps as she returned to the Swiss Miss. As she walked, she prayed for those who'd come into her life recently. She also prayed that Mitzi would find a sense of "home" far away from all that was familiar.

The cold pricked her nose and cheeks as she neared her store, and as she entered she noticed the store was empty. Esther was nowhere to be seen and the pounding had stopped in the office.

"Esther?" Cheryl called out. She moved toward the back office, wondering if the young woman had stepped out for a few minutes.

Yet she hadn't locked up and left the Be Back in Fifteen Minutes sign in the window.

"Over here!" a mumbled voice said. Cheryl stopped in her tracks. She walked around a display table to another table in the back. Esther's head and shoulders were underneath the skirted table. Only her rump, her stockinged legs, and her shoes stuck out.

"Are you okay?" Cheryl paused and bent down.

"I am looking to see if they are down here. If they got knocked off the table."

"They?" Cheryl asked.

Slowly, gingerly, Esther scooted back. Her kapp caught on the table skirt as she paused. Cheryl helped unsnag it, and then she stood to her feet and helped Esther do the same.

A deep furrow marred the bridge of Esther's nose. She looked around at the tables near her and then adjusted her kapp. Her dark hair was slightly messed up around her forehead, but Cheryl wasn't going to mention it. Instead she just wanted to know what had the girl so flustered.

"Did you lose something?"

"I do not think it is lost. I think it is stolen," Esther responded, giving Cheryl a brief glance. "I should have asked Maam to come in and help us today. She offered. I do not think one of us helping customers will be enough."

"What do you mean?"

"We've been robbed again."

"What's missing?"

"Two small handmade Amish baskets and a pile of Amish art coasters."

Cheryl bit down her frustration. "The hand-painted ones?"

"Ja." Esther brushed a strand of stray hair back from her face. "Whoever the thief is has expensive taste. He or she knows what items are small and can be tucked away easily, but still have value. The coasters were sitting right by the cheaper magnets but those were not touched." Esther sighed. "At least that confirms who did it."

"What do you mean?"

"The foster boy. Gavin."

"Gage?"

"Yes, Gage."

"But he didn't. He couldn't have."

Cheryl's thoughts battled. Could Gage have slipped the items into his pocket and also have the cans of dog food in there? And... Cheryl's jaw dropped. And what if he stole the dog food too? Should she go down and talk to the clerk at the market? No, his pouch wasn't big enough to hide the dog food and two baskets and a full stack of coasters. It couldn't be.

"I... Give me a few minutes to think about it." She pressed her fingertips to her forehead. "I'm going to my office. But what I saw after Gage left makes me wonder if we're all wrong about him. I really think we are."

Cheryl walked to the office and noticed something on the carpeted area. She bent down and picked up a small screwdriver. "Is this LeRoy's?" she called back to Esther.

"Oh ja. It must have fallen out of his toolbox. But do not worry. He said that he will be back tomorrow. He put up the new shelving. He said it was all donated. When he returns, he will need help with the file cabinet. He is going to repaint the back wall too. He found extra paint under the sink."

"New shelving? And new paint?"

"Ja, and he will be back tomorrow." Even with the stress of the missing items, Cheryl heard the hint of a smile.

She walked into the office and gasped. The two old shelves on the back wall had been taken down and three shelves put up.

Why hadn't Aunt Mitzi had someone fix up those shelves sooner? She had so much room now. It seemed like such an easy fix.

Of course, that didn't make her decision about what to do concerning Gage any easier.

Cheryl sank onto her office chair. She placed her elbows on the desk and rested her forehead in her hands. "If I were Gage's foster's mom, what would I want someone to do?"

With a baby due any day, she doubted Marion wanted to worry about this.

She thought about going to talk to Chief Twitchell. But if she talked to him, would the chief have to report it to the Department of Job and Family Services? She also thought about checking with the grocery store—to see if he'd possibly stolen that food—but again she didn't know if she could legally do that without contacting the police department.

If she were Marion, she'd want someone to talk to her directly, even if her baby was due. Cheryl took a deep breath, picked up the phone, and invited Marion to coffee. Amazingly, Marion didn't have any questions, and she agreed to meet Cheryl in an hour.

An hour. She needed that hour, to think. To pray.

CHAPTER TWENTY-ONE

The Honey Bee Café was nearly empty. Two other ladies sat at one of the small café tables near the front. Marion greeted Cheryl with a quick hug, as if they were old friends. Cheryl stretched out her arms and returned the hug, joining Marion in a chuckle as the woman's stomach got in the way.

They ordered their coffees and sat, and Cheryl wondered how she should bring things up. She didn't have to worry for long.

"My guess is you want to talk about Gage. I know I do. This transition has been so much harder on him than I'd anticipated." Marion leaned back and rubbed her hard, round stomach. "I hate to think of all he's gone through. And the transition to school is so hard." She took a sip of her coffee.

"You don't have to tell me." Cheryl wrapped her hands around her coffee cup, warming them. "I mean it's really not any of my business."

"There's nothing bad to tell. Gage was raised by a good family, but he lost his parents in an accident."

"An accident?"

"Yes, a car accident. He has an older brother in the military who wants to try to get custody of him. From what we've seen he's a good kid, but you're not the only store owner who has concerns.

I...I don't know what to think." She took another sip. "But I love how willing Gage is to help others. Sometimes I have to prod him, but helping others seems to help him."

Cheryl let the words sink in. "What do you mean?"

Marion took a sip of her coffee. "Most people think all foster kids come from a bad home. Or they have problems that got them in foster care."

Cheryl's view blurred as tears filled her gaze. She wiped a tear in the corner of her eye. "And I'm sure it doesn't help people's opinion of Gage that things started disappearing in stores around the time that he came to town."

"It doesn't." She sighed. "Gage's brother won't get back for four months, so I have to help him find a way to settle in until then."

Cheryl tapped her fingers on the table. "So other store owners have talked to you?"

"Just one." Marion leaned closer. "Agnes from the quilt store came and we chatted. She didn't mention names, but she said at least one other owner was worried. She brought Officer Ortega to talk to me, but I told them I haven't seen any of the missing items. There have also been a few sightings of a person—about Gage's size—who's hauling bags of stuff around town late at night." Marion rubbed her belly again. "Officer Ortega tried to catch the person, and he or she dropped the bag and ran. It was filled with things from Yoder's, cookbooks and such."

"And there was no way it could have been Gage?"

"No. He's not out at night."

Cheryl cocked an eyebrow, and Marion smiled.

"We know because we set up the baby monitor in the hall outside Gage's room. The window in the room is really noisy, and the door needs to be greased. His social worker encouraged us to do that, just in case he gets the idea he wants to head back to Millersburg—where he used to live. But so far he's given no indication he would. And he hasn't left at night. I'm certain."

Cheryl nodded. "I'm the one who talked to Agnes."

Marion's mouth gaped open. "You talked to her even after you and I talked?"

"I'm sorry. I thought it was too much of a coincidence that things turned up missing on the days he was in the store." She sighed. "I'm so sorry I planted a seed of doubt in Agnes's head."

Marion brushed her dark bangs from her face. "Thank you for being honest with me." Her gaze fell to her coffee, and a silent moment passed. "I wish I knew how to make things better for him."

"Keep loving that young man. Hopefully your love will ease his pain. Remind him he's a good kid."

Marion's eyebrows lifted. "Oh, so you think he's a good kid now?"

"Well, I sort of do because I followed him." Then Cheryl told the rest of the story. How she followed him to the next street over, and how she saw him giving dog food to an elderly woman.

"Oh, that's Mrs. Pryce. I had him deliver a book to her last week. He came home and told me her dog was having a hard time because she couldn't get out to give him the food he liked..." Marion's hand covered her mouth.

Cheryl could tell that she was trying to swallow down her emotion.

Marion lowered her hand. "I...I wonder if that's what he's spending his allowance on. Ray gave him twenty dollars last week. He said he spent it on video games, but we've never even seen him play video games."

"Well then I doubly apologize..." Cheryl wished she could sink through the floor. She had to be the worst judge of character. After all, the two people she'd assumed were thieves were actually saints.

"I'm glad he has a friend." Marion smiled. "Even if it's a seventy-eight-year-old woman with a dog and a broken leg. But I wish he could make friends his own age. That he'd settle in and consider this a home, even a little bit."

Two teen girls entered. Their giggles rang out, filling the room. Cheryl glanced over at them, wondering about the friends Gage left behind. She looked back at Marion and could see tenderness in her gaze. "I understand. It's hard fitting into a new place."

"And I suppose that really doesn't help you figure out who's stealing from your store, does it?"

"It's helped narrow down the suspects." Cheryl fidgeted in her seat, knowing that she needed to get back in the store. "That's something."

Then Cheryl got another idea. She leaned closer to Marion, resting her arms on the table.

"You know, I bet he'd love to help around By His Grace too. I'm sure he could stock books or assist customers. That might help him make a few more friends and start to feel connected around Sugarcreek."

Marion's eyes widened, and Cheryl saw she liked the idea.

"You know, I thought about asking Gage if he wanted to help, but I didn't want him to think we decided to open our home to foster care for free labor. But now that we've had a chance to get to know him better, I don't think he'd assume that at all. Instead, I believe he'd see it as a sign that we trusted him." She softly clapped her hands together. "Yes, I think he'd like that."

Cheryl glanced at her watch and then stood. She was glad that she took time for this conversation, but it was time to get back.

Marion stood too and gave her a quick hug.

Cheryl smiled as she felt Marion's round stomach being pressed between them. "Thank you for taking time to talk with me, and be sure you tell us when that baby arrives. It'll be something all of Sugarcreek will be thankful for."

Cheryl sat down on the chair in her office, thinking of Gage. He wasn't the thief, she was certain. She thought about John-John. He'd been suspicious, but he too had just been out doing good deeds. There were reasons why she considered both of them, and John-John even looked the part with his worn clothes, dirty jacket, and frayed shoes. He probably didn't have much, but he gave from what he had. His kindness meant a lot to Violet and the young women and children at the shelter.

She had one person left to consider—Cassie. The young woman was a mystery, and if she was a thief she was doing it in odd ways. She was very obvious in the way she followed people, taking notes and carrying that large backpack. Nothing about that young woman made sense.

Maybe that was the whole point. Maybe her notes were on how she could steal without being caught. Maybe she was paying attention to how many people worked, in what capacities, and the "hidden" parts of the store that were easiest to steal from.

Part of her cringed at the line of her thoughts. Her last two suspects had turned out to be false. She'd have to be careful before she accused someone else or even suggested they might be involved to anyone else. She'd certainly learned that with Gage.

The only problem was that she hadn't seen Cassie since yesterday. Had she taken all she could and left town? Had she hitchhiked to Berlin or Charm, only to start the same process there?

CHAPTER TWENTY-TWO

I t was two days before Thanksgiving, and Cheryl looked at her to-do list. The store would be closed for Thanksgiving, but the day after would be very busy and she had to get these tasks done today.

Cheryl went to her bedside table and picked up the stack of library books. She needed to return them. Pam had been so nice offering her grace, and she didn't want to take more advantage of it.

Out of the seven books she'd checked out, she'd only read three, and all had been easy-to-read inspirational stories. She lugged the books to her car and smiled to think she'd assumed since she didn't have a lot of meetings, dates, or other commitments in Sugarcreek she'd read a few books a week, but that wasn't the case. The work—and the worries—of the Swiss Miss often followed her home. Cheryl was surprised her reading interests had changed too.

She'd picked up a few novels by her favorite authors, but those were too hard to read. It wasn't so long ago when she'd planned a wedding and thought her future was set with Lance. Reading about someone else's happily-ever-after wasn't as enjoyable anymore.

Cheryl walked through the doors of the library only thirty minutes after it opened, but there were already a few people inside.

"Oh, Cheryl," the librarian behind the checkout counter cooed as she approached. "We got a new novel in last week that I thought you'd like. I set it aside." The woman with short grayish brown hair turned to grab a book off a rolling rack. Cheryl hardly remembered talking to the librarian when she was in getting her library card and checking out books—how did Pam remember her taste?

"Uh, thank you, Pam." Cheryl almost told the woman she didn't have the time—or the interest—to read it, but seeing the excited look on the woman's face changed her mind. "*To Dye For*." Cheryl chuckled. "What a cute title. I appreciate this so much."

"Oh, anytime, and if you ever need recommendations just let me know. I love to read, but I love finding the right books for people even more. Just like that young woman over there. She's from out of town." Pam pointed to a table in the reference section. "She is so interested in the history of Sugarcreek. Did you know the original name of this town was Shanesville, and the town grew around the intersection of two Indian trails? It's the most interesting story."

"Really? I'll have to pass that on." Cheryl flipped through the pages of the mystery novel, hoping the ending of this one turned out better than her mystery. "My customers are always asking questions about the area. They love when I pass on interesting facts."

Pam smiled and looked at the book. "Do you have your library card?"

"Oh no. I left my purse at home. I can come back…"

"Nonsense," Pam interrupted. She turned to her computer. "It'll just take me a minute to look you up."

Cheryl nodded and then looked at the young woman sitting at the reference table. She wasn't wearing a hat, and her soft blonde waves fell down her back. It was only as the young woman turned and glanced over her shoulder that Cheryl recognized her. Cassie.

Cheryl drummed on the library counter while she decided what to ask. "Has, uh, she been around a lot? She seems at home here."

"Oh, just a few weeks. I think she's staying in a local hotel, but she must have some pretty important stuff in that backpack because it's always with her."

Cheryl wondered what story Cassie told the librarian . . . if her first name really was Cassie. "Really? Do you know her name?"

"Cassie, but I don't know her last name. I told her we can give her a temporary library card when she's in town, but she's perfectly content to work in here. She looks at the books she needs and then reshelves them. No one ever does that." Then, as if remembering what she had been doing, Pam turned back to the computer to look up Cheryl's library card number.

Cheryl eyed Cassie again. Every time she was in the Swiss Miss she'd worn the bulky jacket and the pink backpack. She looked different with her hair down and wearing a soft pink top. She looked pretty. Trustworthy, which Cheryl guessed wasn't the case. She'd already lied about being a reporter. What else was she lying about?

As she waited and watched, Cassie wrote something in a pink notebook. Then, reading it over, Cassie shook her head, ripped out the paper, crumbled it up, and pushed the paper to the side.

Cheryl's stomach sank. Had Cassie been sleeping in the winter buggy at the Millers' farm?

Like a lightbulb going off, the pieces started coming together. Suddenly it made sense. *The person sleeping in the buggy and the thief are the same person: Cassie.*

What if she'd hidden items around the Miller farm? Could all those items be right under their noses? It made sense. There were plenty of places to hide things. Didn't Seth say that the only reason he found the plastic shopping bag was the peanut butter crackers inside? But maybe there were more items buried in the straw.

"Still looking for your card number," Pam said, interrupting Cheryl's thoughts. "Sometimes my computer is so slow."

"No problem." She pretended to be engrossed with the novel. "I don't mind waiting."

Pam turned back to the computer and continued hitting the Return button, as if that would make things go faster.

Of course there was the fudge. Surely Rover would have found that. Unless Cassie hid it somewhere high, like up in one of the haylofts. She blew out a quick breath, wondering what she should do. Should she go and find Naomi? Should she talk to Chief Twitchell first?

Then, like the sound of a train whistle coming closer and clearer, Cheryl realized that Pam was talking to her.

"Nonfiction, biographies, cookbooks…" Pam's voice trailed off.

"I'm so sorry." Cheryl turned back to the librarian. "What were you saying?"

Pam's eyes widened. "I said that this book is all checked out. You're ready to go. I also asked what other types of books do you like to read?" She smiled, still waiting for an answer.

"Oh, uh…" Cheryl's mind wasn't on the question. Instead she was still watching Cassie out of the corner of her eye. Cassie placed her pencil on the table and stood and walked down a row.

If I can get over there and see the handwriting, then I'll know for sure.

"Dictionaries! I love dictionaries." The words blurted from Cheryl's mouth before she had time to think about them. Cheryl forced a grin. "Oh, I just love looking up new words." She took two steps back. "In fact there was a new word I really wanted to look up today."

"That's so interesting…" Pam's smile stiffened. "I've never heard that one before." She pointed to the area where Cassie had been sitting. "All our books in the reference section can't be checked out, but have you seen the new *Elements of Style Illustrated*? The illustrations are lush and gorgeous, and each illustration is derived from an example quote within the text. It's the perfect book for word nerds. Would you like me to find it on the shelf?"

"Yes, that would be great, and I'll be right over here in the reference section."

Cheryl was thankful the library wasn't too busy today, and thankful Pam thought the perfect book for her would be on the rules of English grammar.

Cheryl spotted a dictionary, pulled it off the shelf, and opened it on the table, right next to Cassie's notebook. She glanced down at the dictionary and smiled at the first word that caught her eye.

"Lubberly. Adjective. 'Of or resembling a lubber,'" she mumbled. "Well, that's not helpful." She scanned *lubber*. "'Noun: a big,

clumsy, stupid person; lout or an awkward or unskilled sailor.'"
She smiled.

Satisfied she hadn't lied to Pam, Cheryl leaned over to look at
Cassie's notebook. Her eyes widened, and she didn't know whether
to smile or to groan when she saw that it was the same scribbly
handwriting that she saw on the papers from the Millers' farm.
Her suspicions were also confirmed by the two words written at
the top of the page. *The Setting*.

On most of the page, Cassie had drawn a map of Sugarcreek.
Cheryl looked closer and noticed a pink star over the Miller farm.

She knew all she needed to and decided to talk to Naomi first.
It was their home that had been intruded. Then after the Millers
decided what they wanted to do about Cassie, they could call
Chief Twitchell together.

She closed the dictionary. Still, none of this made sense. Why
was Cassie here? Why would she stay at the Millers' farm?

Cheryl returned to the checkout counter and pretended to
look over the library's calendar of events, but in truth her eyes were
fixed on Cassie.

The young woman returned to the table and her notebook
with a lightness to her step. The way she bopped along reminded
Cheryl of the sweet and innocent version of Olivia Newton John
in *Grease*.

Cheryl watched Cassie plop into the chair and then discretely
glance around. When Cheryl saw Cassie turning her direction, she
lifted up the library events calendar, holding it over her face. Did
Cassie realize she was being watched?

Waiting a few seconds, Cheryl peeked around the paper. Cassie's attention was again turned to two books and her notebook. She smiled as she set the books up in a pile and then shoved them in her backpack, all of them, even the ones that she'd just pulled off the library shelf.

Cassie swung the backpack over her shoulders, and she innocently walked toward the door and the library security scanners. Cheryl waited for the alarm to sound. Amazingly, it only made a slight beep—the noise of someone exiting—as Cassie walked through. Had Cassie figured out how to disengage the alarm? She wouldn't put it past her. The young woman had slipped the library books in her backpack with such ease and slight of hand that if Cheryl hadn't been watching intently she would have missed it. It would have been easy for Cassie to do the same thing in the stores. And maybe her awkwardness with her notebook made her gain the trust of other shop owners with her stories of her grandfather. The easiest way to rob a person was to gain their trust. And the easiest way to do that was to make oneself a caring, sympathetic character in their eyes.

Cheryl stood there, unsure what to do. She didn't have to wonder if Cassie was the thief now. She'd seen the truth with her own eyes. Cheryl's breath quickened. Every moment of hesitation carried Cassie another few steps away.

Cheryl decided to follow her. She noticed Pam in the distance approaching with the *Elements of Style Illustrated*, but she didn't have time to wait.

She picked up the book that she'd already checked out and hurried toward the door. "I just realized I need to be somewhere," Cheryl called over her shoulder. "I'll be back."

"No problem!" Pam called, completely ignoring the sign that read, Welcome to the Quiet Zone. "I'll just keep it on my holds shelf. You come back when you have a few minutes."

She wanted to respond to Pam, but she didn't want to lose Cassie. If Cheryl followed Cassie long enough, would she catch her going into stores and snatching more things?

But instead of heading to the shops, Cassie turned and walked the opposite direction.

"Where is she going?" Cheryl mumbled.

The young woman continued at an easy pace, not looking around or behind her. The wind whipped Cheryl's hair, and she pulled the collar of her jacket tight around her neck. *What am I doing? Who do I think I am following here?*

Her questions punctuated each step, followed by one more thought. *I think I read too much Nancy Drew growing up.*

A man she recognized from church drove by, and he looked as if he planned to stop and ask if she needed a ride. Cheryl smiled and waved and quickened her pace as if going on a walk in the frigid air were indeed her plan.

She wished she had her car. Or at least knew how to follow someone without being so obvious. So far she was doing a poor job in tracking people. With the way things were going, it would be wise to find an online course on spy tactics. Or go back and dig out all those Nancy Drew books. She'd brought them from Columbus, and they were tucked away in Aunt Mitzi's attic, where she'd put some of her boxes that she didn't need to unpack right away.

As she walked, Cheryl reconsidered calling Chief Twitchell until after she talked to Naomi, and she could almost picture him quoting one of her most favorite Chief McGinnis lines from one of the Nancy Drew books. "It's good to know you're keeping the mean streets of Pancake City free from crime!"

Yet Cheryl doubted Chief Twitchell would be so encouraging. But at least he had to know. She had strong proof that Cassie had been sleeping in the Millers' buggy shed, and she also had reason to believe she was the one stealing.

Cheryl rehearsed the presentation of evidence in her mind, and then she pulled her cell phone out of her pocket and dialed the number for the police station. She'd never known the phone number of the police station in Columbus. Things were different here.

Delores answered the phone, and Cheryl asked for the chief.

"I'm sorry, but he's out on an investigation, Cheryl. I'd be happy to send you to his voice mail."

Cheryl smiled, realizing Delores recognized her voice without her saying it. "That would be great."

A few seconds later the voice mail came on. "Chief Twitchell, this is Cheryl from the Swiss Miss. I know that Agnes has contacted you recently about a lot of items that have been stolen from the stores on Main Street. I haven't talked to Agnes...been a little busy...but I think I have some information you could use." She gave him her cell phone and thought about saying more, but then changed her mind. She guessed the chief didn't like rambling messages, and she'd be able to gauge his response better as she listened to his reaction. She'd learned from past interactions with the police department that pushing too much would provide the opposite effect.

She continued following Cassie as the girl left the Main Street stores behind. Since they were the only two people walking down the frontage road, the fact that she was following Cassie was obvious. Thankfully Cassie didn't turn.

Instead, she walked toward McDonald's. The idea of warming up inside caused Cheryl to quicken her pace. She smiled when she saw the Buggy Parking sign in the McDonald's parking lot—something you don't see every day outside Sugarcreek.

She stepped through the door of the fast-food restaurant, and warm air enveloped her. Sitting inside was a mix of retired men circled up with cups of coffee, young moms with children near the play area, and a few employees eating on their breaks.

Cheryl expected to see Cassie up at the counter placing an order, but instead the young woman headed to the restroom. Cheryl paused just inside the door. Should she follow Cassie into the restroom? Cassie would no doubt recognize her from the Swiss Miss. Then again all types of people visited McDonald's. She waited another minute, and when Cassie did not come out, Cheryl decided to go in.

Maybe I'll just wash my hands.

The bathroom door swung open, and Cheryl approached the sink. On the counter was Cassie's hairbrush. A tube of toothpaste was next to it, and Cassie was leaned over the sink, brushing her teeth.

Cheryl walked to the sink to wash her hands, and Cassie's backpack sat at her feet. It was unzipped and open. Cheryl's heartbeat quickened, and she couldn't help but look down. She expected to see some of the Amish items that had been stolen—maybe even items from her store. Instead, there were only the two books from the library, clothes, and more toiletry items.

Where could she have put the items? Were they all hidden inside the Millers' barn? Cheryl pumped hand soap into her hands and then quickly washed them. Cheryl reached for a paper towel dispenser, and she watched as Cassie pulled another item out of her backpack. She was so busy washing up that she barely glanced at Cheryl, and if she recognized her, she didn't say anything. It was a red handkerchief, similar to the ones Levi used. It seemed he always had one sticking out of his pocket. Had Cassie gotten it at the Miller farm?

It was possible, but seeing the contents of that backpack made Cheryl second-guess whether Cassie was the thief. Even if she was the one sleeping out at the Millers' farm, she may or may not be the thief.

There's only one way to find out.

Cheryl dried her hands and hurried outside. Her phone rang, and when she looked, caller ID said Sugarcreek Police. She knew she'd look like a fool now if she talked to Chief Twitchell. Instead, she only had one other choice.

She'd wake up early and go to the Miller farm herself.

CHAPTER TWENTY-THREE

The alarm clock beeped, and Cheryl's arm swung around, attempting to hit the Snooze button. Why was it so dark? Then she remembered. She sat up and nearly pushed Beau off the bed.

"Sorry, buddy."

Beau stretched and yawned.

"I know it's early," she whispered. "You can stay there for a while longer."

Cheryl quickly dressed in the black sweatpants and black T-shirt she'd set out. She pulled a black crocheted hat on her head and slipped on her jacket. She found herself tiptoeing as she walked to the car.

Her mind spun as she drove to the Miller farm. Discovering the intruder on the Millers' farm was only one of the discoveries of yesterday.

The store had been quiet after she got back from McDonald's. LeRoy had finished the shelves and had repainted her office. It looked wonderful, except that all the things from her desk were piled on the floor. He'd asked for a ride to pick up the file cabinet, but Cheryl had told him that would have to wait. She paid him for the work he'd done, and LeRoy left. He appeared disappointed, but Cheryl didn't need one more thing to think about. Getting the file cabinet, moving the files, and organizing her office would have to wait.

She'd also had a chance to talk to Agnes. As far as Agnes knew, no other items had been stolen from her shop or the other shops in the area. Agnes believed their thief had either moved on to a different town or had gotten nervous. She was troubled to hear the Swiss Miss had been robbed again.

Why me? Why continue to target me?

Maybe if she caught Cassie, she'd have a chance to ask.

Cheryl's eyes blinked slowly as she drove. They burned and felt gritty. There were only a few cars on the road, and no one was walking. It was 3:30 AM, and most people were in bed—where she should be.

She parked her car on the Millers' long driveway, close to the petting farm and hopefully far enough away from the house no one heard her park. In the distance, the farm was completely dark. In fact, everything about the farm was dark and still. It was peaceful though. Was that what drew their visitors? The place was tidy and inviting, even in the gloom of a gray November night. It seemed a safe place despite her mission.

The sliver of moon did little to light Cheryl's way, so she pulled a flashlight out of the driver's door pocket. She walked for a while, the cold air nipping at her cheeks, and then paused in the middle of the road and gazed up at the sky. She spotted Mars left of the crescent moon and again wondered what it would be like to star gaze with Levi, but that wasn't her agenda tonight.

She slowed her steps as she neared the buggy shed. Taking a deep breath, Cheryl opened the latch. Then she hurried inside, focusing her flashlight beam on the buggy.

Unlike when she rode in it with Levi, both of the windshields on the front were closed. She didn't see anything in the front seat and hurried toward the side of the buggy. The side door was open, but when she peered inside, it too was empty.

"What?"

Cheryl looked around the buggy and under it, but no one was there. She'd been so certain she'd find Cassie.

She looked again in the back and saw a small book. It had a plastic cover, and it looked like one of the books Cassie had stolen from the library. Cheryl leaned into the buggy and grabbed the book. She noticed something else too. The seat of the buggy was still warm! Whoever had been there must have heard her coming. But how could she have gotten out?

The creaking of a door startled her. She jumped back, pressed the book to her chest, and focused the flashlight beam on the door. It was a back door that she hadn't seen at first. It was slowly opening.

"Do not worry. I am not going to hurt you." It was Levi's voice. "I just want to talk."

"Levi?" She hurried to the door just as he stepped inside, shining her flashlight on him.

He blocked the beam from his face, and his brow furrowed. "Cheryl? What are you doing in here? Are... are you the intruder?"

"Of course not!" She tilted her flashlight toward the ground. "I came early to see if I could catch the person... and..."

"And maybe you should have let me know? Told me you were coming?"

"I'm sorry. I should have called you yesterday. I have a hunch who it is, and I wanted to make sure that it was her first."

"Her?"

"Yes, it's a young woman named Cassie. She introduced herself to me when she was at the store. She's, well, she's interesting. She's always peeking around and taking notes. She watches people."

"So she can write those stories?"

Cheryl pressed her free hand to her forehead. "Of course. She's researching. She's taking notes so that she can write the stories. She's trying to capture Sugarcreek, me, the people in the Swiss Miss…everything." Cheryl peeked around him. "I just don't know where she went."

"I am not sure either. I had the same idea. I got up early, and I was heading out here. That is when I saw the back door to the buggy shed open. I can see it from the front porch. She must have rushed out in a hurry."

He took a step forward and pointed to the book in her hands. "Is that the book she wrote?"

"No. This is from the library." Cheryl opened it to show him. She lifted the flashlight to read the title page, but was surprised that it wasn't a library book at all.

Levi leaned closer, and he mumbled something.

Cheryl scanned the pages too. The paper was old and crisp. The book smelled of history and age. The ink on the page looked faded in spots. This was no library book for certain.

"It looks to be a journal—a handwritten one."

She turned it over in her hands. "When I saw Cassie with this at the library, I just assumed it was a library book." Cheryl bit her lip. "I've assumed so much…"

She felt her shoulders shivering as she thought about Cassie sleeping out here. How many nights had it been? Too many.

Levi stepped to her side and placed his hand on the small of her back, pressing against her coat. "Why don't we head inside?"

Cheryl stepped out of the doorway, and she looked down the road the way she came. "Maybe I, uh, should drive my car closer. I hate to leave it parked down there, close to the road."

"Sure, I will walk with you, and maybe we will watch for any sign of Cassie on the way."

Cheryl's hand brushed his as she walked by his side. "Do you think we'll find her?"

"I do not think we have to worry about that now." He glanced to the journal in her hand. "We have this. I think she will find us."

CHAPTER TWENTY-FOUR

O nce again, Cheryl found herself sitting around the Millers' table next to Levi. Naomi was up peeling potatoes, and Esther was working on the pies. Were they always up this early working in the kitchen? Cheryl yawned, trying to imagine that.

Her eyes felt tired and raw, and she was still in her black sweat outfit. She took off her black hat and ran her fingers through her hair, sure it looked a mess. Not that it mattered. Not like she needed to impress anyone. Levi sat quietly next to her, glancing through the journal.

She breathed in the aroma of percolating coffee and leaned toward him. "So what did you discover there?"

"From what I can tell, this journal was written by a young man, Walter Schultz, who was riding the rails." He flipped through some of the pages. "In the first ten pages or so he talks about the places he is traveling to as a hobo. Then the dates skip a few months, and he says that he became ill and friends dropped him off in Sugarcreek. A kind Amish family picked him up and took him home."

Cheryl leaned closer to Levi to get a better look. "It almost sounds like that novel—the one with the store owner named Meryl."

Naomi put down the potato peeler and approached the table. "That is interesting that an Amish family took him in. What year did you stay that was?"

Levi flipped back a few pages to look at the date. "It says here 1931."

Naomi fiddled with one of the strings of her kapp. "Does it say the name of the family? That would be interesting to find out—to see if they are still in Sugarcreek."

Levi scanned a few more pages, and then he paused. His jaw dropped slightly. "You will not believe this, Maam. It says here the family's name is Miller."

"Miller?" Seth put down the newspaper and turned to his son. His eyes brightened, and his face looked more animated than Cheryl had ever seen him.

"Ja. It says right here Isaac and Almina Miller..."

"Why, Seth, those are your grandparents," Naomi's words cut off her son.

Cheryl placed a hand on Levi's arm. "So your great-grandparents were the ones who took this man—Walter—in?"

"It appears so."

"Why, I had never imagined such a thing." Naomi turned toward her husband. "Did you ever hear about this? Your grandparents lived in the *dawdy haus* when you were a boy. Do you remember the story?"

"Why, you know my grandparents." Seth chuckled. As he looked toward the ceiling, Cheryl could tell that memories filled his mind. "Could you name someone they did not help? My parents were like that here too, before they moved in with my sister. We often had people staying with us off and on—even Englischers. I can not remember all their names. I am not sure I ever heard the name Walter, but that does not mean it did not happen." He smiled. "And right here on this farm too."

"You might not be able to remember all of them, but this man sure remembered your grandparents." Cheryl looked at the book in Levi's hands, wishing she could read the whole thing. *What an amazing story it must tell.*

But instead of reading more, Levi closed the book.

Cheryl leaned back slightly and eyed him, surprised. "Aren't you going to read more to find out what happened? Did he stay in Sugarcreek for long? Did he go back to riding the rails?"

He ran his hand over the cover and then slid it toward the center of the table. "It is not my property. I am sure if Cassie wants to share it with us, she will."

"It makes sense why she came back here though—why she targeted the Miller farm. She wanted to write about the Amish family who helped Walter." Cheryl's mouth circled in an O. "Do you think this Walter might be her great-grandfather or something?"

Levi stood and moved toward the cupboard for a coffee cup. "That would be my guess."

"But why did not she just talk to us?" Naomi asked. "We would have welcomed her in our home. She would not have had to sleep in the buggy shed." She seemed disappointed that Levi closed the book too. She returned to her potato peeler wearing the slightest pout.

"That's true, but what would you have said if she'd just come out and told you all her plans?" Cheryl asked. "I mean, if someone wanted to come to write a novel and include your family in it, I'm sure you wouldn't have been too thrilled."

Naomi jutted out her chin. "I would have said we are nothing special. I would have told her that..."

"You would have told her that you didn't want that type of attention," Cheryl interrupted again. "Then you would have felt awkward around her."

"We were a little awkward thinking someone was sleeping in our buggy too," Esther finally chimed in, and Cheryl could tell the young woman still didn't know what to think.

"Yes, well," Cheryl said, yawning, "those are only my guesses." She rubbed her eyes. She needed to leave soon, and the idea of heading home and going back to bed sounded wonderful. But instead she needed to dress, shower, and get to the store. Just thinking about it, she yawned again.

"Here is some coffee." Esther brought Cheryl a fresh cup, setting it in front of her. Seth went back to reading his newspaper, and Naomi returned to peeling potatoes.

"Can you tell that I need it?" Cheryl cast her a shy smile. "I'm not a morning person as it is, but especially not after getting up in the middle of the night."

"That is brave of you for getting up and coming out to do that. I suppose you stopped waiting on me to stay up and catch our guest." Levi poured himself a cup of coffee too. Then he sat down across from her.

She looked down in her cup, wishing that Levi wouldn't study her with that intense gaze. She turned to look toward the window, gazing out at the barren fields. Had it looked the same when Walter had been here? No doubt it did.

She thought too about Cassie. She was so young to be out on her own like that. Was she doing it for her grandfather? Maybe as a gift to him.

"Penny for your thoughts." Levi's voice filtered in.

"Oh." She shrugged. "I'm just wondering where that young woman ran off to. And where she's going to hide now. I hope she's okay."

"I am not wondering about where she is going to hide. Like I said before, I am wondering how long it takes for her to come to…"

A knock sounded on the front door, interrupting Levi's words.

Naomi turned, put down her peeler, and wiped her hands on her apron. "It could not be…" She walked to the living room where she might get a better view of the front door.

Seth rose and moved to the door, but Naomi hurried ahead of him. "Let me do it, Seth. You are going to scare that young woman away." She snapped her dish towel at him, and Seth stepped back with humor in his gaze. Naomi moved to the door.

Levi placed his hand on Cheryl's. "Maybe you should talk to her too, since you have talked to her before."

"Of course." Cheryl rose and walked to the door. Naomi was just welcoming Cassie inside. The young woman's eyes were red and puffy. She'd been crying. She was wearing her stocking cap and thick army jacket, but her chin was trembling too. Cheryl didn't know if it was from the cold or from nervousness. Probably both.

"Mrs. Miller, my name is Cassie, and I have something to confess. I've been the one sleeping in your barn. I'm so sorry..."

"I know, Cassie, we have already figured it out," Naomi interrupted. Then Naomi looked to Cheryl. "We have all been concerned about you."

The young woman stepped inside all the way, and Naomi shut the door. "You were?"

Cheryl offered what she hoped was a sympathetic smile, and she hoped her eyes weren't as red as the young woman's before her. "Yes, I was concerned. After seeing you at the library yesterday—and seeing your notebook, I figured it was you, and last night I decided to..."

Cassie placed a hand over her heart. "You're the one who found me this morning?"

"Well, I didn't find you. You'd already slipped out."

"Just barely. I was having trouble sleeping, and I heard footsteps. I got out just in time...and I ran. I'm a pretty good runner."

"It must have been hard." Naomi gazed at the young woman with compassion. "Hiding is never easy. I wish you would have just come to us."

Cassie lowered her head. "I got your note, but I was afraid of what you'd say. I was hoping to finish, uh, my work project before I introduced myself to you."

Cheryl crossed her arms over her chest. "Work project, as in a novel?"

Cassie glanced up, meeting Cheryl's gaze. "So you found my notebook?"

"Rover, our pup, found it." Naomi motioned to the kitchen. "We have all your things. The journal too."

"Are…are you going to call the police? It's fine if you do. I understand… I just have to get that journal back."

Cheryl glanced at Naomi. She knew her friend would offer sympathy, but she wanted the young woman to understand the seriousness of the crime too. "Well, I did leave a message for Chief Twitchell, but no one has talked to him yet. I would like you to talk to him. We can't pretend this didn't happen."

Naomi placed a hand on Cheryl's arm, stopping her words. "From what I can see, no damage was done, except for some jars of peaches."

"I'm so sorry about that. I was hungry and…well, did you find the money that I left?" Cassie looked to Cheryl and then quickly back to Naomi.

"Yes, we found it."

"Did you leave a jar of peaches in a box at the library too?" Cheryl asked, softening her tone. She didn't want to scare the girl away again.

Cassie tucked a strand of hair behind her ear. "How did you know?"

Naomi looked at Cheryl and winked. "Oh, we have a way of finding things out."

"I was guilty that I had those. I was going to put them back in your cellar, but when I heard that man talking about the domestic violence shelter, I decided to put them in. I thought it would be nice."

"It was nice. That man John-John even stopped by yesterday, and I gave him some more. But we do not need to stand here by the door. Why don't you come in and sit at the table? We would like to hear more about what you are doing here. And how we can help."

"Wait." Cassie lifted her eyebrows. "Aren't you mad at me?"

"You did have us concerned at times." Naomi ushered her into the kitchen. Cheryl followed. "And I was worried, but there was really no harm done. If I am going to get upset over a few jars of peaches, then I need to spend more time with God and ask Him to change my heart."

Cassie pulled off her hat, and her blonde hair flowered over her shoulders. "Thank you. I don't know what to say."

She entered the kitchen behind Naomi and paused. Naomi introduced her to Seth, Esther, and Levi. The starstruck look on Cassie's face made Cheryl smile. Cassie had the same look that one would expect from a groupie who'd just seen her favorite movie stars. Cheryl supposed that writing about this family had made them stars in her eyes too.

Esther poured Cassie a cup of coffee.

Levi handed her the journal. "I hope you do not mind, we read a few pages."

She sat in the chair next to Levi. "I don't mind, but I'm sure you hardly got any of the story from just a few pages."

"Can you tell us about it?" Cheryl asked. She glanced at the clock. It was only eight o'clock, and she'd have to leave in thirty minutes in order to shower and get to work by ten, but she didn't want to miss this. "I know you're writing a fictional piece, but that seems to tie into this journal. Does it?"

"Yes, I'm writing my first novel. It's a historical novel set in the Great Depression in Sugarcreek."

"In the Great Depression?" Naomi asked. "I am confused because in the notebook we found it talked about Levi and myself, and it seemed like modern day. So it is not a contemporary novel about the people living here now?"

"Well, I started out contemporary." She looked away shyly. "It starts with Levi Miller, well, finding a time capsule of sorts. Then as he starts looking through the photos and the letters that he finds, the novel slips into the past. Sort of like *Snow Falling on Cedars*. Have you read that story?"

"No, I cannot say that I have."

"Yes, well, we studied it in my creative writing class, except where that novel goes back and forth, mine stays mostly in the past." Cassie bit her lip. "It might go back to contemporary at the end. I'm not sure yet. I haven't gotten that far."

"But I wanted to show you something." She pulled out two thick books covered in clear plastic. They were the library books that Cheryl remembered Cassie slipping into her bag.

"Are those, uh, library books?" Cheryl asked.

"These?" Cassie held one out from her. "Well, I suppose they look like them, but no. They are two more of my great-grandfather's journals. I'm horrible about carrying them around the library. And when I'm doing research, I leave them all over the place. Pam found them after I left them there, and she offered to cover them for me. She did it for free, can you believe it? The covers were starting to fall apart." Cassie placed her hand on the journal that Levi found. "Pam said if I leave this with her, she'll cover it too. But I haven't yet. I've been using it."

"Pam is a nice woman." Cheryl smiled, remembering how Pam even called to remind her of her overdue books.

"These three books are my great-grandfather's journals," Cassie explained. "He was an interesting fellow. He was a college professor at a very young age, and within one year he lost his wife and his job. Not able to cope, he became a hobo for a few years, and he somehow ended up in Sugarcreek in 1931. A few pages in, he mentions staying with the Millers during an illness. They not only brought him back to their home and nursed him to health, but Mrs. Miller ended up introducing him to one of her Englisch friends. They got married a year after meeting." Cassie glanced to Seth and then to Naomi. "If not for the way your family cared for my great-grandfather, I wouldn't be here."

"That is amazing. I have never heard anything like it." Naomi stroked the cover of the journal with her fingertips. "We have some old journals too. They mostly talk about gardening and such. I wonder if Almina ever wrote about your great-grandfather?"

Cassie's eyes widened. "I'm not sure, but that would be cool if she did. My grandpa gave me these journals when he moved into a nursing home. They had belonged to his father."

"When did he move?" Cheryl remembered Cassie saying she was texting her grandfather. Maybe that had been the truth.

"About six months ago. I lived with him before that. I helped take care of him, but it started to be too hard. He needed a lot of care that I couldn't give. Then I moved in with my mom, but she's a mess. That's why Grandpa encouraged me to come to Sugarcreek. He even promised to learn to text if I agreed. Maybe he hoped that I'd find what his father had found here."

Esther came and sat next to them too. "Were you looking for help?"

Cassie shrugged. "Help. Maybe friendship. Maybe a new place to call home. I'm really not sure."

The room grew quiet then, as if everyone were considering Cassie's words.

Cassie glanced around Naomi's kitchen, and Cheryl knew what the young woman was doing. She was trying to take in all the details. The plain wooden cupboards, deep farmhouse sink, and the kerosene lamps and fixtures.

"I've only been here a few weeks, and I really like everyone in town. If it weren't for my grandpa, I might consider staying here." Then she glanced away. "Well, I almost like everyone..."

"Is there someone who has caused you problems?" Levi's brow furrowed, and Cheryl could tell he was quick to step into the role of big brother.

"He hasn't really caused me problems, but I don't care for LeRoy Wagler. I..." Cassie looked down at her coffee cup. "I shouldn't say why."

Levi sat up straighter then, and he ran his fingers through his hair. "Cassie, I know you do not want to gossip, but he has been spending a lot of time with my sister." Levi gestured toward Esther, whose cheeks were turning pink. "If it were your sister, would you want someone to tell you?"

"Yes, very much so." She ran her fingers over the cover of the journal. "It's just that I've been watching, well, I've been watching everyone. And he just doesn't seem Amish to me. LeRoy acts like it when he's around the shop owners and such, but I heard him on his cell phone. He wasn't talking like an Amish person. And he had car keys. He was jingling them while he talked. He didn't know I was there."

"Where?"

"At the gas station at the edge of town. I was there late, getting some food before heading out here. He was leaning outside against the wall. There was a car parked there too, but I didn't stick around long enough to find out if it was his. But that's not the worst part."

Cheryl swallowed, unsure if she wanted to hear. "What?"

"He was laughing and joking and saying that he had everyone fooled."

Cheryl's jaw dropped open. "He's supposed to come back to finish working in my shop after Thanksgiving. He was going to remodel my office..."

"And I bet he would have access to all your business files then, right?" Levi asked.

"He already has, well not completely." A cold chill raced through Cheryl's limbs. "He was in there the other day. He put up some new shelves for me. All my accounts and ledgers are locked up, but I'm sure there are bills and such on the desk that I was sorting through." She pressed her fingertips to her lips. "There isn't information that he can use in those, is there?"

"It depends. If he is Amish, probably not. But from what it sounds like, well, maybe you should call the bank."

"Do you think they will be open today? Tomorrow is Thanksgiving."

"You should try. I will walk you out to the phone shack. I think we need to call the police chief too," Levi said. "I have a feeling this LeRoy is up to no good. And his deception is just the start of it."

CHAPTER TWENTY-FIVE

Cheryl called her bank and credit card companies from the phone shack, and then she decided to do what she should have done in the first place. She drove to the Sugarcreek police department to talk to the chief in person.

Thankfully both Esther and Naomi volunteered to go in and open the Swiss Miss for her. After hearing about LeRoy's deception, none of them doubted that he was behind all the thefts.

Cheryl thought about driving home to shower first, but something inside told her not to dawdle. There was an urgency to get to the station and talk to the chief. She even called ahead and told Delores that she was coming in.

As she climbed out of her car, Cheryl glanced down at her sweatpants. Then she stuck her hat back on her head. She didn't have a smidgen of makeup on, but she supposed that didn't matter.

She entered the station and stopped short. Two women stood in the waiting area talking to Chief Twitchell. She recognized Agnes right away, and the woman standing next to Agnes looked familiar too, but she didn't recognize her in the police uniform. Cheryl paused when she entered, but then Chief Twitchell waved her forward.

"Cheryl, I'm so glad you're here. I have someone who's been wanting to talk to you." The chief turned to the female officer. "I have to run to a meeting, but Officer Ortega wants to hear what you have to say. She's been on this case for a while now, and I believe you have just the information she needs."

The chief hurried off, and Officer Ortega led them to a small room. Cheryl and Agnes sat, and Officer Ortega sat across from them. She wore a soft smile and her purple glasses didn't really match with the style of the uniform, but Cheryl wasn't about to bring that up. Instead she had more important things to say.

Officer Ortega took out a small notebook and a pencil. "Okay, I'd like to hear what you have. I've been watching this LeRoy fellow, and something doesn't seem to add up."

"I have information. It's about LeRoy, that Amish man who's been working in my shop." Cheryl's words released in a hurried breath. "I have reason to believe he's not who—or what—he says he is. I'm not sure why I didn't figure it out sooner. He's been in and out of my shop. I should have guessed it was him. And the other night I saw someone walking down the street with a bag filled with items." She turned to Agnes. "One of your little Amish dolls was found on the street, so I'd guessed that the bag had been filled with stolen items. And…" She pressed her fingertips to her head. "I know that it's LeRoy. I remember how the person was walking. It was the same hunched-over stride that I saw the other day when LeRoy was leaving my shop."

The officer leaned closer and pushed her purple glasses higher on her nose. "But do you know where he was going with that bag?"

Cheryl opened her mouth and then closed it. She hadn't taken much time to think about that.

Without waiting for an answer, the officer held out a printed photograph. "This is our suspect. Look closely and you might recognize him."

Cheryl took the paper from the officer's hands. It was a mug shot of a young man with a buzzed head and a beard. She looked closer and recognized his eyes. "Is this...LeRoy?" He didn't look as handsome in the paper. He looked harder. Harsher. A shiver traveled down her spine.

Agnes smirked. "Yes, well, at least that's the name that he gave us. But did you read the name?"

Cheryl looked down at the paper. "David Dwayne Simons," she read. "So he lied about his name...and he's not Amish."

"He's not Amish, but he must have lived around them because he pulled it off very well. He's wanted in three other counties in Ohio for theft. I suppose he thought he'd try a new scheme."

"But why did he have to steal in the first place?" Cheryl rubbed her brow. "He was actually a really good carpenter."

"We called his dad, and his father owns a construction company near Dayton. The kid does know how to work hard, but unfortunately that isn't enough." Officer Ortega took the paper from her hands. She shrugged. "Who knows why people turn to crime, but if you have any ideas of where he could be..."

"I can only guess. There are some abandoned houses a few blocks from my house. It would make sense if he was keeping stuff inside there. I bet he was carrying stuff in and out of the stores with that toolbox, and then he was stashing them somewhere until he could haul a full load."

"Well, we can go over to those houses and look." The officer nodded as if it were starting to make sense. "We have had a report about a drifter going in and out of them. I just haven't had a chance to check it out—maybe that's LeRoy. Or rather David. And since they are abandoned and are property of the state, we won't need a search warrant."

Agnes clapped her hands together. "Can we ride along?"

"Sure. You can ride in my car. And since both of you have seen LeRoy and interacted with him, I'll tell the chief that I'm bringing you along for identification." She winked. "But I want you to promise to sit in the car until I signal you and let you know that the coast is clear. Deal?"

Agnes clenched her hands together and pulled them to her chest. "Yes, of course."

"Deal." Cheryl gave only a brief nod as if she were used to this type of thing every day. But inside the butterflies turned to sparrows, dancing and fluttering around. Was this really happening?

Officer Ortega led them from the interview room. "Good. I don't want anyone to get hurt. You can never be too safe."

Cheryl sat silent in the back of the police car as Officer Ortega drove across town. She slumped down in the seat and pulled her black hat tighter on her head. She didn't look to the right or the left, but kept focused straight ahead. The last thing she wanted was someone to recognize her. She could almost picture Laurie-Ann spotting her and pointing and waving. And then... Well, it would be all over the prayer chain that afternoon.

Officer Ortega drove to the small abandoned houses not too far from Cheryl's. They'd been rental cottages long ago, but they'd since fell into disarray. Two of them appeared as they always had, but one had an open gate. The maple leaves had been stirred on the front porch, most likely from feet. And something had been hung in the windows—old blankets maybe—to block out the view.

Officer Ortega turned off the engine, and then she looked first to Agnes and then to Cheryl. "Stay here."

Cheryl nodded, and it wasn't until the officer left that she realized she was locked inside the backseat. *Just breathe. I'm okay.* She told herself that if she needed to get out, Agnes could help. For what? To provide backup? No, maybe it was better that she was locked inside.

Officer Ortega walked around the perimeter of the building. She knocked on the front door, but no one answered. When she tried the doorknob, it swung open. She looked back at them in surprise and then walked in.

Even though they couldn't see her, Officer Ortega's voice carried back to the vehicle. "Police! If you're in here, make yourself known."

Minutes ticked by, and Cheryl's heart pounded. Surely the officer wouldn't stay in there that long unless she found something. Or was she in trouble? Cheryl looked to the dashboard. Would Agnes be able to call for help if needed? She hoped she could.

Five minutes later, Officer Ortega exited with a plastic bag in her hand. Cheryl released her breath.

Officer Ortega put the bag in the trunk, climbed into the car, and then turned sideways in her seat to talk to both of them. "The place is stripped clean, but I found a trash bag in the backyard. Inside, I discovered what looked to be invoices for a Web site called AmishCountryGifts.com."

Cheryl pulled out her smartphone and typed in the address. A Web site popped up. "It's an online gift shop. 'Shop Amish Country from Home,' it says." Cheryl clicked on the Merchandise button, and her mouth dropped open. "This is it. This is our stuff! I see my candles, and Agnes, there are quilted items from your store…and fudge! Katie's Fudge is for sale." She puffed out a breath. "LeRoy— or David—whoever he is, has been stealing our things and selling them online. And from what I can see, he's been getting good prices for them too!"

"Why that little crook." Agnes waved her finger. "When I get my hands on him."

"That's the problem," Officer Ortega said. "He's gone. I don't know where he's going or what he's driving. He had a car parked in the back alley." She sighed. "I can ask around, but that might take a while."

Cheryl sat straighter. "I know someone who saw LeRoy with a car—a car that might be his."

"Who?" Officer Ortega pulled out a notebook and a small pencil from her shirt pocket, preparing to take notes.

"It's a young woman. She's in town working on a novel, and she's out at the Miller farm right now."

"She's staying with the Millers?" Agnes tapped her chin. "Are they considering starting a bed-and-breakfast? Because I have customers ask all the time about staying with a real Amish family."

"She was staying there—in their buggy. Sort of uninvited." Cheryl winced and was met with two surprised stares. "Well, it's a long story that I won't go into now. But Cassie said that she heard LeRoy talking on a phone—and he didn't sound Amish at all. She also saw a car. We can go out to the Millers and ask her. I assume she's still there."

Officer Ortega started up the engine. "I suppose it won't hurt." She turned the car around and headed back down the street. "Just doesn't make sense why someone would start an online shop with stolen stuff. Don't they know that we can trace those things?"

"Pretty inventive, I'd say," Agnes chimed in. "And as much as I'd like to go, can you drop me off at the quilt shop? It'll be opening soon, and I need to be there before the tour bus. But you will keep me updated, won't you?"

"Yes, of course." Officer Ortega drove toward Main Street instead. "If it weren't for your help Agnes, I'm not sure where we'd be."

The car stopped in front of Sugarcreek Sisters Quilt Shoppe. Agnes jumped out.

Officer Ortega opened the door for Cheryl. "I assume you'd rather sit in the front?"

"Yes, please."

Cheryl moved to the front seat, and then a shrill filled the air, causing her to jump. A dispatcher came over the scanner. Cheryl didn't understand the woman's lingo, but from the look on Officer Ortega's face, it looked serious.

"I'm sorry, Cheryl, there is a domestic incident across town that I need to get to. I'll come by later, and we can see if I can get a statement from the young woman who you were talking about. Do you mind if I just leave you here at your shop?"

"No, of course not."

She watched as Officer Ortega drove away, and then Agnes hurried into the quilt shop. As soon as the police car left Cheryl's line of vision, the realization hit her. She was in front of her store still in sweatpants and without a car. Her stomach growled, and she realized she hadn't eaten breakfast. The only thing she could do was walk home. She couldn't go into the shop like this. What would her customers think?

Still, Cheryl glanced inside, wondering if she should at least tell Naomi and Esther about the Web site and the information that she found. She peered in, and that's when she saw three faces staring out the window at her. Naomi, Esther, and Cassie. Thankfully there were no early customers. Cheryl had no choice but to go inside now. From the looks on their faces, they wanted to hear every detail.

The shop smelled of evergreen as she entered, and Esther had a handful of pine branches in her hands. Cassie looked at Cheryl shyly, as if wondering if it were okay that she was there. Cheryl barely got through the door when the words spilled out, and she shared all they'd discovered.

As she shared her story, the color drained from Esther's face. The young woman went to sit on the stool behind the counter. "And to think we trusted him. I'd kept my eye on everyone else, but I never once suspected that it could be him."

"I think that's the pride of a good thief." Naomi walked next to her daughter and placed a hand on her shoulder. "He worked to get your trust—to get my trust."

"Can you tell me more about the Web site?" Cassie nibbled on her lower lip. "I wonder if he's been doing this in other areas? I suppose once we tell all the shop owners, they'll be able to see their items. And then we can try to trace back other things that he could have stolen from other areas. Who knows how long this has been going on?"

"Why don't we go back and look it up on my computer?" Cheryl offered. "Four sets of eyes are better than one. Maybe there are additional clues."

Cheryl went to the front and locked the door and put up the Closed sign. The three women followed her back to her office, and she noticed again what a mess it was. Had LeRoy gone through her personal papers while he was "remodeling" her office? She didn't have time to worry about that now. They needed to do what they could to find him first.

Cheryl pulled up the Web site.

Esther gasped, pointing to a photo on the homepage. "Look, those are the little baskets and coasters that went missing just a few days ago. They're already on the Web site for sale."

Cassie wrinkled her nose. "Someone knows how to turn around a product quickly."

"What do you do? Just put in a credit card to pay for it?" Naomi asked.

Cheryl clicked on the Shopping Cart button. "I guess so. Look, it even says it's a secure site. Ha, ha, ha. I bet."

"Oh, good." Esther scoffed. "I was worried about being safe when shopping from a thief."

"Can you scroll down, all the way to the bottom?" Cassie asked. "Sometimes in the footer there is contact information. I think it's required or something."

Cheryl scrolled down, and Cassie pointed. "There, look, there's a PO box in Berlin." She turned to Cheryl. "Should we go check it out?"

"Well, we should probably call the police." She readjusted her hat. *I can't be seen anyplace else like this.*

Cassie stood up straighter. "It's a public building, it's not like we'd be going anyplace dangerous. I doubt he would be there. Maybe if we just ask the postmaster if he's seen LeRoy—I mean David—lately."

"It's a good idea." Naomi nodded. "Didn't you say the police were on another call, Cheryl? Berlin is only a fifteen-minute drive, and it wouldn't hurt to just ask."

"Do you want to come, Naomi? I know how much you enjoy this," she teased.

"Oh, I would, but I'd hate to leave Esther here alone." Naomi smiled and then pointed to Cassie. "I'm sure Cassie would love to help, though. She's very observant."

Cheryl looked to the young woman. Just twelve hours ago she wondered if she might be involved in the thefts too. "Okay, but we're going to have to get my car."

"I don't mind." Cassie perked up. "I'd hate for you to go alone."

Again Cheryl wondered if she should take a quick shower and change, but something inside urged her to forget about that. She needed to get to Berlin. LeRoy had abandoned the house, and it was possible he'd already left the county, but they wouldn't know unless they checked.

They made it to her house, and she quickly changed into jeans, a T-shirt, her UGG boots, and a heavier jacket.

Cheryl's hands gripped the steering wheel as they drove. "Do you remember anything about LeRoy's car?"

"It was older, like an old Mustang, and it had a spot on the car. Like that paint stuff where someone fixed a dent."

"Okay, well that gives us something to tell Officer Ortega. In fact, I should at least call Delores at the station and tell her what we know so far."

The phone rang twice, and Delores picked up. Cheryl was just about to tell her what they discovered when Cassie bounced in her seat and pointed. Cheryl immediately understood, and the words rushed out. "Delores, tell Officer Ortega that we see LeRoy—David's—car at the German Village Market in Berlin. I'm...I'm going to park behind him. Send backup!"

Cheryl hung up the phone and then snickered to herself as she turned into the parking lot. It sounded like she was on the police force now. What was she thinking, getting involved? Yet something didn't let her stop. She had to do what she could to make sure LeRoy was caught.

She pulled into the German Village Market parking lot and for a split second wondered if this really was LeRoy's car. Cassie had seen him by it, but they couldn't be certain. Maybe if they peeked inside, she could see something familiar.

LeRoy's car was parked facing the front of the store. She had to block him in. If she parked behind him, he'd have nowhere to go.

She pulled behind the car and parked illegally. On the far end of the lot stood three Amish buggies, and one Amish man looked at her curiously as he loaded groceries into the back of his buggy. Cheryl turned off the engine and stepped out of her car, ignoring his gaze. As she moved to peer into the backseat, her breath caught. There was the toolbox that LeRoy had made!

"Cassie, look!" She pointed. "Do you see what I see?"

Just then the front automatic doors of the grocery store opened, and LeRoy walked out. He wasn't wearing Amish clothes this time, and he had a bag of groceries in his hand.

He paused and looked at her, obviously surprised to see her there. He must have forgotten that he wasn't wearing Amish clothes, or that he had keys in his hand, for a smile filled his face.

"A beautiful day, ja?" he cooed.

"LeRoy." She smiled, pretending she was surprised to see him. "It's good to see you, and in Berlin of all places." She stepped away from his car toward him. "Are you visiting your brother? I hope he's doing okay."

"My brother? Ja, he gave me a ride to Berlin. I was planning to come back after Thanksgiving to work on your office."

"Oh, good." She clasped her hands in front of her and approached him. "It was a mess before, but I'd hate for my aunt to see it the way it is now." Cheryl was close enough to grab him, but she knew there was no way to overpower him. How long could she stall him? She wondered if Delores had gotten her whole message and had a way to contact the Berlin police. Surely she didn't have to wait for Officer Ortega to make it from Sugarcreek, did she?

LeRoy chuckled. "Yes, things always look like a mess in the middle of a project, don't they?"

"Is your mother doing well, with her heart?" Cheryl forced a smile. "I've been thinking about her."

"Hey, is this your car?" A man's voice called from the parking lot. "It's not legal to park like this." A gangly teen in a parka walked toward them.

She waved to him. "I'm going to park in just a minute. I..." She couldn't think of an excuse for why she'd parked that way but smiled at him instead, hoping he'd get the hint to leave. He didn't.

LeRoy glanced up and fixed his gaze on her car parked right behind his. The smile on his face faded, and then he looked to Cassie. She'd been standing there quietly, not trying to raise suspicion, but he must have recognized her from Sugarcreek. Or maybe from that night at the gas station because his eyes widened as if it were all registering.

Cheryl could almost read his thoughts. *Caught! I've been caught...*

Then, in a split second, LeRoy dropped his bag and began to run. Cheryl lunged, hoping to grab him, but he was too quick for her. Before she could say a word, Cassie darted after him.

"Wait. Cassie, no, don't..."

Her words trailed off, and she watched as LeRoy darted toward the buggies.

"Stop him!" she shouted to the Amish man who'd just untied his buggy.

Without hesitation the man dropped the reins and joined in the pursuit.

Cheryl gasped, watching the scene before her. If she weren't seeing this with her own eyes, she wouldn't believe it.

Just then the sound of a siren split the air. A police car turned into the parking lot of the German Village Market. It had to swerve not to hit her illegally parked car.

She rushed toward them, pointing in the direction of the trio. LeRoy out front. Cassie and the Amish man in hot pursuit.

"They're over there! See him running? He's over there!"

The police officer nodded and then drove their direction. He pulled out into the street and within seconds gained on LeRoy.

The police car swerved in front of him, blocking off his path. LeRoy turned to escape the cop, turning back toward Cassie and the Amish man.

Then, with a tackle worthy of an instant replay in any college football game, the Amish man tackled LeRoy to the ground.

Cheryl gasped, and then clapped, and then laughed. The police car parked, and the officer grabbed LeRoy's arms, taking the Amish man's place. With amazing force, the officer handcuffed LeRoy and held him to the ground. Only then was Cheryl able to truly breathe.

She looked around and noticed the young man in the parka next to her. He was holding up his camera on his smartphone, taping the whole thing. With a chuckle, he stopped recording.

"Did you get that on video?" She gasped.

"You bet I did. Man, I'm going to get a million views on YouTube for this one! Did you see that Amish guy take him down?"

Cheryl took a minute to catch her breath and try to make sense of what she just saw. She walked toward Cassie and the officer. Her knees quivered, and she still couldn't take full breaths.

Is this real? Did this just happen? Did I just help to catch a criminal?

A second police car pulled up, and Cheryl released the breath she'd been holding. Officer Ortega stepped out of the car.

The officer paused and looked to Cheryl. She raised an eyebrow. "And how did you figure this out? Where he'd be?"

Cheryl pointed to Cassie. "She saw the Berlin PO box on the Web site. We headed over here to talk to the postmaster, and Cassie spotted his car. The rest..." Cheryl chuckled. "Well the rest happened so fast I'm not sure I could give you an instant replay. It's a good thing this guy"—she gestured toward the young man in the parka—"caught a video on his phone."

"I usually ask civilians to leave the detective work to the professionals, but nice job." Then Officer Ortega approached the officer who still held LeRoy to the ground. They talked for a few minutes, and then Officer Ortega hauled LeRoy to her police car.

Cassie approached Cheryl, and she could see that Cassie was trying to hide a smile.

Cheryl rubbed her brow. "I bet that's not something you expected to do today."

"No. Not at all, but it's given me an idea." A glimmer of excitement brightened Cassie's gaze.

"Oh yeah, what's that?"

"I was just thinking that as soon as I finish this historical novel, I'd like to start a contemporary one. Maybe that one can also be set in Sugarcreek. And maybe it can be about a man who *pretends* to be Amish to steal from the businesses in town, and..." She flashed an impish smile. "And there is a shop owner who helps to solve the mystery with the help of a handsome Amish bachelor. It can be a romance too."

"A romance?" Cheryl's eyes widened. She groaned with comic exaggeration. "Oh no, don't get me wrapped up in that one."

"Oh, it's not about you." Cassie shook her head innocently. "It would be about a woman named...Carol...and the Amish bachelor named...Leo."

"You're right. No one would ever guess that."

Cassie gently ribbed Cheryl. "Besides, every great book needs to have a hint of romance."

"So solving a mystery isn't enough?" Even as Cheryl asked the question, she remembered that even Nancy Drew had Ned Nickerson. But Cheryl pushed that thought from her mind. *Not this story line.* She sighed. *No hope for that.*

Instead of letting Cassie continue, Cheryl motioned to her car. "Let's get back to Sugarcreek. I'm eager to tell Naomi and Esther that the mystery is solved, and we better do it quick before I'm ticketed for being illegally parked."

"Yes, but can we make one stop on the way?" Cassie picked up her pace.

"Sure, where?"

"Can we stop by Heini's? That's where the fudge comes from, doesn't it?"

"Yes, and you're right. And it's on the way. We're going to need a box or two to celebrate."

Forty minutes later, Naomi and Esther were waiting with expectation when Cheryl and Cassie arrived. Cassie asked if she could be the one to tell the story, and Cheryl sat back and listened as she did. The young woman told it just as if she were writing it in a novel.

"The car stopped, and we jumped out. We were eyeing the car when LeRoy exited. His eyes shifted from me to Cheryl. She plastered on a smile and approached as if she was both surprised and happy to see him. It took him off guard, and that's when I made up my mind that if he ran, I was going to follow him."

Cassie told the whole story in detail, even about how they followed the police car until they saw the sign for Heini's. "We thought about following the police car all the way to the Sugarcreek police department." She smiled. "We thought it would be fun to see him hauled inside. There are just some things that are more important than seeing a crook get put in jail—and that's chocolate." Cassie winked, winning over new friends who laughed along.

After Cassie finished her story, Naomi asked if she could speak to Cheryl in the office.

They entered, and Naomi closed the door behind them. It was then Cheryl knew the talk was serious. "What is it? What's wrong?"

"It is Cassie." Naomi cleared her throat. "I would like to help the young woman, but Seth will not allow her to stay in the house. He says she is too perceptive. He does not want us to give her any more things to write in those novels of hers. Who knows what she will come up with if she was living in the house with us?" Naomi smiled, but then her smile fell. "But still, I would like to help her. We just cannot turn her out on the street. We have to think of something…"

Cheryl noticed the far-off look in her eyes. Leave it to Naomi to try to figure out how to help someone who'd snuck on to their farm, stayed without welcome, and stolen items from their cellar.

"Well, let me think…"

"I know she cannot stay with you, and I would not even ask," Naomi continued. "I wish there was someone in town, an older person maybe, who needs extra help."

"I know someone." Cheryl pointed her finger into the air. "What about Mrs. Pryce? I don't know her that well, but I, uh, know where she lives. Gage was helping her out—taking her dog food and such. And from what Marion said, it's going to be a long road until her leg is healed. I believe those are two-bedroom apartments. I wonder if Cassie would be interested in staying there and helping out?"

Naomi clapped her hands together. "What a perfect idea! I love it! I can talk to Cassie today. I'll even visit Mrs. Pryce. Did you know that she used to be a schoolteacher at the Amish school? She taught Sarah one year. That was ages ago, but I'd love to take her a potpie. I'm sorry to hear about her leg."

Cheryl loved the glimmer of excitement in Naomi's gaze, and she understood that to Naomi showering someone with food was a sign of care. Then Cheryl frowned. Tomorrow was Thanksgiving, and she still didn't have an invitation from her friend.

Taking a deep breath, Cheryl pushed it out of her mind. Too much good happened today to worry about that. She'd focus on what was right and good. She'd center her thoughts on the peace that was being brought back to their community. And for this moment, that was enough.

Chapter Twenty-Six

Cheryl settled onto her couch with a bowl of ice cream, wishing she'd grabbed another box of Katie's Fudge. She'd bought two boxes when they stopped at Heini's, one for her and one for Cassie. She ended up sharing her box with Esther and Naomi, and they had almost finished it in their celebration of both mysteries being solved. Cheryl made a mental note to herself to order more next year.

She kicked her feet up, and Beau took the opportunity to jump onto her lap. Her feet hurt, as if she'd actually been the one chasing crooks all day. She didn't realize how exhausting sleuthing was. In the Nancy Drew novels, no one talked about wanting to go to bed at 6:00 PM after solving a crime, but that's exactly what she wanted to do. Then again, Nancy Drew was a little younger than she was.

Cheryl ran her fingers through her hair, now extra wild since she never did get a shower. But she supposed that there was enough going on that it really didn't matter. No one seemed to care how she looked. Things worked when one felt at home.

She'd deepened her friendship with Naomi and with Esther as they walked this mysterious path together. She'd also gotten to know Agnes from the quilt shop and Marion at By His Grace better too. The seeds of two new friendships were planted, and she couldn't be happier about it. Friendship, she decided, was like an heirloom seed. Once planted, it would grow and produce more seed that also could be planted and shared.

And then there was Cassie. She liked the young woman, and Cheryl hoped she'd stay around awhile. The truth was, Cheryl secretly didn't mind the idea of being written into a novel. Especially if there was a handsome hero named Levi.

Cheryl took a bite of her ice cream, and she considered turning on the television, but she knew she wouldn't last through one episode. She'd had a long day, starting at three this morning.

Tomorrow was Thanksgiving, and she hadn't even bought herself a TV dinner. At least she could sleep in. She probably had enough in the pantry that she could throw a small meal together just for her. *I suppose it's the best I can do.*

She almost let those feelings of self-pity wash over her again. Instead she reached across Beau, who was curled up beside her, and grabbed the pile of mail she'd let accumulate on the side table.

Catalog, catalog, junk mail. A letter from Aunt Mitzi. She smiled and placed the letter on the side table on top of her library book. Then she set her bowl on top.

Cheryl rose to throw the rest of the pile into the trash when a small envelope fluttered out of one of the catalogs. It fell to the ground. She bent down and picked it up and pulled her head back in surprise. She recognized the handwriting and the return address. It was from Naomi, but that made no sense. Why would Naomi send her mail when she saw her every day?

A handwritten note was written on the outside of the envelope:

Cheryl, this was the second piece of mail of yours that
I found in my PO box. I've talked to the postmaster about
it, but I accidentally took this home. I kept forgetting to
bring it to town. I tried to stop you on the sidewalk the
other day to tell you, but you were in a hurry. I hope it
wasn't too important. Laurie-Ann.

She slid her finger under the flap and opened it. It was a piece
of card stock folded in half. On the front Naomi had written,
Happy Thanksgiving.
Cheryl smiled and then read the note inside.

Since you are like family, we would like you to join us
for Thanksgiving at noon. No RSVP needed, we will look
forward to seeing your smile. Please bring your favorite
dessert to share.

She placed the simple invitation back into the envelope, and
then she turned it over and looked at the postmark. The letter had
been mailed over two weeks ago, and all this time she'd thought
she'd been left out. Her heart warmed. The Millers did care for her,
just as she cared for them.

My favorite dessert? She walked to the kitchen, dumped the
junk mail into the trash, and thought of her favorite Oreo pie. She
didn't have any ingredients. Would there be a store open in
the morning? She hoped there would.

With peace settled in her heart and a smile on her face, Cheryl picked up the letter from Aunt Mitzi and then sat down to read. Even her ice cream was abandoned as she dove into her aunt's note.

Dear Sweet Niece,

Thank you so much for the letters. I know that you have plenty to do. It's kind of you to reach out to your old aunt, especially sending words of encouragement. I won't lie and tell you that the last month has been easy. It hasn't been. There are some days I wake up and I feel far too old to be sleeping on a thin mat on the ground or showering under a bucket of cold water, but God has confirmed over and over again that I am exactly where He wants me to be. I have some amazing stories to share, and I'm writing them down in a journal. I want to remember the smiles, the prayers, and the changes that I see. It's the little things that add up.

One fun adventure is that our group was able to visit Port Moresby. And it's there I learned more about William George Lawes. He was the first missionary to Papua New Guinea, and he translated the New Testament into the Motuan language. He moved to New Guinea in 1874, and his family became the first permanent European residents here. He was considered a friend by those in the south coast tribes. He started eleven missions, and he spent the latter part of his life either working to help those in

New Guinea or giving lectures around the world about their needs. Hearing about him made me realize that missionaries have given up so much over time. Hearing about how a man like that stood strong reminds me of where our foundation comes from.

Through the hardships, Cheryl, I am learning to trust God as the foundation under my feet. He will be the strong foundation, whether I am here or there.

It reminds me of an Amish proverb that I once had in a wall hanging in my shop: "A happy home is more than a roof over your head, it's a foundation under your feet." Because God is my foundation, then I suppose wherever I am can be considered home. I'm looking forward to hearing from you soon. I hope the busy season hasn't been too hard on you.

Love,

Aunt Mitzi

Emotion built in Cheryl's throat as she finished the letter and put it back into the envelope. She didn't need to worry about Aunt Mitzi coming back—about her aunt pushing her out of her space. And even if Mitzi did come back, that didn't mean that Cheryl would no longer have a place. Home was where God placed you—whether it was on an Amish farm, like Cassie's great-grandfather. Or in a shelter where women gathered around you and helped you find healing. Or in a foster home where a family called you their own, even as they waited for the birth of a longed-for child.

And now for Cassie, it would be with Mrs. Pryce, who'd schooled so many children and now was getting the help she needed when she needed it. Cheryl smiled, realizing that the two would enjoy each other. And maybe Mrs. Pryce would have some stories to tell.

And for Cheryl, it was in this little cottage with a cat curled on her lap. And tomorrow it would be around a friend's table. She couldn't think of anything she wanted more.

A foundation of love and faith, she decided, did more to build a home than four walls. And somehow all the craziness and conflicts of the last few weeks had taught her that. It was a lesson hard won—but one she wouldn't forget.

CHAPTER TWENTY-SEVEN

It was Thanksgiving morning, and tomorrow would be the busiest shopping day of the year. Even though that had worried Cheryl before, it seemed the least of her worries now. She'd gotten up early to listen to the morning news talk radio and heard that David Dwayne Simons had been officially charged with robbery. Cheryl wished that all the stores' items would be returned, but they were being kept as evidence—at least for now.

The optimistic part of her hoped that LeRoy would repent, make a turnaround, and go on to lead a productive life. He was so young, so talented to keep going down a path of crime.

Cheryl dressed and then drove slowly down Main Street, heading to the grocery store to get items to make an Oreo pie. Good thing it was simple and fast to make.

On the quiet sidewalk, Officer Ortega strolled along in her police uniform, patrolling all the empty shops. She smiled and waved at Cheryl, and Cheryl did the same in return. If the officer hadn't trusted what Cheryl had told her, it was certain that LeRoy would have gotten away. Then who knows what would have happened? He most likely would have started over in a new location— although Cheryl doubted that LeRoy could have pulled off his imitation of another Amish man.

One of the *Budget* scribes had already called Cheryl and asked if he could stop by her shop tomorrow to talk to her and Naomi about the details of finding the thief. The Amish didn't use Facebook or news broadcasts to share information, but one write-up in the *Budget*—in addition to hundreds of sewing circles and barn raisings around the country—and the news would be spread just as easily.

Cheryl drove slowly past By His Grace and thought about Gage. When she'd called Marion last night to tell her about LeRoy's arrest, she'd also asked about the teen. Marion had mentioned Gage would be helping in the bookstore on a part-time basis, starting on Black Friday. He'd already helped her put up some displays of Christmas books, and he'd suggested starting a delivery service for those who couldn't get out of their homes to buy new books.

In the window of the store, Cheryl noticed that a large poster had been taped up. The parking spaces in front of the store were empty, so she pulled over to read:

By His grace, God has given us a new member to our family. Eden Paige was born on November 25 at 3:04 AM, 7 pounds, 8 ounces. Mother and daughter are fine. Daddy and big brother Gage are smitten.

She couldn't believe it. She'd just talked to the woman last evening. My, it must have been an eventful night.

"By His grace," Cheryl whispered to herself. She smiled thinking about what God had given the Berryhills, not one but two new family members. For even if Gage did eventually go to live with his older brother, she had no doubt he'd always be a part of the Berryhill family in a special way.

She pulled back out and continued to the store. It seemed just the way God worked in the way He created a home.

The November sun was high in the sky, casting golden rays over the barren fields as she drove up the driveway to the Millers' farm. Cheryl smiled at the beauty of the scenery as she parked her Ford Focus in front of the Millers' house. The clock on her car read 12:00 PM. Right on time.

Her stomach growled as she opened the car door. Snow had come in the last hour, just a light frosting, but the gravel in the Millers' driveway was a bit slippery. The last thing she wanted to do was to slip and mess up her pie. It was one of Aunt Mitzi's favorite desserts. She didn't want anything to ruin this day of thankfulness.

"Stay right here," she told her older passenger. "I'll go set the pie inside and come right back to help you."

"I can help her," Cassie said, climbing from the backseat. "That's my new job, right, Mrs. Pryce?"

"I told you dear to call me Helen, and I hate to think of myself as anyone's job. A friend and roommate sounds so much better."

Cheryl closed the driver's door, and she took out her pie from the backseat. The slightest wind whispered across the barren fields, greeting her and tugging at her hair. She turned and looked at the Millers' house, and Cheryl had a strange sense of home.

She'd barely made it four steps when the front door opened, and Levi stepped out and then leapt down from the porch.

"Let me help you, Mrs. Pryce. I do not think your crutches were made for this gravel."

Cheryl watched as he walked to the elderly woman and held her arm with tenderness.

Even though she hadn't completely forgotten how harsh Levi had been when he'd told her not to bring her city fears to their farm, her feelings of frustration had lessened, and the tenderness she had for Levi returned. He was so handsome, and most of the time very kind. She'd be worried if he was kind all the time—not even a hero in a novel achieved that.

Cheryl followed behind Levi and Mrs. Pryce, and Cassie fell in step by Cheryl's side. Cassie looked at the roof, the porch, the porch swing as if trying to remember every detail.

"Looks different in the day." She chuckled. "It's much prettier in the light than in the shadows."

"Isn't that the way it always is?" Cheryl said. She sighed. "I'm guilty of that too—staying in the shadows. Sometimes I focus so much on the questions, the worries, and the misdeeds that I forget that the dark doesn't always last."

Instead, light follows the night, she wanted to say. *And in the light one's true home is revealed.* But Cheryl decided to keep those thoughts to herself. And maybe she'd even find a journal to write them in.

It was easy to put the buggy before the horse, to do things in the wrong order. To worry before trusting. To hide before opening one's heart.

But in the end, God was good—or goot as Naomi would say. It was God who held not only the answers to every mystery, but also the hearts of His people in His palms.

Home in His palm was a good place to be. For whether in Columbus, Sugarcreek, or Papua New Guinea, God's palm laid a firm foundation on which any man or woman could stand.

It was something to be thankful for. She *was* thankful for it. And as Cheryl walked inside and saw all the smiling faces, she knew this day of Thanksgiving was something to be thankful for too—God bringing them together as only He could.

AUTHOR LETTER

Dear Reader,

I know, like me, you've enjoyed Cheryl's first months in Sugarcreek, Ohio. With new friendships, an influx of customers, and curious mysteries that she's helped solve with her friend Naomi, Cheryl hasn't had much time to catch a deep breath. Yet as someone who's moved into a new community twice, after a few months the reality of living in a new place hits one's heart hard. The newness wears off. Questions begin to emerge such as, *Is this really where I belong?*

I remember well the lonely months after moving from Northwest Montana to Little Rock, Arkansas. Exploring the city became more of a chore than an adventure. Unfamiliar, local customs often made me feel like an outsider, and there were days I wished for what I'd left behind.

In *The Buggy before the Horse,* Aunt Mitzi feels the same. While slogging through the undeveloped areas of Papua New Guinea, Mitzi longs for a hot bath and her friends back home, and Cheryl wonders if she'll need to turn back the store and her home to her aunt. Will Cheryl have to leave new friendships behind?

If there's one thing that's certain in life, it's this: things will change. Another certain thing is that God can be with us in these changes. I hope that as you journey with Cheryl and Naomi through the pages of this novel, you'll discover more than the answers to a curious mystery. I pray you'll also be pointed to the truth of what a foundation in faith is all about.

No matter where we are in life—and what we find ourselves wrapped up in—there is always one place we can find "home," and that is in the arms of Jesus Christ. May your life be built on the foundation of God's love. His love alone is a foundation that can never be shaken, no matter what unexpected challenges come.

With hope,
Tricia Goyer

About the Author

Best selling author Tricia Goyer has published fifty books and more than five hundred articles! She is a two-time Carol Award winner as well as a Christy and ECPA Award nominee. In 2010, she was selected as one of the "Top Twenty Moms to Follow on Twitter" by SheKnows.com. Tricia blogs at ForTheFamily.com, TheBetterMom.com, and NotQuiteAmishLiving.com. She is a mother of six, grandmother of two, and wife to John, and they make their home in Little Rock, Arkansas. To learn more, visit TriciaGoyer.com.

Fun Fact about
the Amish or Sugarcreek, Ohio

Whenever I research an area, I love to dig into the history of a place. Why? Because where a town came from often becomes the firm foundation of the people who live there.

The history of Sugarcreek is fascinating. The Amish have farmed the area for decades, and they have also passed down family farms. This township was first named Shanesville in 1814, and a town sprung up where two Indian trails crossed. Many German and Swiss immigrants settled there because the landscape and the climate were similar to the homes they left in the old country. The name "Shanesville" was changed to "Sugarcreek" in the mid-1800s, after a nearby creek called Sugar Creek. Due to the heritage of the first settlers of the area—and the families that remain who carry on their ancestors' traditions—it's known as the "Little Switzerland of Ohio."

Many of the traditions of the first settlers continue on today through the Amish, such as farming, cheesemaking, and woodworking. More importantly, Christian values are passed down too, with hopes of those being carried on to future generations. As one Amish proverb says, "The kind of ancestors you have is not as important as the ones your children have." So while the history of Sugarcreek is important, it's even more important to take the lessons we've learned from the Amish of Sugarcreek and pass them on.

Something Delicious from Our Sugarcreek Friends

Katie's Amish Fudge

6 tablespoons butter (salted preferred)

½ cup heavy cream

½ cup dark brown sugar

⅛ teaspoon salt

⅓ cup ground sweet chocolate (for extra flavor, add 1 tablespoon of dry cocoa)

1 teaspoon pure vanilla

1⅔ cups powdered sugar (sifted works best)

Pecans

In a double boiler, combine butter, cream, sugar, salt, and ground chocolate, and cook over medium heat, stirring frequently until boiling lightly.

Reduce heat to a low boil for five minutes, stirring constantly.

After five minutes, remove from heat and stir in vanilla, then powdered sugar (a little at a time). Beat until smooth. (If you didn't sift your sugar, it won't be smooth.)

Add pecans (toasted are always better), and pour into eight-inch-by-eight-inch pan.

Cool for thirty minutes or until set.

Read on for a sneak peek of another exciting book
in the Sugarcreek Amish Mysteries series!

A Season of Secrets
by Elizabeth Adams

The door of the Swiss Miss flew open just as Cheryl Cooper finished hanging handblown glass balls on the small fir tree by the front window. She put the ornament box down on the small table and turned to see Lydia Troyer walk inside and slam the door against the cold November wind.

"I am sorry," Lydia said as she unbuttoned her heavy woolen coat. She crossed the floor and hung her coat in the office at the back. She came back out as she tied a red Swiss Miss apron around her waist. "It is very chilly out there today." Lydia warmed her hands in front of the potbellied stove for a moment.

"It definitely feels like winter is on its way," Cheryl said. Thanksgiving had just passed, and she was looking forward to the cheer and warmth of the Christmas season, but she was not looking forward to the cold that came with it.

Lydia pulled her cell phone out of her jeans pocket and looked at the screen. Then she put it away and turned to Cheryl. "What should I do?"

Cheryl had to laugh. Lydia—the best friend of her other part-time employee Esther Miller—was Amish, but she was on *rumspringa*, her running-around years where the rules were relaxed and Amish teens could experience the outside world. Lydia had embraced that freedom wholeheartedly. She dressed *Englisch*—not in the traditional Amish style—and carried her cell phone with her everywhere, just like most regular teenagers in America. And, like a typical teen, she checked it constantly. But Lydia was a hard worker as well as bright and outgoing, and Cheryl was glad to have her around.

"There are some boxes I was going to unpack behind the counter," Cheryl said, gesturing to the back of the shop. "Maybe you could inventory those and set them out?"

"I will start there," Lydia said and headed off. With the holiday season upon them, Cheryl had asked Lydia to pick up some more hours. Lydia was eager to make some extra money, while Cheryl was thankful that she'd have more help around the shop in the busy coming weeks.

Cheryl turned back to the small Christmas tree, adjusted the placement of a few of the ornaments, and then looked around the store. The shelves were well stocked with handmade soaps, candles, jams, and cheese, as well as hand-carved wooden toys and other small souvenirs. Cheryl ran the Swiss Miss, a gift shop right in the heart of Ohio Amish country, and she tried her best to make the shop warm and welcoming as well as fill it with the finest merchandise she could find. And now, with the holiday season in full swing, Cheryl knew that it was especially important for the store to look its best. The Amish may not be extravagant in celebrating the holiday, but the tourists who came through Sugarcreek would be looking for gifts, and Cheryl was happy to help. A few customers were currently browsing the candy bins, but they seemed quite content selecting between pastel-colored saltwater taffy, spicy peppermints, and bitter horehound.

Satisfied that all was in good order, she carried the empty box toward the back of the shop and set it down on the counter. She'd take the box back out to her car, and then she'd spend some time working on putting together a care package for her aunt Mitzi, who owned and had run the Swiss Miss before she moved to Papua New Guinea to follow God's call to the mission field earlier this year. Aunt Mitzi's latest letter had said that everything was going well, but she missed some of her favorite things from home, like peanut butter and Greta Yoder's famous cinnamon rolls, so Cheryl had decided to put together a care package filled with her aunt's favorite things. She'd include some of Naomi Miller's jams for sure, and also a bag of the taffy Rebekah Byler made that Mitzi loved so much, and…

Cheryl looked up as Lydia gasped.

"What's wrong?" she said.

Lydia was staring down at her phone, her long black hair falling down around her face. "What could this mean?" she muttered.

"What is it?" Cheryl's heart beat faster. Could something be wrong with one of Lydia's family members?

"I just got this weird text," Lydia said and held out her cell phone.

Cheryl looked down at it and squinted to read the letters on the small screen: *I know what happened to Mark.*

She looked back up at Lydia, trying to make sense of the words. Lydia's face had drained of color.

"Who is Mark?"

"My cousin," Lydia said. She pulled the phone back toward herself and read the message again. "He disappeared a little over three years ago. No one ever knew what happened to him. Except now"—she looked up at Cheryl, her eyes wide—"it looks like someone does know after all."

Cheryl studied the cell phone Lydia held out and considered what she had just told her. Lydia's fingers flew across the screen, typing a response: *Who is this?*

"Wait, what do you mean your cousin Mark disappeared three years ago?"

They both stared at the screen, waiting for a response, but none came.

"Just that. He left his job at Weaver Lumber one night, in late September three years ago, and he never made it home. The police were brought in, and there were all kinds of theories about where he went, but they never found out what happened to him."

Cheryl's thoughts raced around in her head. She had only lived in Sugarcreek a short time, and she had never heard about this before. How had an Amish boy simply disappeared? Wasn't this the kind of thing people still talked about years later? What could have happened to him?

"Back up. Tell me more about what happened," Cheryl said.

Lydia took a deep breath and nodded. Her eyes were wide, but Cheryl could see she was trying to stay calm. "Mark was eighteen, in his running-around time, but still very devoted to his family and the church. But then one night he left his job to drive home, and that was that. He vanished. They found his car outside the bus station in Columbus a few weeks later."

Cheryl tried to make sense of this. "What did the police say?" she finally asked. She looked down at the phone, but there was still no response.

"They say he ran away. That he took a bus somewhere and just left." Lydia sent another text back asking, *What happened?* "They talked to a few people and found out that he was interested in art, which is true, and that he liked many things about the Englisch life, which is also true, and they said he must have driven to the bus station, gotten on a bus, and run away."

She set the phone down gently on the counter. "But he did not run away. He would not have. Not without saying good-bye."

Lydia could be a bit flighty, but Cheryl heard nothing but earnestness in her voice.

"Mark *was* pretty interested in the Englisch life, and yes, he was trying to decide whether to join the church or not..."

This, Cheryl had come to understand, was the purpose of the running-around time, or rumspringa. The strict rules the Amish lived by were relaxed so that kids could see the outside world and make an informed decision about whether they wanted to remain Amish and join their church, or whether they would leave the church behind and become Englisch. An overwhelming number did choose to stay Amish in the end, but each teenager had to make the choice for themselves.

"But just because Mark was interested in the Englisch world, it does not mean he just left. Mark would have told me if he was planning to go somewhere. We were close. And he would have said good-bye to his parents. He would never have just vanished like that. I am positive."

Cheryl could see Lydia was getting worked up, and she could certainly understand why. Lydia felt very strongly that Mark hadn't run away. But that only left one alternative...

"So what do you think happened to him?" Cheryl asked.

Lydia shook her head. "I do not know. I do not—" She broke off. "I hate to think about it, but I wonder if something horrible happened to him. I hope not, but I do not know what else it could have been. Especially with the bloody shirt they found behind the Honey Bee. I mean, what else could..."

"The bloody what?" Goodness. This was getting gruesome.

Lydia stopped. "Oh, right. I am sorry, I forget you do not know any of this." She took a deep breath and then continued. "They found one of Mark's shirts in a trash bin behind the Honey Bee the day after he disappeared. It had blood on it. So it seems likely..."

Lydia gulped, taking in air. She was getting worked up again, so Cheryl waited a moment. Lydia was sure something bad had happened to her cousin, but Cheryl didn't know what to believe. But whatever the truth was, someone out there now knew, or claimed to know, what had happened to Mark. But who was it?

She looked down at Lydia's phone, lying on the counter. It was a standard cell phone with a touch screen. There was still no answer. "Do you have any idea who could have sent the message?"

"I do not know." Lydia pointed to the number at the top of the screen. It was a local number, but not one she had stored in her phone, so there was no name attached to it. "I do not recognize this number."

A text like this would most likely have come from someone Lydia knew; after all, whoever sent it must have known that Lydia and Mark had been close. But it hadn't come from someone whose number Lydia was familiar with. Since it was a text, it could only have come from a cell phone or tablet, and as only teens on rumspringa were allowed to use such devices, the number of potential senders was limited.

Unless it came from an *Englischer*, of course. In which case, it could be just about anyone.

But even if someone really did know what had happened to Mark, why send a text about it? If this was real—and Cheryl wasn't sure it was—why not simply tell Lydia directly?

And if this wasn't real…Cheryl shook her head. If this wasn't real, it was a very cruel joke.

"This person is not responding to my questions," Lydia said, looking at the screen again. "Is there any way to discover whose number this is?"

"Probably," Cheryl answered. That challenge didn't seem too difficult. How hard could it be to learn who a specific phone number belonged to? If they found that, they'd find the person who sent the text, and, if that person was telling the truth, it would hopefully lead to answers about Mark. "I'm not sure how, but I bet there's a way."

"Oh, Cheryl, if there is a way to find this out, it would mean so much. Could you help me?"

Cheryl didn't know what to say. She already had plenty going on with the store during holiday season and getting a gift box ready for Mitzi, but then she saw Lydia's pained, earnest face and realized there was only one thing she could do.

"Of course I'll help you."

A Note from the Editors

We hope you enjoyed *Sugarcreek Amish Mysteries*, published by the Books and Inspirational Media Division of Guideposts, a nonprofit organization that touches millions of lives every day through products and services that inspire, encourage, help you grow in your faith, and celebrate God's love.

Thank you for making a difference with your purchase of this book, which helps fund our many outreach programs to military personnel, prisons, hospitals, nursing homes, and educational institutions.

We also create many useful and uplifting online resources. Visit Guideposts.org to read true stories of hope and inspiration, access OurPrayer network, sign up for free newsletters, download free e-books, join our Facebook community, and follow our stimulating blogs.

To learn about other Guideposts publications, including the best-selling devotional *Daily Guideposts*, go to Guideposts.org/Shop, call (800) 932-2145, or write to Guideposts, PO Box 5815, Harlan, Iowa 51593.